THE
LAWLESS ONE
AND THE END OF TIME

LONNIE PACELLI

PUBLISHED BY PACELLI PUBLISHING
BELLEVUE, WASHINGTON

Pacelli
PUBLISHING

THE LAWLESS ONE
AND THE END OF TIME

Published by Pacelli Publishing
9905 Lake Washington Blvd. NE, #D-103
Bellevue, Washington 98004
PacelliPublishing.com

Cover design by Rachel Ronan | Kiwi Creative
Interior design by Pacelli Publishing
Author photo by Trevor Pacelli | TrevorsViewonPhotography.com

Printed in the United States of America

ISBN-10: 1-933750-93-6
ISBN-13: 978-1-933750-93-4

"And then the Lawless One will be revealed…"
2 Thessalonians 2:8

By 2030, American culture had permeated the rest of the world in its pop art, lingo, fashion, education structure. English had become the primary language among the world's inhabitants, native tongues being less popular with younger generations. Older generations tried to keep their customs alive, but youth wanted everything American.

Since the 1950s, scientists and politicians had debated the existence and effect of global warming. The debate raged into the 21st century on whether global warming was real and its impact on the world. In 2020 the world got its answer. Rice, wheat, corn and soy production began dropping due to increased carbon dioxide, heat, and ozone exposure. By 2022, production had dropped by 20 percent, triggering worldwide panic over food supplies. The member nations of the Group of Ten (G10), assembled to discuss how to solve the dwindling food supply problem. The G10 arrived at two conclusions: food rationing was necessary to ensure the survivability of all people groups; and a singular world currency was necessary to ensure individual currency fluctuations didn't create unfair rationing.

The G10 proposed consolidating the 196 countries into ten ethnarchies: Africa, Asia, China, Caribbean, Central America, Europe, North America, Russia, Oceania, and South America. Each ethnarchy elected a chairperson to manage the transition from a sovereign country to an ethnarchy, ensure fair food-rationing within and across ethnarchies, and manage the transition to a single world currency. The second recommendation, a singular world currency, was no easier to implement. The United States wanted the dollar, Europe the euro, China the yuan, and Russia the ruble. Because there was no compromise reached on an existing currency to use, the G10 decided upon a new currency, the hera. The G10 set a timeline of January 1, 2025 for the ethnarchy consolidation and hera conversion to be complete, with one hera worth one U.S. dollar. The ethnarchy consolidation and single world currency was unpopular with most of the countries but was also viewed as necessary for equitable world survival. Both went into effect in 2025 as planned.

Some countries ultimately came to accept the consolidation, others harbored bitterness. Those troubled with the consolidation never forgot it and vowed to right what they saw as a great injustice. Making matters worse was a polarizing chairperson loved by millions of followers but despised by his enemies. His actions, foretold by scripture, would usher in the end of time.

THREE SHOT
2066

The Israeli-Palestine peace treaty had been in place for three and a half years. With Israel and the Palestinian countries of Jordan, Syria, Lebanon, and Egypt's Sinai Peninsula under Europe's control, a peace was realized that hadn't existed since Israel's establishment as a state in 1948. Europe established its embassy in Jerusalem which was regularly visited by world dignitaries and leaders.

It was a rainy day on March 1, 2066, not the best weather for the dedication that was to follow later in the day. A motorcade of four black cars stopped in front of the embassy. From the third car, three of Europe's highest-ranking officials emerged and began walking up the stairs to the embassy. The sideways rain blew to their backs, the security detail pointing their open umbrellas into the wind to keep them from blowing inside-out. Then came the muffled *thump thump thump* of bullets hitting flesh, the three collapsed on the stairs, those near them splattered with blood. No gunshot sounds contributed to the confusion of the stunned onlookers as they watched the men drop. Paramedics reached the men in moments. Two of the three lay face down on the steps, bleeding from the head, the third sitting on the steps, bleeding from the arm.

A paramedic approached the man on the left, face down on the stairs, his body already soaked from the rain. What was left of his jaw was in a bloody mass a meter away from his body on the wet steps--bone fragments, teeth, and flesh left in a trail from the man to his mandible. He turned the man onto his back.

"Can you hear me sir?" the paramedic asked.

The paramedic saw his chest heave, then heard a gurgling sound, the air from his lungs flowing across the little bit of his tongue that he had left. Another paramedic came to him to prepare the man for transport while a third gathered what he could of the man's jaw.

Another paramedic approached the man in the middle, face down on the steps and unconscious. Blood flowed from a single bullet hole above his right ear. The paramedic pressed on his carotid, feeling for a pulse.

"He's still alive!" he yelled.

Two more paramedics carrying a stretcher ran to the man. They'd seen injuries like these before and fully expected the man would be dead within an hour, but they proceeded undeterred despite the odds.

A paramedic approached the man on the left, sitting on the stairs, bleeding from his right forearm. He was alert but bewildered at the commotion and the sight of the other two men on the ground.

"Sir, can you hear me?" The paramedic asked.

The man just stared at him.

"Sir?" The paramedic asked again.

"My arm," he said as he looked at the wound on his arm. He then looked at the other two men. "Are they alright?" he asked.

"We're gonna take care of them," the paramedic said.

"Take care of them first."

"We are."

The man watched as the other two were put on stretchers and transported to waiting ambulances. He looked at the wet bloody steps, where the men's bodies lay just seconds ago. Those who came to see him and his two colleagues had cleared the area, and Israeli Defense Force and embassy security swarmed the area looking for any clues as to who the shooter was. He watched the two ambulances leave the area, sirens blaring, racing to Jerusalem Health.

The paramedic put a triangle bandage on the man's forearm.

"Let's get you to the hospital," the paramedic said.

The man got up and walked on his own to the waiting ambulance, got in, then saw a man in a suit follow him onto the ambulance before he heard the loud *slam* of the ambulance doors close.

"Sir, are you OK?" The man in the suit asked.

"Yes."

"Any idea who did this?"

"I've got a good idea," the man said, blood beginning to soak through his bandage.

SAL CARLOTTA
2030

At 14, Sal Carlotta was already six feet tall with a lean swimmer's physique. His facial features were perfectly symmetrical with piercing blue eyes, angular chin, high cheekbones. His hair was uniformly short, and he sported a neatly trimmed five o'clock shadow with no bald patches. He easily passed for someone much older, an advantage he exploited when hooking up with girls.

His father, Gene, was born in Naples, Italy. He graduated with a 4.0 grade point average in finance from Harvard University. He was recruited by nine companies after graduation, choosing to work at investment banking firm Miconal as a financial analyst. He steadily rose through the ranks to become its youngest chief financial officer at 35. His drive and determination permeated his entire life. Whether it was business, sports, or politics, Gene viewed his relationship with others as, "For me to win you must lose." He craved being a winner, wanting his son to be just like him.

Sal's mother, Marie, was born in Dublin, Ireland and met her husband at Harvard where she also maintained a 4.0 grade point average as a finance major. She had fiery red shoulder-length hair, sky-blue eyes, a milky white complexion, and freckles that gathered around her nose. Marie and Gene started dating while at Harvard and married just before graduating. Like her husband, she was heavily recruited by several companies, choosing Miconal for both the career opportunity and to be close to Gene. She saw them working, living, and loving together as the ideal marriage. Feeling threatened by her at work, Gene treated her as if she was a competitor first and lover second. Marie didn't want to compete, she wanted to be adored by a loving husband. When she got pregnant with Sal, she decided to leave Miconal and be a stay-at-home mom to escape the stress Gene was creating in their marriage. While she enjoyed her role as primary caretaker for Sal, she also felt bitterness toward her husband for selfishly putting his career aspirations over hers. After Sal was born, she poured herself into him as his nurturer and protector. Their relationship was very close, much closer than either had with Gene.

Gene and Marie decided to enroll Sal at Naples Academy in central Naples. The Academy was renowned for its disciplined approach to learning, top-shelf academics, and reputation at colleges worldwide for churning out the highest-quality students. Gene wanted Sal to prove himself as the best of the best, while Marie wanted Sal to have a well-rounded educational experience. Sal was never asked what he wanted, but he accepted the school choice because it would help him prove himself to his father. He also knew that if his father were happy there would be less stress on his mother, which further motivated Sal to excel.

Sal got up at 6:30 each morning and began with push-ups, sit-ups, squats, and lunges, then held a plank position for five minutes, looking at himself in the full-length mirror during his routine. Then a quick shower and back to his bedroom which looked like a well-stocked trophy shop, filled with his academic and athletic achievements. Despite his age, Sal had amassed more awards than most received in a lifetime. Competing to win was his *modus operandi*. And there were never enough trophies for him.

He reached into his closet, pulled out some of his favorite clothes, every one having some designer label. His outer appearance needed to exude confidence, it was how he masked is inward insecurities that were fueled by his father's sky-high expectations of him.

He gave his trophies a quick glance, took one last look at himself in the mirror and made his way down the hallway to the kitchen.

Marie had yogurt and croissants already at the breakfast table. It was an identical breakfast every day, just as his father liked. Gene was on a conference call with Miconal's senior management team. Another breakfast with conference calls, where Gene was physically present but mentally and emotionally somewhere else. For Sal, seeing his father there but ignoring him was worse than him not being there at all. Yet another reminder that Sal was not a priority to Gene. Marie was sitting at the table sipping her Americano. He heard her throwing up through the night, something she'd been doing a lot over the past month. He kissed her good morning and sat.

Gene finished his conference call, put down his phone, and continued to eat breakfast. Sal searched for something to say to his father to get his attention.

"Problems at work, Dad?" Sal asked.

"There's always problems," Gene said. "What classes are you taking?"

This was the fourth time in the past two weeks Gene asked about Sal's classes. Whether he forgot the answer or wasn't listening didn't matter to Sal or Marie. Not remembering was indication that Gene didn't care.

"Gene he's already told you three times about his classes," Marie said, which only agitated him.

"So tell me again."

"Calculus, advanced placement history, chemistry, world literature, and football," Sal said.

"You're capable of more," Gene responded.

"Gene, he's already got a full workload," Marie said in defense of her son. Already not feeling well, her eyes welled up with the escalating conversation.

"Those classes are for average students. Top-notch colleges don't accept average. Step up your game."

Sal knew to keep quiet. His father would rant for a minute then get preoccupied with something else. Marie wasn't having it.

"Stop already!" Marie got up and went to the sink, her back to the kitchen table. Her outburst was out of character, surprising Sal. Gene picked up his phone again, not wanting to deal with Marie's flare-up. Sal got up from his chair and went up to his mother.

"Mom what's wrong?" Sal asked as he put his hand on her shoulder.

"I'm OK, you need to get off to school." Sal knew that she wasn't OK, but it was clear she didn't want to talk or be consoled. He looked back at Gene who was already engrossed in something on his phone.

"I love you Mom," Sal said as he kissed his mother on the cheek. He looked back at Gene, still staring at his phone, his thumb swiping up and down on the screen, oblivious to Marie's distress.

Sal grabbed his backpack, kissed his mother again, gave his father a polite good-bye, and left the apartment for the 15-minute walk to the Academy bus stop. The Carlottas lived in an exclusive apartment building in the Naples highlands with expansive views of the Bay of Naples. Scooters, pedestrians, and litter filled the narrow streets. Naples' city infrastructure had been crumbling for years, with graffiti and garbage overtaking the once-charming landscape. Its residents simply got used to it; living, working, and shopping like any normal city. Sal made it a point to walk by his favorite *pasticceria* each morning where freshly-made *tiramisu*, *sfogliatella riccia,* and *cannolis* caught the attention of each passer-by. Sal's favorite was the *sfogliatella*, with its stacked, flaky pastry layers and sweet creamy ricotta cheese filling. Some mornings he would stop and get one to enjoy on his walk. On this particular morning, not even his favorite pastry could lift his mood: inadequacy in the eyes of his father, feeling like he would never be able to meet his astronomical expectations; fear of being anything less than number one; pity for his mother and her unhappiness in her marriage; gratefulness to her for standing up for him against his father; concern over Marie's frequent puking, then her atypical outburst. And then there was her yellowing skin and getting so skinny. His mother always kept a slim figure, but she'd never been gaunt like this. She never spoke of it, and Gene never seemed to notice.

Sal saw the empty bus stop ahead, still thinking about his mother as he walked. "Is she sick?" he thought as he reached the bus stop.

Paul Ambrosi

2030

Paul Ambrosi learned to read at the age of three. Despite being only 14, he had read books on topics such as macroeconomics, game theory, political history, and mathematics. His father, Joseph, was a fifth-generation Ambrosi living in Naples. He owned and operated a family supermarket which was passed down from his father. Despite working hard at the supermarket, he always managed to find time for his wife Ida and children Paul, Alberto and Anna. Whether it was a school musical, football game, or parent-teacher meeting, Joseph was always there lending an encouraging hand to his family. He and Ida went on dates every Friday, frequenting nearly every restaurant in Naples, saving up two-for-one coupons to enjoy inexpensive dinners together. What or where they ate wasn't as important as spending time together. Just as important for Joseph was that he set an example of how his sons should love and respect a woman, which he modeled to a tee.

Ida was raised in Athens, Greece and met Joseph at just 13 when her family was vacationing in Sorrento. The two met on a ferry ride from Sorrento to Naples, talking non-stop as if they were long-time friends. Joseph told her of the family supermarket which she visited the next day with her parents. They exchanged phone numbers before Ida and her family left to go back to Athens. Ida and Joseph kept in regular contact, including Joseph going to Athens each summer to spend time with Ida. When they were both 18, Ida came to Naples and married Joseph. She seamlessly fit into the family supermarket business, no job too hard or beneath her. At age 20 she gave birth to Alberto, then to Paul at 22, followed by Anna at 24.

Even with three small children under the age of five she managed an orderly home, worked at the supermarket, and kept family blowups to a minimum.

At five-foot-eleven with a slim build, Paul looked like a boy that most any girl would want to take home to meet the parents. He was a bit on the quiet side but was inwardly comfortable in his own skin and exuded an air of humble confidence rarely seen in a 14-year-old. Despite his confidence, he was uncomfortable around girls and made no effort to build relationships with them beyond platonic chit-chat.

Joseph and Ida transferred Paul to Naples Academy after one of Paul's teachers talked with them about the Academy's program for gifted students. Academy tuition would be a huge financial drain, but they felt it was important to give their son the opportunity to fulfill his potential. Several of Joseph's well-off long-time customers heard of Joseph's financial struggle to send Paul to Academy and banded together to pay for a large portion of the tuition. With the supplemental funds, Joseph and Ida were able to send Paul to Academy without the other children having to sacrifice. What Paul didn't know at the time was the impact one of the customers would have on him later in life.

Paul shared a bedroom with Alberto. Two twin beds, two dressers, and two desks were about all that fit in the room. There was only one closet with two rods; Alberto got the upper rod and Paul the lower. Despite the close quarters, the brothers peacefully coexisted. They really had no choice as there was nowhere else for either of them to go. Three bedrooms, one bathroom, an eat-in kitchen, and a living room made up the entire Ambrosi home.

On his first day of Academy, Paul waited his turn for the bathroom, quickly did his business, then went back to his bedroom to get dressed. Looking at the lower closet rod, Paul wished he had a better choice of clothes. "Just make do," he thought as he decided on his outfit. He pulled out a light blue button-down oxford shirt with an off-brand emblem on the pocket. The shirt was neatly pressed and fit his slim physique well. He slipped on neatly-creased beige khakis and his only pair of nice dress shoes. The look was simple, but he thought it worked.

Paul shut the light off in his bedroom and made his way down the short hallway to the kitchen. As a child Paul would count how many "big-boy" steps it took for him to get from his bedroom to the kitchen. Now he could do it in three big strides, which he playfully did each time he left his room. He smelled warm croissants that Ida had just baked. *One, two, three*, he stepped. The rest of the family was already at the table.

"Hey all," Paul said.

"Good morning, Paolo," Ida said as she put a basket of croissants on the table. Paul sat down at the table, his mouth ready for a croissant with honey-fig jam. He reached across the table to get a still-warm croissant, tore it open, and slathered it with the jam. He took a bite and savored the flaky, buttery, and sweet breakfast as Anna, Alberto and Joseph all made their way to the table.

"Paolo when are you going to be home?" Ida asked as she sat down with her espresso.

"Debate ends at six, should be about seven."

"OK, dinner at seven." Ida was insistent that the family eat together as much as possible. She was raised in a household where the entire family ate together and saw the importance of connecting at the dinner table. She wanted the same for her family. "Remember, I need some help at the store tonight after dinner." Joseph said.

"Cool."

Paul got up from the table deciding to finish his croissant on the 10-minute walk to the Academy bus stop. He put on a light jacket, grabbed his backpack, kissed his mother and headed out.

"Later"

"Don't break too many hearts today!" Anna said. Anna's friends loved to come over to the Ambrosi's apartment just to get a glimpse of Paul's good looks. She admired her brother not only for his brains, but for how kind he was to other people.

Paul walked out of the apartment into the cool morning air, reflecting on how fortunate he was to have this opportunity to attend Academy. He was humbled by the supermarket customers choosing to help pay for his tuition with no expectation of anything in return, other than Paul using the experience to do something great later in life. He thought of his father's example of the perfect father and husband and the seemingly perfect marriage that his parents shared. He remembered how one of Anna's friends fawned over him the day before, how cute she was, but how he didn't see her as anything more than a nice girl. He then playfully mused about how many big-boy steps it would take to get from his apartment to the bus stop. Doing the math subconsciously triggered him to take big-boy steps as he walked. His pace was brisk, purposeful and straight as he counted one-and-a-half-meter lunges. He was big-boy stepping as he approached the bus stop and saw the boy already there eyeballing his strange gait. Embarrassed, Paul caught his gaze and realized how ridiculous he looked. He quickly adjusted his stride, walked up to him and extended his hand.

"I'm Paul," he said.

CALEB TODD
2030

Caleb Todd hated history, math, science, and everything else school. "Some of the richest people in the world were college dropouts," he would justify to his parents. Despite being 14, Caleb displayed the maturity of a 10-year-old and the stubbornness of a child going through the terrible twos.

Caleb's father, Aidan, was raised in Dublin in a blue-collar household. Being uneducated, Aidan learned early on that survival meant hard physical work. He applied at the Guinness brewery on his 16th birthday, starting work the week following. He enjoyed traveling around Europe when he could get time off from the brewery and had a love for Italy. He met his wife Gloria while in Naples. He went in for a sandwich at the supermarket where she worked and talked with her for only a few minutes, but that was all it took. He was so smitten that he went back each day to buy random items as an excuse to talk to her. After he left Naples he called and messaged her daily. He ultimately quit his job at Guinness, moved to Naples, and got a job at the Naples shipyard. Eight months after first meeting they married.

Gloria Ambrosi was raised in Naples. She worked at the family supermarket along with her brother Joseph. From the moment she met Aidan she felt in her heart they were going to marry. Every conversation, date, and kiss further confirmed her feelings. Gloria stood about four-foot-eleven but had the imposing disposition of a burly, six-foot tall man. She feared no one and had no problem at all putting an unruly person in his or her place. She could hit a fly on the wall at five paces just by flicking the slipper from her foot. She dearly loved her husband and children and served the role of protector well. If anyone in any way threatened Aidan or the kids, they would experience Gloria's wrath. She ruled the roost, and Aidan was fine with that.

Caleb was the third of five children, with older brothers Philip and Frank, younger brother Luigi and younger sister Carolina. Philip and Frank teased Caleb mercilessly, they thought it fun to see their younger brother squirm and cry. They became expert at doing it behind Gloria's back, their physical and emotional bullying creating deep fissures in Caleb's personality--craving attention, lashing out at others, obsessively seeking positive reinforcement.

Caleb was five feet, two inches tall with wavy black hair, brown eyes, and a baby-face complexion. When he was around others his age, he looked more like one of their younger brothers than a peer. They towered over him and frequently teased him about his diminutive stature. The worst part for him was not having gone through puberty yet. Changing clothes in gym class was torture, with others openly laughing at his hairless features. Even though he coveted attention, this was not the type he wanted. He loathed it, and it led to deep-seated insecurities and bitterness which stayed with him the rest of his life.

Attending Academy was not a privilege for Caleb, it was meant to instill discipline. He had already been kicked out of two other schools for bad behavior. In one he set a bag of dog poop on fire in one of the classrooms, setting off the sprinkler system and forcing the entire school to evacuate. In the other he threatened to kill a teacher if she gave him a failing grade. With each expulsion, Aidan and Gloria tried everything they could to get their wild child to behave. Their last resort was a special program at Academy for students with disciplinary issues.

An Academy program called "tiering" had a 90-percent success rate of rehabilitating problem students into productive, law-abiding adults. The program had two tiers. Tier one was for less-serious offenders who attended Academy during regular school hours. Tier two was for more serious offenders that Academy referred to as "guests." Guests lived at Academy for the entire semester. Guests were told when to eat, sleep, shower, attend class, exercise, and relax. Guests wore standard gray uniforms and electronic ankle bracelets which tracked movement. Because guests attended classes with other Academy students, the uniforms made the tier two students obvious to the others. Tier two looked and felt like prison and putting it on display to the other students only added to the shame.

Caleb was admitted into tier one under probation; if he demonstrated good behavior he would stay there. His conduct was reviewed weekly by a three-person review board for infractions that, if committed, could get him "guested" to tier two. The only way for Caleb to graduate from tiering and attend as a regular student was if he received at least a 3.0 grade point average for two semesters and committed no infractions during that period. Caleb was happy that no one knew he was in a disciplinary program. Caleb hated tier one, but tier two scared him nearly to death. The only saving grace about Academy was knowing that his cousin Paul was also attending, even though Paul wasn't in the tiering program.

On this first day of Academy classes, Caleb jumped down from his top bunk, showered, and returned to his room to dress. His brother Luigi was still sleeping on the bottom bunk. Caleb intentionally made noise while dressing just to get under his little brother's skin, a warped kind of payback for how his older brothers treated him. When Caleb slammed the dresser drawer loudly, Luigi shook, looked at his brother and gave him a "what the heck?" look. Caleb mocked, "Sorry, dude," and continued banging around the room. Recognizing he wasn't going back to sleep anytime soon, Luigi got up and headed to the bathroom, bumping Caleb with his shoulder like a hockey player checking an opponent into the wall. Caleb looked in his closet to decide what to wear. Being so fearful of tier two, he refused to wear anything gray to avoid someone thinking he was guested. He chose a bright yellow shirt that hung off his bony frame, looking about the same as it did on the hanger. Blue jeans and dark shoes completed the outfit. He made his way down the hall to the breakfast table of yogurt and Nutella-filled croissants. Aidan and his older brothers Philip and Frank were already at the table.

"Hey, Squirt," Philip teased. Not saying a word, Caleb gave Philip the evil eye.

"That's enough!" Gloria the matriarch piped in.

Aidan ripped open a croissant, the Nutella gently oozing from the flaky crust. After taking his first bite, he looked over at Caleb. "Academy's a great opportunity for you, Caleb. It's got what you need to straighten your life out before it's too late. You need to make the most of it."

"Making the most of being stuffed in lockers!" It was Frank's turn to tease Caleb.

Aidan continued, "Caleb, take this seriously. Tier one is a gift right now. You don't want to end up in tier two, right?"

"Right."

"Good. Let Paul help if you need it."

Caleb took two croissants, grabbed his backpack, and headed out the door for the ten-minute walk to the Academy bus stop.

"Try to stay out of lockers, little one!" Philip got in one last jab as Caleb left.

"Screw you!" Caleb muttered so his mother couldn't hear.

Caleb stormed out of the apartment down to the street entrance. As he hit the first of three steps at the apartment front door he lost his footing and fell face-first to the street below. No broken teeth, but he split his chin and grazed both his palms trying to break his fall. Better that he just kept going to the bus stop with a bloody chin and scraped palms than go back to the apartment and be ridiculed by his brothers. His walk to the bus stop was a tornado of angry thoughts about Academy, the tiering program, being teased about his size and delayed puberty, and his relentlessly mean brothers. He had been in the eye of this storm many times before. His escape from the storm was an imaginary world he had cultivated over the years. In his world all the people who were mean to him were forced to follow his orders. He was bigger and stronger than everyone else, and millions of people worshipped him. Women wanted to be with him and men wanted to be like him. In his world he had more money than he would ever need, lived in a huge mansion, and drove the nicest cars. As he saw the bus stop with two guys standing there, he came back down to the reality of who he really was--the son of a shipyard worker, incessantly teased by classmates and brothers, and one bad report away from being guested as a tier two ankle bracelet-wearing Academy prisoner.

Paul saw his cousin Caleb coming and met up with him before he got to the bus stop.

"Hey, Cuz, you alright?" Paul said as he looked at Caleb's split chin.

Caleb just looked at him and rolled his eyes.

"Sorry, man." Paul knew that look. He wished Caleb's family would ease up on him. They walked up to the bus stop where Sal was already standing. Paul introduced the two. "Caleb this is Sal. Sal this is my cousin Caleb."

"Hey, Caleb," Sal said.

Caleb nodded his head backwards, not saying a word.

BERT WINN
2030

At 7 each morning, 14-year-old Bert Winn got out of bed. He typically woke up earlier, but he had to stick to his routine. After a bathroom stop, he went downstairs to breakfast. At 7:10 he ate a breakfast of three ciabatta slices with ricotta cheese and a glass of milk. He prepared his own breakfast every day even though his mother was already awake and completely willing to do it for him. If she interrupted Bert's routine in any way it created unnecessary stress for him. She stood by while he executed his routine the same way at the same time every morning.

Bert was a happy baby. His six, nine and 12-month check-ups indicated he was developing exactly as expected. At 18 months, Bert would only say "ball," which he used to describe just about anything or anyone he saw. This concerned Bert's mother, Hayley, as her older daughter Morgan was using many more words and forming short sentences at 18 months. Bert's pediatrician said to "give him time" and that "girls typically talked more than boys." At two years of age Bert was only using a few words and appeared to just mimic others. If Hayley said, "Do you want me to carry you?" Bert would respond, "Carry you." He would spend hours doing things over and over again, his favorite being puzzles. He had a wooden puzzle of the United States that he would do repeatedly, seemingly never getting bored of the activity.

He had difficulty maintaining eye contact, as if it were painful for him to look others directly in the eye. He didn't like to be cuddled, which upset Hayley. She discussed Bert's symptoms with her pediatrician again, who this time recommended she have Bert tested at the Children's Hospital Autism Center at Naples. The test results came back conclusive; Bert had Autism Spectrum Disorder.

Bert's father, Ryan, was a cybersecurity naval officer at Naval Support Academy Naples Military Complex. He participated in many strategic initiatives during his career, the most important being the peacekeeping assignment during the ethnarchic consolidation. He loved his career with the Navy and saw to it that he obeyed orders from his superiors, so he could continue his climb up the chain of command. He used the right words, "family first" when asked about his priorities, but his actions unfortunately didn't match his words. With Ryan, it was "Navy first, family distant second." With each set of relocation orders, Ryan was quick to justify to Hayley why it was so important that they move. The Winn family had lived in each of the ten regions at one time or another, and while Hayley wanted to be a supportive wife, she was getting tired of the relocations and the stress that went with them.

The stress was even more pronounced with Bert, who required much more preparation and expectation-setting than his neurotypical sister. While Ryan was an attentive and responsible father, he didn't really understand why things were so much harder for Bert. Though he loved both his kids, he related better to his daughter. Thus, more of Bert's caretaking and nurturing fell on Hayley.

When Bert was diagnosed with ASD, Hayley immediately began learning as much as she could about autism. She took copious notes on Bert's actions, what made him happy, what agitated him. She worked hard at creating as much stability in Bert's life as she could, particularly considering their frequent moves. Each time they were given orders to move to a new location, she took detailed pictures of their current home to record what was in each room and where it was located, as well as the wall colors and flooring types. When setting up the new home, she would diligently recreate these elements of the previous home to try to reduce the impact and stress of the move for Bert. He was agitated by changes, so she would do all she could to alleviate his stress. Hayley dutifully accepted this responsibility without complaint or making her daughter feel as if Bert was favored over her.

At 7:25, Bert went upstairs to his room to make his bed and get ready for his first day at Academy. As with prior moves, the first day of school in a new place was always stressful. He had been through it so many times, though, that the change in routine almost felt like routine itself. He began to accept that each September he would start a new school, and while it was trying, expecting the change each September helped alleviate the stress. After showering at 7:30, he brushed his teeth at 7:45, and headed back to his room at 7:50 to get dressed. His room was sparsely appointed with a bed, nightstand, dresser, and closet. On his nightstand was a lamp he had since he was five. On his dresser were three pictures lined up like soldiers; one of his family, one of the family cat that died when he was ten, and one of him when he was eight. Each evening before bed he would lay the clothes he planned to wear the next day on the floor at the foot of his bed. The shirt, pants, socks and shoes looked like someone had been lying there, then suddenly melted into the floor leaving his clothes behind. Bert always wore button-down shirts because he hated how it felt to pull a shirt over his head. Because he was sensitive to certain fabrics, all his shirts were cotton. It was important to him to follow the same dressing routine every morning. At 7:58 he left his room. He grabbed his backpack and approached his mother to kiss her goodbye. Being careful not to get too close, he and his mother followed their ritual of pretending there was a beach ball between them when they kissed hello and goodbye. It was a compromise that Hayley had to negotiate with Bert; she wanted him to kiss her but had to respect his discomfort with being touched. They created an imaginary beach ball that gently squeezed between their chests, which caused them to extend their necks over it to peck each other on the cheek. Though it looked peculiar, it was the closest Hayley could get to her son.

"Have a good day, Bert."

"OK."

"I love you, Bert."

"OK, bye."

Out the door by 8:00, right on schedule for the seven-minute walk to the bus stop.

Bert started down the narrow Naples streets. He and Hayley had practiced the route three times to ensure Bert could make it to the bus stop without getting lost. During his practice runs, he memorized many of the sights, sounds, and smells along the way. He walked by a bakery and smelled warm crusty bread. He looked at the loaves in the window and imagined a jack-in-the-box wearing a rainbow wig popping out from the center of a loaf. He walked by a *salumeria* and heard the *chop chop chop* of the meat cleaver cutting into a marbled rib roast. He saw the different cuts of meat and imagined re-assembling them to create a cow version of Frankenstein's creature. This imagery was typical for Bert. He would see something, then imagine something that to neurotypicals would be completely bizarre. To him it was completely normal, and he thought it was fun to have such a vivid imagination. At the same time, if he was interested in a topic, he could apply acute focus and describe even the most minute details of the subject. There was a tree on the way to the bus stop that fascinated Bert. From memory, he could tell you all the carvings on the tree, the dent from where a scooter hit the tree years ago, and the branches that were trimmed away so people could walk unobstructed. He didn't understand why others didn't have the same attention to detail he did.

"Take a right at the *gelateria*, then the Academy bus stop is ahead 200 paces on the left," he thought as he approached the *gelateria*. He turned right and started counting steps. He could see the bus stop with three boys standing there. He walked up to the bus stop and sat at the bench, not saying a word. Paul, Caleb, and Sal stared as Bert quietly sat. Paul introduced himself then introduced Bert to Caleb and Sal. Sal attempted to pat Bert on the shoulder in his greeting, But Bert backed away to avoid being touched.

"What's wrong with you?" Sal asked.

"I don't like being touched."

"Whatever, dork." Sal shook his head at being rebuffed by Bert.

The bus could be seen coming up the street, the words *Naples Academy* in red above the windshield. The bus came to a stop and the door opened. The leather-faced bus driver had a half-smoked unlit cigar in the corner of his mouth. "Get in boys."

FIRST DAY AT ACADEMY
2030

The four boarded the bus. Caleb sat down in a seat near the back of the bus and Paul next to him. Seeing how upset his cousin was, Paul tried some light conversation with Caleb to lift his spirits. Bert sat in the empty front seat right behind the bus driver, slid over to the window, and cast his gaze outside the window. He reasoned that sitting behind the bus driver would be the least popular seat, reducing the likelihood of someone sitting next to him. Sal sat in the cool kids section, the back of the bus.

The ride from the bus stop to Academy was about 30 minutes from Naples' Chiaia quarter along the southern edge of Villa Comunale Park to the Capodichino district. The bus traveled eastbound along the Port of Naples Seaport, picking up students at four stops. With each opening of the door, a waft of salty sea air entered the bus. Sitting right behind the bus driver, Bert would turn his head toward the door each time it opened and take in the cool salty breeze. He closed his eyes and imagined a man made of sea salt boarding the bus and blowing the breeze on his face, then leaving the bus before the driver shut the door. After hearing the door swoosh shut, he would imagine Sea Salt Man waving at him until the next stop where he would board, blow, and leave again. At the central point of the seaport, the bus turned north on its way to Academy. The cool salty air was quickly replaced by the smoggy warmer air of the city center. The streets were bustling with cars, scooters, bicycles, and pedestrians all making their way to work, school, and errands. Row after row of drying laundry pinned to clotheslines flapped in the wind. The traffic was the usual stop-and-go for a weekday morning, allowing plenty of time to take in the sounds, smells, and sights of the city.

As the bus reached Academy, the students unloaded the bus, congregating at the front of the school. Bert had practiced a couple of times with his mother the week before to make sure he knew where his classes were and what to expect. A tone, then a deep-throated voice over the PA system, "Welcome students, it's now 9:00. Please report to first period class by 9:10." The students dispersed: Bert to world history, Caleb to remedial math, Sal to advanced chemistry, and Paul to macroeconomics. They had six periods of classes with an hour for lunch. Extracurricular clubs and sports began at 4:10, sometimes continuing as late as 7:00 p.m. Times were strictly adhered to, with demerits given to students who broke Academy rules, which included fighting, swearing, and tardiness. For regular students, demerits affected class ranking. For students in the tiering program, demerits translated to infractions which pushed a tier one guest into tier two. Neither Paul nor Bert were concerned about demerits, they were rule-followers and weren't concerned about consequences. For Caleb, demerits meant infractions that would lead to guesting into the dreaded tier two. For Sal, demerits could impact his class ranking, and jeopardize the number one ranking he so craved. They were both motivated by fear; Caleb the fear of embarrassment and Sal the fear of not being number one.

At lunchtime, Bert sat at a table by himself eating his homemade lunch of ricotta cheese and tomato on *friselle* bread. Seeing Bert, Paul came up to the table with his potato-filled pasta with garlic olive oil and sat across from him. "Hey, Bert." Paul said.

"Hi."

Caleb approached with his Neapolitan pizza and sat next to Paul.

"These classes suck. I hate this place!" Caleb said

"Give it time Caleb, you need that 3.0 to get out of you-know-what." Caleb forgot Paul knew he was in the tiering program and that the only way out was no infractions and a 3.0 grade point average.

"They still suck."

Sal came over with his spaghetti and seafood sauce and sat next to Bert, intentionally sitting close enough to him so their shoulders were touching, "Hey, dork," Sal said.

Bert shuffled his chair away from Sal. "Don't touch me!" Bert blurted. As Sal started to inch his chair toward Bert to continue his teasing, Paul calmly got up and stood over Sal.

"Back off, Sal." Paul said while looking down at the still-sitting Sal.

Sal stood up and faced Paul. "What're you gonna do about it?" Sal's nose was nearly touching the bridge of Paul's, him being an inch taller, wanting to intimidate Paul.

Paul wasn't having it. "Don't do anything that'll get you demerits. Be cool."

Demerits. Sal hated the thought of demerits. It wasn't worth getting into a tussle with Paul. "All good, man." Sal said as he backed down. Paul quietly went back to his chair and continued eating. Sal moved his chair away from Bert to avoid their shoulders touching.

"Thank you," Bert said to Sal.

The rest of lunch consisted of idle small talk, first about football, then about girls. "Check her out." Sal said pointing to a blonde-haired girl sitting at the table next to them.

"I'd tap that!" Caleb said.

Caleb and Sal continued their adolescent banter, Paul and Bert didn't engage. Bert was reciting facts he had learned from the morning's history classes under his breath in between bites. Paul could have played along but didn't find chattering about girls, particularly locker-room talk, the least bit interesting.

The 1:00 tone rang, lunch was over, off to fourth period. Before leaving, Bert approached Paul.

"Thank you," Bert said putting out his clenched hand to fist-bump Paul.

Paul fist-bumped Bert, "No problem."

Extracurricular activities started after sixth period. Buses left Academy starting at 4:15 then every hour until the last bus at 7:15. Sal went to football practice, then home on the 7:15. Paul went to debate club and left on the 6:15. Bert attended history club and caught the 5:15. Not wanting to spend any more time at Academy than necessary, Caleb left promptly at 4:15.

Caleb's bus ride home was awash with anger about the tiering program, his small and hairless stature, and the incessant teasing from his older brothers. He knew that when he walked in the door his older brothers would be there, ready to harass him. His mind flashed back and forth between hating Academy, hating his home life, hating his appearance. He decided to get off the bus and hang out at Villa Comunale Park until dinnertime at 6:00. This became his routine almost every day, rain or shine. He slowly walked around the park, made his way along the pathway flanked by knee-high grass, empty liquor bottles, and strewn rubbish that littered the once-beautiful park. He knew every graffiti marking on every statue and took note of freshly-painted tags which seemed to show up weekly. He thought about his life, dreading the thought of being nothing more than a shipyard worker like his father. He believed he was meant to be more, but he had no idea what "more" meant. He wished that dinner was later in the evening to minimize the time he had to spend with his brothers, but also knew his mother was adamant about eating at 6:00 and didn't want to experience her wrath for being late. Caleb made his way to their apartment, arriving at 5:55. Philip was there waiting for him.

"Hey, Tiny One!" Philip said.

Not saying anything, Caleb thought, "Here we go again."

After debate club, Paul got on the 6:15. On the bus ride home, he stared out the window and thought about how much he loved debate club. Getting into sparring matches, looking for argument angles, and coming up with winning discussion strategies was a real rush for him. This coupled with his humble exterior made him a wolf in sheep's clothing for debate opponents. He knew he needed to maintain a mild-mannered exterior to keep his opponents off-balance, skills he wanted to hone in debate club. As the bus approached his stop, he remembered he promised to help his father after dinner at the supermarket. He got off at his stop and walked home, enjoying the warm dusk of early evening. He walked in the front door to find his mother preparing dinner.

"Paolo!" his mother said, kissing him on the cheek.

After football practice, Sal showered and caught the 7:15. On the bus ride home Sal thought about his father's high expectations and what he would say at dinner to please him. He thought about telling him about the difficulty of his classes and how he was planning to ace them, how he would graduate number one in his class and not get any demerits. He then thought about how he backed down to Paul at lunch and how that would not make the list of dinner topics. He knew his father would see that as a sign of weakness, further feeding the inadequate narrative. As he got off the bus and walked home, he thought about his mother, and if this would be another night of puking. He opened the door and went into the kitchen where she was making pizza.

"Hi honey, pizza tonight."

"Great. Is Dad home?"

"Just you and me for dinner. He's working late."

Sal felt the relief of not having to face his father and enjoying a peaceful dinner with just his mother. Hopefully she'd be able to keep the pizza down.

Bert boarded the 5:15 bus after history club. Knowing that dinner was at 6:00 sharp every night, he knew that the 5:15 bus would get him in the door just in time for dinner. On the ride home Bert recited history fact after fact. He absorbed them like a sponge, it was as if he had unlimited capacity for remembering details and could recall information like a computer retrieves information from a database. Riding along the seaport, Bert thought about Sea-Salt Man each time the bus door opened. He kept watching the time to make sure he could be home in time for dinner at 6:00. Knowing his walk was seven minutes and needing two minutes after arriving home to get ready for dinner, that meant the bus had to be at his stop no later than 5:51. With each minute Bert watched the time to ensure the bus would get to his stop by 5:51. He felt himself getting agitated out of concern that the bus might be late, but was relieved when it arrived at 5:50. Bert walked home in seven minutes and arrived at his front door at 5:57. His mother was setting the table.

"Hi, Bert," his mother said leaning forward to kiss Bert in her beach ball stance.

"Hi," Bert said meeting his mother's kiss with the imaginary ball between them.

"How was Academy?"

"I like my history classes, one guy is nice, one guy is a jerk, and one guy is short." Bert gave his blunt assessment of his day. "Maybe the nice guy will be my friend." Bert's mother gave a warm smile. She had been praying for years that Bert would finally have a friend, his first ever. Perhaps this would be the year.

MARIE
2031

Marie had been losing weight, her skin and eyes getting more and more yellow. She hated doctors and hadn't seen one since Sal was born. It was the pain in her stomach and back that changed Sal from concerned to scared, and convinced Marie to see a doctor. She scheduled an appointment for January 6 at 9 a.m. When the doctor saw her skin and eyes and rapid weight loss he had an idea what it was but needed confirmation. "Marie, I want you to have a CT scan, we need a better look at what's going on." Marie went for a CT scan that afternoon. That evening the doctor called her.

"Can you come in tomorrow morning at 8:30?" he asked.

"Yes, what's the problem?"

"There are some abnormalities showing up in the CT scan, we'll discuss what I'm seeing and treatment options tomorrow."

"I'll be there. Thank you." Marie hung up.

Gene had just finished a conference call in his home office and saw Marie sitting at the kitchen table, expressionless. "Who was that?" he asked.

"The doctor, he wants to see me again tomorrow morning."

"I'm sure everything is alright, Gene said."

"If it were nothing, he wouldn't want to see me again so soon."

Gene had noticed the changes in Marie's appearance, but also knew how much she hated doctors. He chose to say nothing, which made Marie feel that he didn't care about her. His "everything is alright" comment fueled her feelings. She was scared and felt alone in her dismay.

Sal came home from Academy to find his mother sitting at the table, staring into space and looking upset. Gene had already gone into his home office to start another call with his staff in Chicago.

"What's wrong, Mom?"

Marie needed a sympathetic ear. "I went to the doctor today and he sent me to get a CT scan, now he wants to see me tomorrow morning." Trying best not to alarm Sal, Marie spoke in a sobering tone, avoiding crying but also not taking the situation too lightly.

"What else did he say?" Sal asked.

"Just that he wants to talk about what he saw and treatment options." The gravity of events caught up with her. "I'm so scared, Sal." She dropped her head down on the table, trying to keep her sobs to herself. Sal pulled his chair next to her and held her as she cried. Sal just sat there holding her, hearing his father's muffled conference call in the other room as backdrop to his mother's quiet weeping.

Sal insisted on going with Marie to the doctor appointment. She didn't bother asking Gene, as she knew he was giving a presentation to Miconal's board of directors that he couldn't miss.

Sal and Marie sat down at the desk in her doctor's office, waiting for him to come in. The room was completely quiet except for the *tick tock* of a vintage clock that hung on the wall. The two sat there, neither saying a word, trying to prepare for whatever the doctor might say. The door opened, the doctor came in wearing a white coat with a stethoscope around his neck.

"Hello, Marie."

"Hello, this is my son, Sal."

"Hi, doc," Sal said as he shook his hand.

The doctor sat down at his desk, Marie's file already sitting on top. He opened it to the CT results. He spoke calmly but got to the point.

"Marie, the CT scan suggests you have cancer of the pancreas. I've already made an appointment for you to see our practice's oncologist today at 9:00 to discuss next steps. I'm concerned enough that we need to move quickly."

"How long do I have?" Both Marie's mother and father died a very slow and painful death due to cancer, and she had been the primary caretaker for both. The experience of watching her parents suffer through cancer contributed to her hate of doctors, not because of who they were as people, but because of the news they brought with them.

"It's too early to tell, which is why I want you to see the oncologist right away."

Marie and the doctor continued to talk about Marie's diagnosis. Sal's own thoughts drowned out their conversation, remembering how his mother cared for her parents as they fought cancer. He had watched her try to keep a strong face in front of them, then break down when they weren't around. He hated seeing his grandparents suffer and the emotional toll it took on his mother.

"Sal, do you have any questions?" the doctor asked, waking Sal from his brief daydream.

"Can it be cured?"

"We'll do our best, Sal," the doctor said.

Sal nodded in response. *We'll do our best* was no better than a *no* to Sal.

"Dr. Sciortino is one of the best oncologists out there. He'll take good care of you. His office is just down the hall, he's expecting you."

The doctor got up, shook both Marie's and Sal's hands and led them out of his office.

Marie saw Dr. Sciortino, who ran more tests that confirmed Marie's cancer was at stage III. She was immediately scheduled for surgery to remove part of her pancreas, then chemotherapy treatments would follow. Sal had to watch her fiery red hair fall out in clumps as she continued chemo treatments. When she was home, nurses cared for her during the day, but in the evening Sal assumed the role of primary caretaker. Gene was in denial and poured himself into his work rather than deal with Marie's declining condition. Sal watched his once-dignified mother suffer the shame of having her son clean her up after getting sick and using the toilet when nurses weren't there. She would hold her hands to her face in embarrassment as Sal tended to her, distraught at Sal seeing and touching her most private parts. Despite the chemo, her condition progressed to stage IV. She was in and out of the hospital, with Dr. Sciortino trying all he could to counteract the aggressive cancer. After Marie was admitted to the hospital for a fifth time in May, Dr. Sciortino came into her room while Sal and Gene were sitting with her. He laid out the facts as best he could.

"Marie, right now we need to keep you comfortable." Marie remembered that term--it meant she was going to die. She'd been preparing for him to say the words and was ready to accept it. Sal wasn't.

"What does that mean?" Sal said.

"It means we need to minimize her pain."

"Does that mean she's going to die?" Sal's anxiety escalated.

"Yes."

Sal looked at his mother, who was lying in the bed, a comforting smile on her face, being strong for her son, having accepted her fate. He then looked at Gene, expressionless, looking at Marie, finally acknowledging she was going to die. Sal couldn't hold himself back.

"Why weren't you around more for her? Why didn't you care for her? She needed you and you weren't there!" Years of frustration came out of Sal toward Gene, the self-absorbed man who put his career in front of his family, set impossible-to-achieve expectations for Sal, and let Sal step in as caretaker when it should have been him doing it. For the first time in his life Gene just sat there--no snappy retort, no snide comment, no *you're not good enough* critiques. Worst of all, no apology. He just sat there quiet. And it made Sal livid.

Marie lived for three more weeks then died on June 2, 2031. She had an open-casket wake followed by a graveside service. Before they closed her casket, Sal put a note in her hand, a promise he was determined to keep for the rest of his life: *The day will come when no one dies from cancer and I'm going to make it happen. I just wish I could have helped you. I'm so sorry, Mom. I love you.*

GRADUATION
2034

Sweat started to well under Paul's black graduation cap. Already a humid 32 degrees Celsius at 9:30 a.m., Paul wished he hadn't worn a jacket and tie under his long black gown. He stood with the 240 Academy graduates waiting outside the campus football stadium. "Where did the time go?" he thought. Their first day at Academy seemed like yesterday, now after four years they were graduating.

Caleb spotted him and came over.

"We're out of here!" Caleb said as he gave his cousin a huge hug, not bothering to contain his enthusiasm.

"Good job, Caleb."

"Yeah, thanks for the pep talks."

Pep talks between Paul and Caleb were a regular occurrence during the four years at Academy. With the continued threat of tier two looming over Caleb, he was constantly on edge that he would do something that would get him guested. When Caleb was agitated over some perceived act of unfairness toward him, Paul's smooth, reassuring words were the perfect antidote to Caleb's flustered demeanor. It only took a few minutes for Caleb to calm down after talking with Paul. Had Paul not been at Academy, Caleb would have most certainly been guested into tier two.

Sal stood by himself, looking out over the infield grass and into the stands where parents and guests were sitting. He spotted his father, then noticed an empty seat next to him. He teared up at the sight of the empty seat. It didn't matter to him that his father was there.

She wasn't there, that's what was killing him.

Bert gazed out over the infield, preoccupied with the seat and stage configuration. He looked out over the 240 white chairs--one for each graduating student--perfectly lined up on the infield grass in ten rows of 24. He observed the black stage with 30 white chairs for faculty and special guests behind a large podium. He imagined a man made of flames arising from the podium, generating the sweltering heat of the morning. Flame Man's arms thrashed in concert with the orchestra's dissonant toots and plucks as the musicians warmed up. His flailing stopped when the musicians quieted at the raising of the orchestra conductor's baton, then Flame Man's arms fluidly moved in conjunction with the conductor's baton when the orchestra began playing.

At 9:45 the students began their entrance to the stadium, followed by faculty and special guests. Academy's dean of students then approached the podium, signaling to the conductor to stop the music. He began his welcome address. "Students, parents, friends, families, guests, and faculty; welcome to the Naples Academy 2034 graduation ceremony!" He barely finished his sentence before being interrupted by clapping and whooping from the students. The dean continued with his welcome, introduced the special guests, then invited the student with the number one academic ranking to approach the podium and be recognized. Sal seethed as Paul rose from his chair, walked up the stairs to the stage, shook the dean's hand, and accepted a silver plaque recognizing his achievement. Paul and Sal were the only two students with 4.0 grade point averages, but Sal received two demerits due to fighting at football games. Because Paul had received no demerits, he was ranked number one. He hated not adding that plaque to his trophies, but he would have given up all his trophies just to have his mother there.

Three special guests added their congratulations and provided their advice to the graduating students. The dean then approached the podium to begin handing out diplomas. Paul stood with the first row of alphabetically arranged students. They exited their row to the right and walked to the stairway at the right end of the stage. One by one, they ascended the two stairs and waited at the top until their name was called. Paul was fourth in line. As he made his way to the stage, he flashed back over his four years at Academy. Aside from having a perfect grade point average, Paul continued to display a remarkable ability as a debater. It didn't matter the topic, Paul could structure and execute a winning argument regardless of whether he personally believed in the position. Paul had a knack for knowing what to say and just as importantly, what *not* to say. He never went on a date. He wasn't anti-girl, he just had better things to do. During his third year at Academy Paul decided that he wanted to be an economist. He applied and was given a scholarship to the London School of Economics. The scholarship was another blessing for his family, allowing Paul to go to an elite school his parents couldn't afford otherwise.

"Paolo James Ambrosi," The dean announced. Paul walked up to the podium, accepted his diploma, shook the dean's hand, descended the left stairway, and returned to his seat. From the moment his name was announced, he could hear people cheering for him, most of all his parents and siblings. At 14, he didn't pay attention to public accolades, but at 18 he was much more aware of people cheering. And he liked it.

Sal's row stood up to get diplomas. After Marie's funeral, Sal and his father became more like roommates than father and son. Gene continued to focus on his work, paying less and less attention to Sal. His once-high expectations of Sal gave way to indifference. Sal responded by modeling his father's behavior, putting his all into his Academy experience. Sal learned to be completely self-sufficient, not expecting or getting any help from his father. He became obsessed with the vicious disease that took his mother from him so suddenly. Except for football, his classes and extracurricular activities all had a singular focus--to eradicate cancer.

"Salvatore Eugenio Carlotta," the dean announced. Sal walked toward the podium, accepted his diploma, shook the dean's hand, and left the stage. As he walked back to his seat he could see his father talking on his phone, oblivious to Sal getting his diploma. "God, I hate him." College at Columbia couldn't happen fast enough for Sal. He was so done with his father, the further away from him the better.

Rows three, four, five, then six left their seats in single file to receive their diplomas. In row nine, Caleb was counting the minutes until he didn't need to step foot at this hellhole of a school again. During his four years at Academy he grew eight inches, topping out at five feet ten. Puberty sprouted in year two, with Caleb growing a wispy mustache that he filled in with mascara to help him look older.

Caleb succeeded in steering clear of tier two. In four years, he never committed an infraction that caused him to be guested, but because he never achieved a 3.0 grade point average, he remained in the tiering program. Knowing he was always one infraction away from being guested to tier two motivated him to behave, and hung over his head like a looming storm.

History, math, science, they all were a waste of time to Caleb. "Just get by," he would think as each semester started. In his second year at Academy, he decided to take an introduction to holograms class. This was nothing like he experienced in any of his prior classes. The class was so easy for him, the concepts made sense, and he could see how his knowledge of holograms could be useful later in life. He aced the class, the first time ever doing so. Holograms became his obsession, and he learned everything he could about them. He sat by himself each day after school leaning against the Enrico Pessina statue at Villa Comunale. He talked with imaginary holograms, fancying a world where lonely people would never be lonely again. His hologram friends would be loyal. His hologram friends wouldn't judge. His hologram friends would be supportive. His hologram friends would be there when he wanted them and go away when he didn't. In his world, hologram friends were the elixir to loneliness.

Row nine stood up. Caleb made his way to the stage. "Caleb Devin Todd," the dean announced. Caleb walked to the podium, accepted his diploma, gave the dean the finger, and walked off the stage back to his seat. That would have gotten him guested into tier two. Small victory.

Row ten stood up. Bert was the third from the last student in the row. During his four years at Academy, Bert excelled in anything and everything related to history. In his mind there was no changing history, and no interpretation of history, it either happened or it didn't. It just made so much sense.

Prior to Academy, Bert never lived in one place more than a year. His father worked at NSA Naples without new transfer orders for four years, allowing Bert to stay at Academy. This was the longest that Bert had been in any one place in his entire life, and he loved the stability and predictability. It also allowed him to build a friendship for the first time. From the first day at Academy, Paul defended him and proved himself to be a loyal and trusted friend. Paul and Bert went to movies together, shared an occasional Neapolitan pizza, and just hung out. Paul understood that Bert would get overwhelmed after about two hours of socialization and timed his visits with Bert to stay within the two-hour window. Paul also modeled positive behaviors on how to interact with others, how to use judgment in what to say, and when to not blurt out whatever was on his mind. Paul was Bert's only friend, but there was no better friend he could have had.

Bert made his way up the stage stairs. "Bertrand Allen Winn," the dean announced. Bert walked to the podium, accepted his diploma, extended a guarded handshake and walked off the stage. Ryan and Hayley Winn were both in tears seeing their son graduate from Academy. As Bert walked back to his seat, Paul left his seat, walked up to Bert, and fist-bumped him.

"Good job, man!" Paul said.

"Thank you."

After the final diplomas were awarded, the dean announced, "Ladies and gentlemen, let me be the first to present to you the Naples Academy graduating class of 2034!" Joyful hollers filled the stadium with the launching of sweat-soaked graduation caps being thrown in the air. It was a race run well, but much more difficult races awaited the four.

COLUMBIA
2034

T he girl sitting next to Sal on the plane had red hair and blue eyes, reminding him of his mother. While he did not discriminate on who he hooked up with, he had a penchant for red hair and blue eyes. She had just closed her book and shut her eyes. Now it was time to make his move.

"So, what's taking you to New York?" Sal asked.

She opened her eyes and looked over at Sal. "Finally, he's talking to me," she thought.

"NYU," she answered.

"Cool, Columbia."

Awkward pause. She didn't know anyone in New York, but she thought he was so cute. She kept the conversation going. "What's your major?" She asked.

"Biomedical engineering with an emphasis in oncology."

"Political science then law school." She hoped they would have a common interest through their major, but it wasn't happening. A question would keep him talking. "What's oncology?"

"The study of cancers." Sal said. He liked that she asked him a question and wanted to keep the conversation going.

"How did you get interested in that?" She asked.

"My mother died of cancer." Sal rubbed his eye as if to wipe a tear away to continue his act.

"So sorry about your mom," she said. Cute and sensitive, someone she might want to get to know better. They chit-chatted through the rest of the flight.

"Here's my number, coffee sometime?" She asked as the jet pulled up to the gate.

"I'll message you later this week." Sal said.

Mission accomplished. He said and did all the right things to get her number. That's all that mattered to him.

Getting women to sleep with him was a competition. He kept pictures of women on his phone with notes on how long it took him to get them to bed, his electronic "notch-on-the-belt" triumphs. Like his trophies in his bedroom, he regularly perused the pictures, reveling in his conquests. Even though he had the pictures, he had long forgotten most of their names. The redhead with blue eyes he met on the plane would make it into his collection, her name soon to be forgotten like so many others.

Most students attended college within their home ethnarchies. For Sal to attend Columbia, there would typically be a process of filing for student visa applications, interviews, and waiting for months with no guarantee of approval. That is, unless you were well connected with a fat checkbook. Sal's father knew how to work the system and grease the palm of the right bureaucrat who approved Sal's student visa in one meeting. Sal wanted to be away from his father, and his father was content for Sal to be away from him.

A Ph.D. in biomedical engineering took a typical student eight to nine years to achieve. Typical wasn't in Sal's lexicon, he set his sights on finishing in seven. Extra classes during the school year, summer sessions, schmoozing the professors. Doable for Sal. What else would he spend time doing? His mother was dead, he hated his father, and he had no one else in his life who meant anything to him. He decided to fast-track his bachelor's degree in three years, then an additional four to get his Ph.D. He scheduled time with his biomedical engineering advisor Dr. Allen to talk through his plans.

"Sal, good to meet you," Dr. Allen said.

"Nice to meet you as well."

"So, I see you are entering Columbia from Naples Academy with a 4.0 GPA. Impressive."

"Thank you."

"I understand from your email that you want to be on a seven-year Ph.D. program, is that right?"

"Yes."

She removed her glasses and placed them on the desk. "Sal, no one has ever graduated the program in seven years. Even at eight years the work is intense. What's your rush?"

"Did you say no one has ever graduated in seven years?"

"That's right."

"I'll be the first."

Dr. Allen was taken aback by Sal's arrogance. "Sal, it took me eight years of intense study to get my Ph.D. You're a brand spanking new freshman who thinks he's going to school the rest of us and get it done in seven. Time for a reality check, young man."

Dr. Allen's condescending tone reminded Sal of his father. Seeing he wasn't going to get anywhere with her, he grabbed his backpack, forced a polite, "Thank you Dr. Allen," and left her office. Another person for Sal to prove wrong.

MASTER OF FAILURE
2034

Caleb couldn't get the words "shipyard worker" out of his head. He had no glamorous plan to attend a prestigious university, travel the world, or meet interesting people after graduating from Academy. He was destined for the shipyard, just like his father and brothers before him. He despised the thought but had to make money, so shipyard it was.

"I'm Caleb Todd, shipyard worker." He imagined being in a bar trying to pick up girls. "Who would be interested in a shipyard worker?" Caleb thought. While there were plenty of shipyard workers who earned an honest and happy living, for Caleb it was the lowest of the low. Yet unless something drastic happened to change his future, the best Caleb would achieve was becoming a shipyard foreman. "Caleb Todd, shipyard foreman" sounded like he wasn't an apprentice failure anymore, he was a master failure.

"Caleb, get the forklift and bring that pallet of rice to the loading dock," his foreman said.

"Rice pallet, check." As Caleb walked to the forklift, he imagined a hologram friend walking next to him. He started a conversation with his imaginary buddy.

"Hey Caleb Todd, shipyard failure," his imaginary friend said.

"Yeah, has a real ring to it," Caleb said.

"On your way to foreman failure."

"I can see it etched my headstone now, 'Here Lies Caleb Todd, Master of Failure.'"

Caleb reached the forklift, started it up, drove to the pallet staging area, and loaded a pallet on the forklift. His imaginary friend was sitting next to him.

"You're meant to be more than a shipyard worker," his imaginary friend said. "You're meant to be more."

'You're meant to be more' echoed in his head as he drove to the loading dock with his pallet. Then he heard the foreman's voice. "I said rice pallet! This is wheat! Come on Caleb, stay focused!" Caleb took the wheat pallet back hearing his imaginary friend repeating, "You're meant to be more."

That phrase.

It haunted him constantly. Every time he clocked in to work, every time he faced ridicule from his brothers, every time he saw a guy driving a convertible sports car with a beautiful woman sitting next to him, her hair blowing in the wind. He believed he was meant to be more, he just had no idea what or how.

LSE

2034

This wasn't Paul's first time in London. While at Academy, Paul and the debate team he led traveled there for a debate competition. He had very fond memories of London and looked forward to coming back. Paul deplaned at Heathrow and boarded a bus to his dormitory at London School of Economics. Paul sat down next to a man about his age. The man tried to push himself toward the window, reminding Paul of Bert and his not liking to be touched. Paul leaned toward the aisle to give him space. The man continued leaning away from Paul, his eyes cast out the window. As the bus headed east on M4 towards LSE, Paul pulled a bag of Bavarian pretzels from his backpack, opened it, and crunched down on one. He then tipped the open bag toward him. "Want one?" Paul asked.

"Yes," the man said, pulling one pretzel from the bag. There were no words uttered the rest of the bus trip, just Paul tipping the bag towards the man, the man grabbing a pretzel, then the synchronous crunching of the two men eating. Yes, he was just like Bert, and Paul knew how to make him feel comfortable.

The bus pulled into the LSE dormitory stop, and Paul offered the man one more pretzel, then stepped off the bus. About an hour later after he had settled into his room, the door swung open. It was the man from the bus. He had gotten off at the wrong stop so had to find another bus to take him back to the dormitory. Paul extended his hand, "I'm Paul."

"I'm Harry, your roommate."

"Yes, we're roommates, and we both like pretzels. I guess we're both a bit twisted." Paul joked, wondering if Harry would get the pun.

"Good one!" Harry chuckled. Roommate relationship off to a good start.

Deciding to give Harry time in the room by himself to unpack and get used to his surroundings, Paul went for a walk around campus. Despite the campus being in the middle of bustling central London, many of the streets around campus were pedestrian-only. As Paul walked the campus in the cloudy damp weather, he thought about his parents back in Naples, his time at Academy, his new roommate, his friend Bert, and his cousin Caleb. He was worried about Caleb and his unhappiness about working at the shipyard. "I need to stay in touch with Caleb," Paul thought. Walking by the library, he thought about how many big-boy steps it would take to get from the library to his dormitory. He started the calculation in his head and elongated his gait, to the amusement of onlookers.

DORM AT HOME
2034

Bert looked at the schematic he had drawn for his new study. "Do you want your desk over here?" Bert's father asked. One square on the graph paper equaled eight centimeters of floor space. The desk was 24 squares long and must be 12 squares from the wall. He got out his tape measure and measured 96 centimeters from the wall. "It goes here," pointing to the 96-centimeter mark on the tape measure. "Oh, and remember Paul is going to call me from LSE at 2:00."

Throughout his last year at Academy, Bert and his parents had talked a lot about what Bert would do after graduation. He had the grades and aptitude to attend university. The concern was the magnitude of change and how Bert would adapt. They discussed many options, including Bert going to LSE to be with his pal Paul. They decided that Bert should attend Naples University which was a 30-minute bus ride from home. He would attend classes, clubs, and social activities at NU but would live at home. A new study was set up in their home which simulated a dorm room. They decided to move Bert from his old room at the apartment to teach him to improve his skills at adapting to change, ensuring the study was laid out differently than his old room. Bert accepted the change and painstakingly laid out how his new study would look on graph paper, ensuring everything would have its place. His new study even had a small refrigerator, which Bert thought was a great addition to the room. To ensure stability during his college years, Bert's father accepted early retirement and became a cybersecurity consultant. With Bert's older sister already at university in Germany, Bert and his parents settled into their new normal of life.

Along with their discussions about where to attend college, Ryan and Hayley talked with Bert about what to major in. He clearly loved history and was exceptional at recalling facts, but what would a history major do in a post-college career? It was more important that he get a degree to build confidence in a subject he was passionate about. So Bert became a history major and took classes to help him with life skills and social interactions.

At 2 p.m. sharp Bert's phone rang. Paul's picture showed on the screen. "Hey, Paul!"

Her Name is Laura

2037

Bert and Paul talked every Sunday at 2 p.m. Naples time since starting college three years ago. Paul always called Bert, and Bert would make sure he was prepared for Paul's call. Bert had the same routine. He would go into his study at 1:55, get a bottle of water from his mini-fridge, sit in his beanbag chair, and wait for the call. Paul knew how important it was to Bert that he be on time and not miss a Sunday call, and Bert was thankful for Paul's dedication to their friendship. The calls were mostly small talk about classes, family, and clubs. Then Bert threw in a curve.

"I have a girlfriend; her name is Laura," Bert said.

"Dude! Tell me about her!"

"She's 21, just like me. She was sitting by herself eating lunch at the student union. I sat down at the table next to her and she started talking to me—it was more like she was talking *at* me. She went on and on for 15 minutes, then told me her autism made her nervous around people, which caused her to talk too much. She must have been real nervous, but I didn't mind. It was easier on me to not have to talk so much."

"What's she like?" Paul asked.

"Short brown hair, brown eyes, a little shorter than me. She's a math major and wants to be a math teacher. She found out she had autism at 17. She never had friends growing up, she has never been to a birthday party other than her own."

"That's sad, Dude."

Bert continued. "She was teased a lot growing up. Her parents didn't understand her, they wanted her to be normal. She said she could tell I was like her and just knew I would be nice to her and wouldn't tease her. I told her I knew what it was like to be teased and to me she was perfectly normal. I thought about how you were so nice to me. I was nice to her like you were nice to me. On Saturday I asked her to be my girlfriend and she said yes."

"That's amazing! Happy for you, man."

"She's coming over for dinner tonight at six. Mom and Dad are meeting her for the first time. They're excited to meet her. Dad is making eggplant parmigiana. I'm making tiramisu."

"Sounds great. Let me know how it goes!"

"OK, I should go now. Talk to you next week," Bert said.

"Good luck with Laura!"

Choosing to live at home and go to Naples University was a winning formula for Bert. In the three years since starting at NU, he maintained a 3.8 grade point average and took a part-time job at the school library. At the urging of his parents, he did something in his freshman year that he thought he'd never do. He joined speech club. His first speech assignment was to deliver a five-minute presentation about any topic he wanted. With his love of history, he decided to talk about the September 1943 Four Days of Naples battle. He prepared for 12 hours and wrote out extensive notes, fearful he would forget facts. He tossed and turned the night before the speech, worried about messing up his speech and being embarrassed. The next day he showed up at speech club with notes in hand and butterflies in his stomach. He was third in line to go. As the first two speakers went he felt the anxiety build and the slight drip of sweat roll down the side of his face onto on his collar. Then it was his turn. He slowly walked to the podium and looked out over the 30 classmates comprising the audience. As he panned left to right he remembered a Bible verse his mother told him the night before, *Psalm 46:10: Be still and know that I am God.* He imagined himself being still, calm and quiet standing in front of God, sensing that God would be with him through his speech. He felt a quiet peace come over him, the butterflies in his stomach dissipating. He then delivered a perfect speech on what happened during the 1943 uprising in Naples against the German forces occupying the city. He never looked at his notes; only relying on his memory. He finished in exactly five minutes, then heard an enthusiastic round of applause from his audience. For Bert, this five-minute speech was a turning point in his life. It was five minutes of him being the center of attention and speaking authoritatively on a topic without stammering or panicking. It was the first of many outstanding speeches he would give in his lifetime.

HARVARD

2037

Paul had encouraged Bert to join speech club for weeks. Paul knew how good it would be for Bert to conquer his paralyzing fear of public speaking, and that it would open up opportunities for him later in life. Paul saw potential in Bert that most others didn't see. He just needed support and encouragement which Paul was gifted in supplying.

Paul maintained a 4.0 grade point average in his first three years at LSE, culminating in a BSc in economics and politics. Paul was active in debate club, continuing to hone his ability to craft arguments and deepen his ability to influence others through his use of words. He did private tutoring for fellow LSE students in math, history, and political science. He regularly volunteered at a local shelter for homeless teenagers, tutoring them in science, technology, and math as well as serving meals and offering encouragement. He went on dates, but after a couple of times out with a girl he would lose interest and break it off. His ability to develop and maintain close one-on-one relationships was his Achilles heel. Bert was his only real friend; others were just acquaintances. He simply didn't care.

Paul's interest in politics continued to grow through his three years at LSE. While he didn't consider himself a politician, he was drawn to make the world a better place. He was deeply concerned with the ten-ethnarchy world structure and saw it as being ripe for corruption, with so much power being consolidated in so few people. He decided that if he were ever to enter politics, he needed a law degree, and he needed to get experience outside the Europe Ethnarchy. He'd always been fascinated with the idea of living in the

United States. He applied to five law schools but one was his favorite. He wanted to be a Harvard man, and Harvard was where he ultimately went. Going to Boston, it turned out, would be an ideal choice for what he was to do after he graduated.

SOLVING LONELINESS
2037

The phrase "You're meant to be more" haunted Caleb for three years since graduating from Academy. His life was shipyard worker by day, partier at night. Sometimes he partied with friends and acquaintances, sometimes at home with his imaginary friends. While he enjoyed his time out with other people and the occasional female conquest, he loved his world of imaginary hologram friends most. In his hologram world he controlled everything; who he was friends with, when and where they would appear, what they would do.

What he cherished most was unconditional acceptance, even by people who only existed in his imagination.

Caleb looked up to his cousin Paul, he was someone who was going to make something of his life. They occasionally talked on the phone, mostly about Paul reassuring Caleb that he was not a failure at life and if he wanted to do something other than being a shipyard worker, he should pursue it. Caleb talked with him many times about his fascination with holograms. Paul encouraged Caleb's fascination, but also saw warning signs that Caleb was slipping more and more into an imaginary world, one he seemed to prefer over the real world. During one of their discussions, Paul decided to probe deeper on Caleb's obsession.

"What do your hologram friends give you that real friends don't?" Paul asked.

"They like me for who I am. They don't judge me. They are around when I want them and gone when I don't. I could be in a room full of real people and still feel lonely because no one pays attention to me. I never feel lonely with my hologram friends."

"I can see how you'd feel that way. I feel lonely at times too. It's painful."

Paul had an idea. "We've talked about how you're not happy at the shipyard. You're fascinated with the idea of hologram friends. There are certainly other lonely people in the world. How can you use hologram technology to help others who struggle with loneliness?"

The question gave Caleb pause. He never thought about creating something that would help others overcome loneliness. And how could he make money at it? Could this be the answer to his 'You were meant to be more' dilemma that had haunted him for years?

After about a minute of silence, Caleb responded. "I never thought of it like that. I need to think about it."

Once again Paul knew just what to say to his cousin. "OK, let me know if you want to talk more. Talk to you later, Cuz."

"Later." Caleb hung up, still rocked by Paul's question. He typed, "How do I solve the problem of loneliness and make money at it?" on his phone and set it as his screen saver. He grew determined to find the answer.

DOPPIO TIME
2037

S al looked at the clock in his room, 10 p.m. Time for a doppio espresso with two teaspoons of sugar. Sal was studying for his last final before graduation. He put two scoops of kopi luwak coffee beans in the grinder. He liked the eccentricity of drinking kopi luwak, the beans being harvested from the feces of the civet cat and 20 times more expensive than average coffee beans. Sal drank kopi luwak coffee partly for the taste, partly for the image. He ground the beans to a fine consistency, dumped the grounds into the espresso machine basket, tamped the grounds, added two teaspoons of sugar, and brewed the sugar and coffee mixture. The espresso dripped into a waiting cup, forming a beige crema head on the brew. He brought the cup to first his nose, smelled the nutty aroma, and then to his mouth. He closed his eyes and tilted his head back as the mix of bitter, sweet and velvety crema slowly trickled across his tongue and down his throat. Like a Pavlovian dog drooling at the sound of a bell, his doppio was a signal that he would be up another four hours studying.

For three years at Columbia, Sal survived on four hours of sleep a night, thanks to his Sunday through Thursday evening doppio fix. Friday and Saturday evenings were reserved for drinking and adding pictures of women to his phone, which now numbered over a hundred. None more than a couple of hookups, then off to the next.

As Sal wrapped up studying for his last final, he recalled the meeting with his advisor at the beginning of freshman year; how she condescendingly told him there was no way he would get his Ph.D. in seven years. Getting his bachelor's in three years was the beginnings of proving her wrong, which he desperately wanted to do. He aced every class, attacking the hardest classes like a bull seeing a red flag. He was out to prove himself as the best. His father, whom he so despised and hadn't talked to in three years, lived in him. The person he hated the most was precisely who he was turning into.

In his second year of undergrad, Sal took an elective class on organ-on-a-chip technology. OOC was a microfluidic chip that simulated a human organ's function. Originally used in drug testing, OOC technology had advanced to the point where a chip could be implanted in a person's body to replace lost functions in major organs. The technology and its possibilities fascinated Sal. What if this technology had been available when his mother was diagnosed with pancreatic cancer? Could it have saved her? Could she still be alive today? He couldn't get the questions out of his mind, and they fed his determination to be the person to find cancer's cure.

ORGAN-ON-A-CHIP
2041

Columbia's department of biomedical engineering was preparing a public relations piece to tout the groundbreaking research its faculty and students were conducting. Sal's organ-on-a-chip project was one of three featured projects. During Sal's four years of graduate work in biomedical engineering, he passed all the required classes in biomedical signals and controls, biomedical measurements, and statistics just fine. Organ-on-a-chip technology, though, captured his fascination ever since he first studied it in undergrad. He read everything about OOC that he could get his hands on. He received a grant to further study OOC, resulting in research findings that caught the interest of the medical community.

At 2:45, the interviewer and her cameraman showed up at the lab. "Are you Sal?"

Sal looked up and saw his interviewer, a striking brunette in her late twenties, and no wedding ring. Sal nodded.

"I'm Elise Thompson. I'll be interviewing you for the biomedical engineering PR video."

"Nice to meet you." Sal said.

"Here's how it'll work. We'll stand at this counter together with your rat subject in front of us so viewers can see it. Does it have a name?"

"He."

"Excuse me?"

"It's a he, not an it." Sal took a strong affinity to his lab subjects. He also liked putting Elise off balance with the trivial correction.

"Sorry, does he have a name?" She didn't see the point in making a big deal about 'he' versus 'it' but didn't make an issue of it.

"Gene."

"I'll ask you a few questions about your research, then ask you how the department helped you make it all possible. Just give me honest answers, OK?"

"No problem." Sal knew just what he was going to say. The cameraman pulled his camera out of his bag, set up two lights, and put the camera on its stand.

Elise asked her cameraman, "Ready?"

"Good." The cameraman said.

Elise looked quickly at her notes. "three, two, one. I'm Elise Thompson with Columbia University and today I have the distinct pleasure of talking with Sal Carlotta, a doctoral candidate in the biomedical engineering department. He's been doing groundbreaking research on organ regeneration. Thanks for joining us today, Sal."

"Thank you, Elise."

Elise gave a quick glance at the cameraman. He responded with a "thumbs-up."

"Sal, tell us about your research." Elise continued.

"My research involved creation of a microfluidic chip, that, when coupled with genetically-engineered synthetic cells, could repair organ defects. In my project, I created a chip which was attached to a rat's damaged liver. I then injected a saline solution into the rat's bloodstream which included genetically engineered dormant liver cells. When the saline solution came in contact with the chip, the dormant liver cells in the solution were activated and went to work on replacing the unhealthy liver cells. After two days, the damage to the liver was completely repaired. What was once a damaged liver became a healthy functioning liver with no trace of damage."

"And your rat's name is Gene, right? How did he get his name?"

"I named him after my father."

Elise was thrown by the answer but recovered quickly and continued with the interview.

"Your dad, how interesting. When did the experiment with Gene start?" Elise asked.

"Two years ago."

"So, your research is two years old and it's now just coming to light? Why so long?"

"Actually, two years is a very short time in the research world. I wasn't sure about the longer-term effects of the experiment, so I decided to keep the research need-to-know until I had better data. More research needs to be done."

"And how's Gene today?"

"We've tested Gene every week since the experiment, and his liver is healthy."

"Are there follow-up treatments required?"

"None."

"Impressive work, Sal! I should note that Sal is not only one of our top doctoral candidates but is also, at 25, the program's youngest candidate." Elise teed up her plug for the biomedical engineering program. "How has Columbia's biomedical engineering program helped make your research a reality?"

"Not one bit."

"I'm sorry?" Elise wasn't expecting *that* response.

"Just kidding." Sal liked watching Elise get flustered on camera. "Dean Andrews and the rest of the department totally supported me. This project would have gone nowhere without the department's support."

Elise composed herself and continued the interview. "That's great to hear, Sal. We're all looking forward to seeing the great things that come of your research. Thanks for your time, Sal."

"My pleasure, Elise."

The cameraman signaled that the recording had stopped.

"Hey, that was fun," Sal said.

"Why did you do that?"

Sal gave a mischievous grin. "Just having a little fun." Sal turned to the cameraman. "You can edit it out. right?"

"Yeah," the cameraman said as he was packing up his equipment.

"See, no harm done. Sorry for putting you on the spot, Elise."

Elise was still ticked but showed Sal some grace. "Apology accepted."

"Let me make it up to you." Sal teed up his move. "How about dinner tonight on me?"

"Sorry, can't." A little grace was all Sal was going to get from Elise.

The cameraman finished packing up. "OK, let's go," he said.

"Thanks for the interview!" Sal said while holding out his hand to Elise.

"Good luck, Sal." Elise shook his hand and walked out of the room.

The cameraman waited for Elise to leave then approached Sal. "You got balls, man," smiling as he fist-bumped Sal.

Sal fist-bumped him and smiled.

Sal's OOC research was widely published in medical journals, garnering the attention of the medical community, biomedical companies, and investors. There was no shortage of job opportunities for Sal, particularly with biomedical device companies. He could work anywhere he wanted, and knew he was in a position to take advantage of his rock star status. He just wished his mother was there to see it.

Sal had a hologram recording of his mother from his tenth birthday party that he would play when something or someone reminded him of his mother. Her fiery red hair lightly bounced as she walked from the kitchen to the dining room table with Sal's birthday cake. He would play that five-second snippet in slow motion over and over again, standing in front of her as if she were walking towards him with the cake. The lit candles glistened in her blue eyes as she led the happy birthday chorus. He always muted the hologram recording right after the singing ended because that was where his father said from behind the camera, "Blow out the candles, Sal!" Just hearing his father's voice made him cringe, and he'd rather hear nothing than that domineering voice. He'd seen the hologram recording hundreds of times, and knew every movement his mother made, even her crooked smile after he blew out the candles. He couldn't watch it without tearing up.

Sal's job decision criteria were basic; make as much money as possible, focus on cancer's cure, and stay as far away from his father as he could. Gene had remarried while Sal was in graduate school and later accepted a position as CEO of an investment banking firm requiring a move to Tokyo. Sal would take a job anywhere.

Except Tokyo.

MR. & MRS. WINN
2042

Bert and Laura were both 26 when they married, almost five years to the day from when Bert first told Paul he had a girlfriend. During their courtship they learned about each other's likes and dislikes, how they wanted to be touched, when they needed time apart from each other. With the help of a pre-marriage counselor who specialized in counseling people with autism, Bert and Laura planned out strategies for how they would respect each other's preferences, establish clear expectations of each other, define a daily schedule they both could agree to, budget their money, and help with being intimate. Neither of them enjoyed being touched, but they both understood the importance of intimacy in a relationship. They also planned out their spiritual life. Since they were both Christian, they decided to attend church on Sunday mornings, join a small group that met every two weeks for two hours, and donate ten percent of their salaries to their church. Their counselor was impressed, "You're doing a great job laying out expectations," she said. "Lots of couples spend years trying to figure out what you've already accomplished." To Bert and Laura, this was completely natural, they couldn't understand how other married couples got by without knowing what to expect of each other.

During Bert's senior year as an undergrad, he decided he wanted to be a history professor. The concreteness of historical facts was such a natural fit for him. He had overcome his fear of public speaking and actually enjoyed teaching others. He liked the predictability of a teaching schedule and felt comfortable in a classroom. He practiced his lectures in front of Laura, who gave him blunt feedback but also encouraged him. After receiving his bachelor's degree in June 2038, he immediately began graduate studies at Naples University, completing his Ph.D. in four years. He had become well-known at NU during his eight years and was admired for his work ethic, ability to focus, and reliability. In the last year of his Ph.D. program he was offered an associate professorship at NU, which he enthusiastically accepted. Attending Bert's graduation ceremony where he became Dr. Bertrand Winn was yet another milestone his parents never envisioned Bert achieving. At each turn Bert surprised his parents with what he could accomplish, demonstrating how someone with autism was "normal" in so many ways. Now as a married man with a Ph.D., Bert continued to exceed his parents' expectations for the life he would lead.

Bert and Laura held a simple ceremony at their church. About 30 attended, mostly family members. Paul was his best man and Laura's sister Amy her maid of honor. Laura's parents, like Bert's, had questions about what Laura's life would be like as an adult. Seeing her in a white dress, becoming Mrs. Bertrand Winn was something they doubted would ever happen for their daughter.

They had a reception at their church with eggplant parmigiana and tiramisu, the same meal they had at their first dinner together. After about two hours, Bert and Laura said their goodbyes, and left for their wedding night suite at one of Sorrento's finest hotels, followed by a two-week honeymoon in Greece. Paul helped send them off, then took a late train back to Rome. His client was expecting him the next morning, the client no one said no to.

BEDSIDE CHATS
2041

In October of Paul's last year at Harvard his father was diagnosed with stage three pancreatic cancer, the very same that took Sal's mother. He had surgery in November followed by intense chemo. The thought of losing his father agonized Paul. He wanted to quit Harvard to be by his father but Joseph wouldn't hear of it. His son was going to be a lawyer, and nothing, not even his cancer, was going to slow it down. Paul worked out his schedule to allow him to spend one week a month in Naples with his father, and the rest of his time in Boston. The cancer had progressed to a point where his father couldn't work, so Paul's mother, brother and sister covered time at the supermarket. Paul moved a bed into the living room where his father would rest during the day and put a desk right next to the bed so he could study. Some days his father wouldn't say much, but sometimes he had periods of clarity, talking about random topics. He'd talk about when he was a child growing up in Naples, how the world was such a different place. There was no rationing or ethnarchy structure. He'd talk about meeting Ida at such a young age and how he was so taken by her. He'd talk about the four greatest days of his life, his wedding day and the day each of his three kids were born. Paul asked him questions about his childhood, his hopes, his fears. His father would lie in his bed and tell Paul things he had never revealed about himself before. How he at one time hoped to be an attorney just like Paul was going to be. How he couldn't believe Ida would be interested in a man like him. How Joseph's father was an alcoholic who would beat his mother until the day Joseph at age 13 stood up to his father and threatened to kill him if he ever touched her again. Paul recorded their conversations to have after his father's passing. One particular bedside conversation moved Paul more than the rest.

"Dad, looking back at your life what's the single most important piece of advice you would give to someone?" Paul asked.

"Hmm." He looked up and to the right as if the answer were stuck in his brain's right hemisphere. After a minute he stared back at Paul, having found the answer.

"Don't let life get in the way of love." Joseph gave the answer with a clarity and conviction that surprised Paul.

"Did you let life get in the way of love?" Paul asked.

"Sometimes. Things got so busy with the supermarket, paying bills, and all the other busy-ness that, at times, I wasn't as attentive to you kids and your mother as much as I could have been. Sometimes loving you all wasn't top of mind, and I took you for granted."

Paul was a taken aback by his father's admission. Growing up he saw his father as very loving and always putting others before himself.

"Dad, I didn't feel like you put life before love. I always felt loved by you." Paul said.

"Good. I tried my best, but it took work and constant reminders of what was important to me, you kids and your mother. Love takes work, and life can't get in its way."

The two of them sat there quietly for a minute, then Joseph nodded off. Paul turned off the recorder, thankful that he captured that particular conversation.

Paul graduated with his Juris Doctor degree from Harvard in June. His father was too ill to make the trip, but his mother, brother and sister attended. Caleb stayed with his uncle Joseph and together they watched a live hologram of the graduation ceremony. Joseph drifted in and out of sleep during the ceremony, but was awake enough to let out a, "Good job, son" when Paul was handed his diploma. After the ceremony Caleb called Paul.

"Congrats, Cuz!" Caleb said.

"Paolo, I'm so proud of you." Joseph's voice was weak, Paul heard wheezing with each breath Joseph took.

"Thanks, Dad. We're catching a plane back to Naples tonight, I'll see you tomorrow afternoon."

"OK. I love you, Son."

"Love you too."

Paul, his mother and siblings went straight to the airport to catch their flight back to Naples. Two hours after the flight left Boston Paul got a message from Caleb, "Call me as soon as you can."

SUPER CHECKERS
2041

Caleb was there when his uncle Joseph took his last breath. He died just a few hours after watching Paul get his law degree. Caleb wasn't particularly close to his aunt and uncle, but Paul asked him to stay with his dad while the rest of the family was in Boston for his graduation. Paul had done so much for Caleb through the years, including encouraging Caleb to pursue his passion for holograms. There was no way Caleb could refuse Paul's request.

When Paul got the message from Caleb, his mother was sleeping in the seat next to him, his brother and sister reading in their seats five rows back.

Paul called Caleb back from his plane seat. "He's gone," Caleb said.

"My gosh." Paul whispered, so his mother wouldn't hear him.

"I'll call the funeral home and have him taken away." Caleb said. "You don't want to see him like this."

Paul trusted his cousin's judgment. "Thanks. We'll be home in about ten hours."

"I'm so sorry, Paul."

"Bye." Paul hung up.

Paul chose not to tell his mother and siblings on the plane; he waited until they landed in London for their connection to Naples to save them reacting to the news with a plane full of people watching. Paul sat in his seat for the remaining four-hour flight, keeping his father's death to himself, watching his mother sleep in the seat next to him. He watched her deep breaths, her head slightly bobbing with each breath she took, looking so peaceful, knowing in a few hours he'd give her the worst news she'd ever gotten. He thought about the times he had observed his father demonstrating how much he adored his mother, and how she respected him. He smiled as he thought about his father faithfully taking his mother out on dates every week. He remembered how, when he was a kid, his father was so attentive to him and his siblings, reading to them, playing games with them, encouraging them when they were down. Tears welled as he thought about the "Don't let life get in the way of love" bedside conversation he had with his father just months earlier. He turned off his overhead light to hide his tears, occasionally taking a napkin to his face when a tear made its way down his cheek. "Thank God she's asleep," he thought as he wiped his face, not wanting her to see him crying.

The plane landed at Heathrow where they had a four-hour layover before their Naples flight. Paul had talked with the flight attendant and arranged a private room at the airline's lounge. After they disembarked and went through customs, Paul suggested to his mother and siblings they go to the lounge while they waited for their flight. "How nice, Paolo," his mother said. The concierge had been briefed they were coming and was waiting for them.

"Mr. Ambrosi, we have a room for you, this way please." The concierge led them into a room with two sofas facing each other and a table in between. Drinks and snacks were already on the table waiting for them. "Paolo, they're treating you like royalty!" Ida said. This was the first time she had ever been in an airport lounge, let alone one with a private room and refreshments.

"Sit down, Mom." His mother was struck with Paul's serious tone despite being in such luxury.

Ida, Alberto and Anna sat on the couches. Paul sat next to his mother, facing his siblings. He took Ida's hands and held them.

"Paolo?"

Paul took a deep breath "Dad's gone."

She knew Joseph was sick and that his time was probably near, but she still wasn't prepared to hear those two words. She lowered her head into her hands that Paul was still holding and started weeping. Always wanting to be strong in front of her kids, she quietly sobbed, her hands covering her face. Paul let go of her hands and gently hugged her, his own tears starting up again. Anna was crying, leaning on Alberto, her face buried in his chest. Alberto leaned back on the couch, looking up and crying, his chest bouncing up and down with each sobbing breath. The four of them continued for five minutes, with Ida quietly saying, "My prince is gone!" over and over between sobs. Ida didn't ask how or when Paul found out, none of that mattered. It wasn't going to bring Joseph back.

"He was the . . ." Paul started then had to stop to compose himself. "He was the best dad." Anna's silent sobbing then turned into full-on crying, tears and mascara leaving black wet spots on Alberto's white shirt. After another five minutes, Paul started in again. He took a deep breath and exhaled.

"Caleb's staying at the apartment until we get there. He's already called the funeral home to take Dad, we'll see him again at the wake."

Ida looked up at Paul and nodded. She did her best to compose herself. "Do you kids remember how Dad would say he always made his dentist appointments at 2:30? You know, tooth-hurty? Your father loved to make us laugh." Seeing his wife and kids happy was the most important thing in the world to Joseph, and he would stop at nothing to make them laugh.

"Yeah, do you remember how Dad would switch shirts with Paul when he was little?" Anna added. "Dad's shirt would be swimming on Paul and dad looked like he was wearing a corset in Paul's."

"Or how about the games dad made up, remember super checkers?" Alberto said. Super checkers was just like normal checkers, except that a dice roll dictated how many consecutive moves a player made.

"Yeah, and remember how you'd cry when he won a game?" Paul said to Alberto. "When he asked you why you were crying you'd say, 'I'm just so happy for you!'" That one got more laughs, Ida then shared something her kids never knew about Joseph.

"When each of you were born, your father insisted he be the first to hold you as soon as you came out. He then brought you over to me with tears in his eyes and said, 'Thank you for giving me the most precious gift I could ever receive.' He kissed you on the forehead, handed you to me, and kissed me. He so adored each of you, from the very moment you were born." Ida looked lovingly at each of her kids as she was telling them. Alberto and Anna came over to the couch where Ida and Paul were sitting, and the four just held each other.

For the next three hours they laughed and cried as they relived wonderful memories they had of their husband and father. The concierge came in and told them their flight would be boarding soon. They packed up, thanked the concierge, and left for their gate for their three-hour flight to Naples.

The empty bed where Joseph had laid just hours earlier was in the living room. Caleb had stripped the bed sheets, leaving just a bare mattress. He came up to his aunt Ida and hugged her.

"I'm so sorry, Aunt Ida."

"Thank you, Caleb." Ida had cried herself out, now she was just tired.

"He died peacefully. The funeral home picked him up earlier today. They're waiting for your call on arrangements."

Ida nodded. "I'll call them."

"I'm gonna go, Aunt Ida, let me know if I can do anything." Caleb hugged his aunt again.

"I'll walk you out," Paul walked out with Caleb and thanked him again for his help. "Certainly, Cuz," Caleb said.

Joseph's wake was two days later. Hundreds paid their last respects. Ida and her children heard story after story about how Joseph had touched their lives in some way. How he once gave a family free groceries for a month when both the father and mother were out of work. "Don't worry, you pay me back when you have the money," Joseph would say to them. Then another family told them of how he gave their troublemaker son a job when no one else would hire him. "Joseph was the only one who trusted our son, he set high expectations of him, and encouraged him to succeed. Because of Joseph, our son went on to graduate from college and became a youth counselor." Ida remembered the boy but had no idea he was troubled, or that Joseph loved and encouraged him like one of his own. At the funeral, Paul eulogized his father, telling everyone about his bedside chat with Joseph, about not letting life get in the way of love. It was a beautiful tribute to his father's legacy, one which filled the room with smiles, sniffs, tears. After the funeral, attendees were invited to a reception hall downstairs for some light snacks and conversation. Before going, Ida and her three children went up to Joseph's casket to pay last respects. They just stood there, none of them wanting the moment to end as they would never see him again.

After a few minutes Paul broke the silence, "There are people waiting for us downstairs." Alberto, Anna, and Paul all started toward the reception hall, while Ida stayed with her prince.

"Just give me a few more minutes. I'll be down soon."

"Take your time, Mom," Alberto said. They left her there with the only man she ever loved, not ready to say her goodbyes.

The reception hall was arranged in a simple manner, with folding chairs around folding tables with paper tablecloths. Two large rectangular tables in the center of the room held plates of Italian meats, cheeses, breads, and condiments. A bartender served drinks in one corner of the room. Despite the food in the room, the distant smell of formaldehyde permeated the air, a constant reminder that they were still in a funeral home. Paul, Alberto and Anna came down to an already-full room of friends and family. Alberto and Anna made their way to the food table, thanking people for coming. Paul went to the bartender, got a glass of Merlot, and started chatting with several of Joseph's customers from the supermarket. A handsome older man with silver hair, wearing a gray sharkskin suit which hugged every line of his body, approached Paul.

"Hello, Paul."

Paul didn't recognize the man. "Thank you so much for coming, how did you know my father?"

"I came in the store almost every day to get lunch. He was the kindest, most wonderful man. The last time I saw you I think you were about 16."

Paul was still perplexed as to who the man was. "I'm so embarrassed but I don't recall us meeting."

"My name is Ed Carloni." Paul knew that name. Carloni was one of the people who helped fund Paul's attending Naples Academy. Paul was mortified.

"Oh my gosh, Mr. Carloni! I'm such an idiot for not recognizing you."

"Not at all, Paul. It's amazing how gray hair and wrinkles can disguise someone."

Paul smiled at Carloni and took a nervous sip of Merlot, still humiliated for not recognizing someone who generously funded his schooling.

Carloni continued. "Your dad couldn't stop bragging about you. London School of Economics, then Harvard Law, very impressive."

"Thank you, Mr. Carloni. Your generosity helped me so much, I don't know how to repay you."

"It's truly been my pleasure, you were well worth the investment." Carloni got to the real reason he had approached Paul. "Have you taken a job with anyone yet?"

"No, with Dad being sick I put off looking."

"I have a law firm with offices in Naples and Rome. There's a particularly interesting client in Rome that I'd like to talk with you about. What do you think?" Paul was caught a bit off guard with the question. Carloni apologized for being so abrupt. "Sorry to spring the question on you. You've got things to do to help your mom get settled. When you're ready, give me a call." Carloni handed Paul his card. "Take your time, I'll be here when you're ready." He kissed Paul on each cheek and headed to the food table. Paul looked down at the card. How peculiar someone would offer him a job at his father's funeral. "Even in death, Dad supports me," Paul thought as he looked at the card. He then heard Ida coming, so he slipped the card in his pocket and went over to his mother and kissed her.

"They just took him to the mausoleum," she said. "They asked if I wanted to go. I can't watch him being stuffed into a wall."

"You need to eat, let's get some food." Paul put his arm around his mother, escorting her to the food table.

Paul continued to mingle with guests into the evening, occasionally putting his hand in his pocket and rubbing the raised letters on Carloni's business card. "Who's the interesting client?" he thought.

Interesting Client

2041

For the next month Paul focused on helping his mother adjust to life without Joseph while Alberto and Anna ran the supermarket. Each morning they would walk to the newly-constructed mausoleum at Villa Comunale to visit its first occupant Joseph. Ida would bring a thermos of coffee and Paul would carry a folding stool for his mother to sit on. They would enter the mausoleum at one end and walk down along the wall of empty plots until they got to Joseph's plot, every sound echoing as it bounced off the stone walls and floor. Paul would set the folding stool in front of Joseph's plot and Ida would sit, pull a cup from her purse, open the thermos, pour some coffee, look at Joseph's name on his plot, then chat about whatever came to mind. She talked about things that happened yesterday, fun things they did when they were young, what she was going to do later on that day. Paul sat on a bench out of earshot of his mother, respecting the privacy of her chats with Joseph. Sometimes he'd walk the length of the mausoleum, observing if there were any new tenants since the last visit. One thing he hated about the mausoleum was seeing his mother's name underneath Joseph's with a birth date but no date of death. When she died the plot would be reopened, her casket would be put in end-to-end with Joseph's and sealed shut. It didn't seem to bother her as she knew her body would be next to Joseph's for eternity. Paul despised seeing it, a constant reminder that someday he would lose her too.

After about an hour, Ida would take a last sip of coffee, put the empty cup and thermos back in her bag, wipe Joseph's name with a tissue, and gently kiss the etched letters. Paul knew the routine, when he saw his mother put the cup in her bag and close the thermos, he would make his way over to her, getting there just as she was kissing Joseph's name. He would then fold the stool and they'd walk back home. Ida so appreciated Paul's help, but she also realized that Paul had his own life to live. On the one-month anniversary of Joseph's passing, Ida and Paul were leaving the mausoleum for their walk back home. It was an unseasonably cool and cloudy summer day, very comfortable for walking.

"Paolo, did you call Mr. Carloni?" Paul had told his mother about Carloni approaching him at the funeral during one of their walks to the mausoleum.

"Not yet."

"You should call him."

Ida was Paul's first priority; he wanted to make sure she was well-adjusted first. "You still need help, Mom." Paul said.

"It's time, Paolo. I'm fine. Call him."

"Are you sure?"

"As sure as I'll ever be. I have to adjust to life without your father. Now's the time to do it. Call him."

"I'll call today." Paul gave Ida the only answer she'd accept.

Later that day Paul pulled the business card from his wallet and called Ed.

"Hello, Mr. Carloni, this is Paul Ambrosi."

"Paul, good to hear from you. How's your mom doing?"

"She's a tough woman."

"Yes, she is." Carloni had known Ida for years through his daily visits to the supermarket. "Tough but loving."

"She'd like hearing that." Paul said.

"Are you at a point where we can talk?"

"Yes."

"Can you come by my office tomorrow at nine? I'm just down the street from the supermarket. Same address that's on my card."

Paul hesitated for a moment. He knew that his mother was going to the mausoleum at nine. Then he remembered what she said. "Nine works."

"Good. See you tomorrow at nine. Take care."

"You too." Paul hung up. He was excited about the meeting with Carloni, but deep down was concerned about his mother.

The next morning Paul got up, showered, dressed in the same suit he wore to his father's funeral, then started making his way down the hallway to the kitchen. Even though he was a grown man he still took three big-boy steps to get from his room to the kitchen. Ida was already up sitting at the table drinking an espresso and eating a croissant.

"Paolo," she said.

"Hi Mom." Ida already had an espresso ready for Paul. He sat at the table next to her.

"You going to see Dad this morning?"

"Of course, I have to tell him about you going to meet with Mr. Carloni. Your dad always liked him."

"Can you carry the stool?" Paul took a bite of his croissant.

"I'll manage; if I get tired along the way I have a stool to sit on." Ida said smiling at her bit of wit.

Paul smiled at his mother's quip. "Just don't push yourself. Dad isn't going anywhere."

"I won't, Paolo. Don't worry about me, focus on Mr. Carloni."

"OK." Paul finished his espresso. "I wanna get there early and spend some time preparing. Tell Dad I love him."

"I always do." She said with a reassuring smile. "I'll be fine, Paolo."

"OK, Mom."

Paul got up, kissed his mother, grabbed his half-eaten croissant and a folder with his resume, and headed out the door for the 20-minute walk to Carloni's office. Paul had walked the path thousands of times, because the office was close to the supermarket. It was a warm summer morning, so Paul took off his suit jacket to fend off breaking a sweat. He thought about his brother and sister taking over the supermarket, so his mother wouldn't have to worry about it. He pictured his mother sitting next to Joseph's plot on the folding stool, talking about what happened that day and reminiscing about their life together. He thought about his buddy Bert and how he had found happiness with Laura. He walked by the supermarket and saw his brother unloading produce in the back. "I'll stop by later," he thought, not wanting to interrupt Alberto. He got to Carloni's office 30 minutes before their meeting time. He lost the sweat battle on the walk so decided to sit in a *pasticceria* across the street to cool down and think about what he was going to say to Carloni. Paul sat by the window looking at Carloni's office, thinking about the questions he would ask, but one kept coming to mind, "Who's the interesting client?" he thought. "Maybe a senator, or some CEO, or wouldn't it be funny if it were the Vatican!" Paul laughed and shook his head at the ludicrousness of it being the Vatican. Ten minutes before the meeting, Paul saw Carloni walk into his office, and gave him a few minutes to settle in before going over.

Paul got up from the table, put on his jacket, gave his brow a quick wipe with a napkin, and walked to Carloni's office. Carloni's assistant was seated behind a desk in the lobby when he saw Paul enter.

"Mr. Ambrosi?"

"Yes."

"Mr. Carloni's been expecting you. His office is just down the hall, last door on the left."

"Thank you." Paul walked down the hall, reaching Carloni's office. He was sitting at a small round table with two chairs looking at his phone and sipping coffee. His crisp white shirt perfectly pressed, black shoes shined to a mirror finish, not a silver hair out of place. Paul quietly knocked on the open door.

"Paul, good to see you again." Carloni got up and shook Paul's hand. "Can I get you something?"

"Water would be great, thank you." Paul settled in the chair at the round table, sitting on the edge of the seat, back straight, Carloni got a bottled water from the fridge in his office and sat down across from him, legs crossed, relaxed in his seat.

"How's your mom today?"

"She's good. She goes to the mausoleum every morning to see my dad. This is the first morning she's going by herself."

"She's a tough cookie," Carloni took a sip of his coffee.

Paul opened his folder and handed Carloni his resume. He already knew Paul's credentials; he just scanned the resume for any interesting tidbits.

"Debate club--handy skills for a lawyer," Carloni continued reading, "Perfect GPA at both LSE and Harvard. Volunteered at a homeless shelter. Tutored other students. You're the full package."

Paul looked down, embarrassed at the compliment. "Thank you, Mr. Carloni."

"It's Ed." He wanted to make Paul feel a bit more at ease.

Paul looked up and smiled. "Then thank you, Ed."

Carloni continued the discussion he started at Joseph's funeral. "Remember the interesting client in Rome? Well, it's the Vatican."

Paul was mid-sip of his water and did all he could to keep from choking when he heard Vatican. His joke was now reality. "The Vatican. What's your statement of work?" Paul asked, trying to stay cool despite being surprised about the mystery client.

"Ever since the Archdiocese of Boston sex abuse scandal over 40 years ago, the Catholic Church had been defending cases worldwide, some legitimate, some fabricated, but all taking up time and resources. In 2030, Pope Pius XIII personally engaged in the issue, hiring our firm as a global general contractor to qualify law firms, manage caseloads, provide assistance on cases where needed, and report directly to Pius XIII on the status of cases, particularly those where the abuse was confirmed. Pius XIII was determined to clean up abuses in the church until his death in 2040." Carloni stopped to take a sip of his coffee while Paul sat across from him on the edge of his seat taking in every word. Carloni continued. "The next pope was elected by the elector cardinals who took the title Pius XIV, adopting the name of his predecessor, to symbolize the continued annihilation of abuse in the church. We continued as role of general contractor with the transition and meet with Pius XIV monthly to report on cases."

Paul was familiar with Pius XIII and XIV, and knew about the abuses in the church, but had no idea Pius XIII and XIV were so involved. On one hand, he was happy the church was taking such a strong stand against abuse but was also disappointed the church had so many cases to deal with in the first place. Carloni revealed to Paul what he wanted him to do, "Paul, I'd like you to be on our Rome team working as liaison to our subcontract law firms in the United States. You would be based out of Rome and travel about once a month to the United States to review cases, certify subcontract law firms, and raise issues back to the Vatican. We have an office in Boston, so Harvard would be a plus. You'd be part of the team that gives Pius XIV monthly status reports and advise him on actions he should take. How's it sound?"

Rarely had Paul been caught speechless in his life. Working with the Vatican on high-profile cases, advising the pontiff on actions to take, traveling to the United States every month. Paul tried to think of a downside but couldn't come up with one.

"Awesome," Paul said.

"Great," Carloni said. "I should let you know there is one particular requirement the Vatican insists upon."

"Here comes the downside," Paul thought to himself.

"Are you a practicing Catholic?"

Paul was born into a Catholic family and went through all the tollgates required of Catholics, but as an adult church meant weddings, funerals, Easter, and the occasional Christmas Eve midnight service.

"Define practicing," Paul said.

"You just gave me my answer," Carloni said. "The Vatican requires everyone working for the Vatican to be practicing Catholics, attending mass every Sunday, going to confession at least once a year, receiving weekly holy communion, not eating meat on Fridays during Lent. Tithing is strongly encouraged but no one will check on your tithing habits. Is this a problem?"

In his years at Harvard he never imagined being accepted or rejected for a job because of his worship habits. He took a sip of water, stalling for time while he thought about his answer. The opportunity was just too good to pass up. "No problem," Paul said.

"Good. I want you to go through an interview loop with some of my associates, then after I get their feedback, we'll make a final decision and discuss offer terms. Any other questions for me?"

"Just one," Paul said. "Will I have direct interaction with the pontiff?"

"Plenty."

"That's great, thanks." Paul knew that the pontiff was the head of the executive, legislative, and judicial branches of government in Vatican City, whatever he said was law. Being in a position to advise someone with such sanctioned power over not only Vatican City but millions of Catholics around the world was an adrenaline rush for Paul.

"Very good, I'll get back to you with an interview loop schedule and when you should plan on being in Rome. Pleasure talking, Paul." Carloni arose from his seat, smoothed the front of his slacks, and kissed Paul on either cheek.

"Thank you, Ed." Paul reciprocated the kiss. Carloni went back to his desk as Paul walked out of his office, down the hall, gave the assistant a quick wave, and out the door.

Paul decided to stop at the supermarket to see his brother and sister. On the walk he thought about his meeting with Ed, the opportunity to work with the Vatican, the peculiar requirement of being a practicing Catholic. His family rarely attended church together growing up. He didn't have anything against the Catholic church but going to church just wasn't that important. What he did admire, though, was the charisma the current pontiff Pius XIV possessed, how he captivated audiences with his speeches, and the power he possessed. Pius XIV was able to get a meeting with any world leader and could sway opinion seemingly at will. He saw it at the 2041 annual ethnarchy chairperson meeting in London. Pius XIV addressed the leaders on corruption in food rationing and called for an independent council on fair rationing across the ethnarchies. He successfully influenced the ten chairpersons to form the council with the pontiff as its head. These were the ten most powerful people in the world of different religious beliefs, but they saw Pius XIV as a man who loved people for who they were, not who they worshiped. Having the ability to observe Pius XIV and learn from him was a priceless education.

Paul got to the supermarket, opened the door, and caught the familiar whiff of cheeses and Italian meats. Alberto was slicing salame, Anna was stocking shelves.

"Hey, sibs!" Paul said.

Anna got to Paul first and kissed him. Alberto waved to him from behind the meat slicer, finished his slicing, and hugged his brother.

"How you doing, bro?" Alberto asked.

"Great, Mom is doing well; she's going to the mausoleum on her own this morning."

"Really? She's OK with going by herself?" Anna asked.

"She insisted on it," Paul said. "I think she was kind of happy to do it on her own, maybe it's an independence thing."

"I'm sure she'll be fine," Alberto said. "So, what were you doing this morning?"

"I talked with Ed Carloni about a job in Rome."

"What did you think of the job?"

"Amazing opportunity. If I get it, I'll get to work with the Vatican and travel to the United States every month."

"The Vatican?" Alberto asked as he grabbed some prosciutto and put it on the slicer. "What would you do there?"

"Work on the abuse case backlog."

"Ooh, interesting stuff," Anna said. Alberto was just about to turn on the slicer when his phone rang. His heart jumped when he saw the name.

DENTED FOLDING STOOL
2041

Alberto took another quick glance at the phone. "It's Naples Hospital," Alberto said to Paul and Anna. Alberto took a deep breath and answered the call. "Hello?" He said.

"Mr. Ambrosi?"

"Speaking."

"This is Ellen Giannini at Naples Hospital Emergency Department. Is your mother Ida?"

"Yes."

"She was involved in an accident, she's in the ED. Can you come right away?"

"Is she OK?" Paul and Anna could see the concern on Alberto's face.

"We need you to come to the ED right away please." The fact that she didn't answer Alberto's question led him to think the worst.

"We'll be right there."

"Thank you." Giannini hung up.

"It's Mom, we need to go to Naples Hospital."

"Is she OK?" Anna asked.

"She wouldn't say. Let's just go."

Alberto, Anna and Paul quickly closed the supermarket, got into Alberto's car for the five-minute drive to the hospital. None of them said a word in the car; not knowing their mother's condition conjured up worst-case thoughts in their minds. They arrived at the hospital, the car screeching into the lot and parking in the first spot they could find. The three ran into the hospital up to the reception desk.

The Lawless One and the End of Time ◆ 91

"I'm Alberto Ambrosi, my mother Ida is here. Can we see her?" Alberto asked the receptionist.

"Just one moment." The receptionist picked up the phone, "The Ambrosis are here." She hung up.

"Ms. Giannini will be with you in a moment," the receptionist said.

"Thank you," Alberto said. He turned to his siblings. "This can't be good."

Anna was already crying, Paul trying in vain to comfort her with a brotherly hug. They then heard the echoing *click click click* of a woman's heels on a tile floor, the sound getting louder as the woman approached them. "Mr. Ambrosi?"

"Yes, I'm Alberto Ambrosi, my sister Anna and brother Paul." They each shook Giannini's hand.

"Let's talk for a minute," Giannini said.

"Where's my mother?" Anna asked through sobs.

"You can see her in a moment," Giannini said in a quiet, reassuring tone. She led them into a small room with four chairs and a table, a box of tissues on the table and a blue button on the wall by the door. Giannini closed the door behind her and pulled out a chair to sit, the rest following suit.

"Your mother was hit by a car this morning." What the Ambrosis didn't know was that Giannini was a grief counselor. "She was in a crosswalk when a driver ran a red light and hit her. Paramedics responded within five minutes and transported her here. She had multiple internal injuries, a broken hip, and concussion."

"Had? She used the word had?" Paul thought as Giannini was talking. "Is she dead?"

"We did everything we could for her, but we couldn't save her. She passed away at ten past ten this morning."

"Ten past ten," Paul thought. "She was coming back from the mausoleum. This wouldn't have happened if I were with her."

The three were at a loss. First Joseph died in June and now Ida in July. Two parents lost in two months. Anna's sobs turned into loud wails, her face buried in Paul's chest. Paul and Alberto silently cried. Giannini sat there patiently, available for any questions.

"Can we see her?" Paul asked.

"Of course, but she is badly bruised."

"I don't want to see her, not that way." Anna said.

"I'll go," Alberto said. "Paul?"

Paul nodded. Anna stayed in the room while Giannini led Paul and Alberto to their mother. She was still in the trauma room where a technician was cleaning up. They walked in, Paul noticing his mother's bag, heavily scuffed from being scraped along the pavement during the accident. Leaning against the wall, next to the bag was the folding stool, the top of it dented from being driven over by the car that killed her. He walked over to the bag and picked it up, hearing the clinking sound of the broken cup and thermos inside. He picked up the folding stool that he had carried for his mother each morning. He looked over at her in the bed with Alberto holding her hand. Paul was sure she died because he wasn't with her. He could have seen the car coming and held her back. He went over to his mother, held her other hand and stroked her hair. The two sons just stood there in silence for ten minutes, looking at her, stroking her hair, holding her hand, wiping their tears. Alberto then broke the silence. "We should go back and be with Anna."

Alberto, Paul, and Giannini walked back to find Anna, her wailing subsiding to somber sobs. As Alberto and Giannini went into the room, Paul noticed another room across the hallway. "Can I go in there for a minute?" Paul said, still clutching the folding stool.

"Of course," Giannini said.

Alberto and Giannini went back to be with Anna, while Paul went into the room across the hall and closed the door. The room had the same four chairs, table, tissue box and blue button. Paul put the dented folding stool on the table, pushed one of the chairs aside clearing a place on the floor, dropped to his knees, and fell forward onto his forearms, his head in his hands. It was just him in the room, allowing himself to let loose, not caring if people outside the room could hear him. He never allowed himself to openly grieve when his father died; he wanted to be strong for his mother. This was his time to grieve for both his parents. His thoughts were all over, oscillating between blaming himself for her death and being angry at God for allowing this to happen. He decided it was time to blame God.

"Why did you let this happen? Both of them in two months! She didn't deserve this! He didn't deserve the pain you put him through! What kind of God does this?"

He then thought about Carloni telling him he needed to be a practicing Catholic to get his job.

"You do this, then you expect me to worship you? What kind of egomaniac are you?"

Paul got up off the floor and started pacing in the small room, like a tiger pacing around his cage, his tears of sadness turned into full-on rage at God.

"She did nothing to you! You took her for no reason! FOR NO REASON! You put him through so much pain! You're not a loving God, you're a narcissist! I'll never forgive you!"

Paul continued his pacing and yelling for 15 minutes, then slumped in one of the chairs, completely drained. He said what he needed to say and meant every word. After a few minutes he composed himself to be strong for Alberto and Anna.

He walked out of the room back into the room where Alberto and Anna were hugging, exhausted from crying. Giannini had left earlier, telling them to hit the blue button on the wall if they needed anything. Paul went over to his siblings and the three hugged each other.

"Let's go home," Paul said. They left the hospital, Paul still holding the folding stool with its fresh dent.

The next day, Paul, Antonio and Anna went to the same funeral home that handled Joseph's arrangements for Ida. The directions to the funeral home director were simple. "Do the same for Mom as you did for Dad," Alberto said. After making the quick arrangements, Alberto and Anna went to the supermarket and Paul went home. He decided to do his walk to the mausoleum one more time. He wanted to feel like his mother was with him, so he carried the dented folding stool. He walked along the same route, then came to the intersection where Ida was killed. He didn't know anything about the driver or what had happened. He noticed fresh skid marks in front of the walkway and a stain on the street that could have been blood, he wasn't sure. It really didn't matter, knowing wasn't going to bring her back. He arrived at the mausoleum and started the long walk toward Joseph's plot. He noticed a man standing in front of the plot and heard a grinding sound. As he got closer, he saw what the man was doing--etching the date of Ida's death into the plot's cover. Not seeing a date there when Ida was alive bothered him but seeing a date of death made him furious all over again. He turned around and walked out, banging the dented stool on the door jamb as he left.

Ida's funeral was a surreal repeat performance of Joseph's. Same people, same format, except this time, Alberto gave the eulogy. The reception was in the same downstairs location with the same food and same faint formaldehyde smell. Some attendees gave the standard "sorry for your loss" line to the Ambrosis, others just came and hugged them, not knowing how to console someone who lost both their parents a little over a month apart. Carloni approached Paul.

"Paul, I am so incredibly sorry," Carloni said.

"Thank you, Ed."

"Let me know if I can do anything for you."

"You can." Paul was expecting Ed at the funeral and was ready to talk to him. "I want to continue forward with the interview loop as soon as possible."

"You don't need to do that, Paul, we can give you some time."

"No, I want to push ahead. Let me know when you can have the loop set up and I'll be there."

Carloni saw the determination on Paul's face. "I can do that, but if you want to defer just let me know."

"I don't want to defer." Paul didn't want to sit home wallowing in guilt or seething in anger. Pushing forward with his career would keep his mind off losing his parents.

"OK then. You'll hear from me in a couple days. You take care, Paul."

"Thanks, Ed."

"Paul, it's time to go to the mausoleum," the funeral director said. In the funeral instructions, Paul told the director he wanted to be at the mausoleum when Ida was put into the plot with Joseph. Alberto and Anna didn't want to watch, so Paul went alone in the hearse.

"Just a minute," Paul said. He went to the coat room in the reception hall and grabbed his mother's bag and the dented stool. "Let's go."

Paul sat in the front seat of the hearse as they drove to the mausoleum, his left arm over the seat back, his hand on Ida's casket. When they got to the mausoleum, attendants helped unload the casket onto a rolling cart, then into the mausoleum. Paul followed the casket, dented stool in hand. He looked at the door jamb seeing where the stool left its mark the last time he was there. Squeaking wheels from the rolling cart and echoing footsteps accompanied the long walk to the plot. Joseph noticed the freshly-filled plots, seeing those that had two names, one with a death date, one without. They got to Joseph's plot, the cover already removed. He looked in and was hit by the pungent stench of decomposing flesh before seeing

Joseph's casket. His casket was pushed to the back end of the plot, making room for Ida's casket at the front. The attendants adjusted the rolling cart's level so the casket could slide from the cart into the plot.

"Do you want a minute before we put her in?" The funeral director asked.

"No, but can I put something in between Mom and Dad?"

"Sure."

Paul placed his mother's scuffed bag in the plot. The bag still had the broken coffee cup and thermos she took with her to the mausoleum each day for her talks with Joseph. He then started to put the dented stool in but stopped.

"Just the bag," Paul said. He didn't want to part with the stool.

The attendants slid the casket in, pushing the bag into the plot so it rested between Ida and Joseph's caskets. Two of the attendants then lifted the stone cover and secured it to the plot. The attendants left, with only the funeral director and Paul remaining.

"You OK, Paul?" The funeral director asked as he put his hand on Paul's shoulder.

"All good, I'm going to stay here for a minute. I can walk home from here."

"Alright, take care of yourself, Paul."

The funeral director made the long walk to the mausoleum entrance, his footsteps echoing until Paul heard the bang of the front door close. The mausoleum was silent--just Paul, his parents, the other plot occupants. Paul stared at the death dates of both his parents on the plot cover, still shocked at the short time between their deaths. After a few minutes he made the long walk to the front door, lunging his steps and counting the number of big-boy steps from his parents' plot to the front door.

SHAME
2041

The next day Carloni sent Paul the interview loop, three attorneys and two Vatican Cardinals all on the following day. That morning Paul took a train from Naples to Rome's Termini Train Station. One of Carloni's associates was waiting there for him and took him to their offices in Vatican City. One after one the interviews happened, the interviewers vetting Paul for understanding of the law, integrity, communication ability, and project management capability. Each asked about Paul's willingness to be a practicing Catholic. He came across as if he were eager to worship and willing to be a practicing Catholic. The thought of worshiping a figure he so detested made him want to vomit, but he was able to fool his interviewers into thinking there was no issue. He got a thumbs-up from each of the interviewers and Carloni offered him the job at 250,000 hera a year. Paul asked if he could start in a month so he could go back to Naples and help his siblings finalize his parents' affairs. On September 8, 2041 Paul joined Carloni's law firm, working in Vatican City.

For the next three years Paul thought about nothing but his work. Each month he traveled to the United States, visiting every diocese at least once a year, more if there were known abuses or allegations. He personally met with every accused minister. He had a sixth sense about whether each one truly committed abuse or was wrongly accused. If he smelled guilt, it was only a matter of time before his interrogation skills wore down the abuser to admit wrongdoing. The abuser was immediately dispatched to Vatican City where he met with the pontiff one-on-one to explain his actions.

There were over a hundred meetings between the pope and confessed abusers during the three years, always ending with the abusers leaving the pontiff crying in shame. The guilty abuser would then stand in front of the *Apostolic Signatura*, the Vatican City's legislative body, to be further shamed and sentenced, then be interred for life in a Vatican-run prison just north of Vatican City, commissioned by Pius XIII. Each prisoner's physical health was of utmost importance, they were well-fed, clothed, and medically cared for.

The prison was all about shame.

There were two buildings in the prison complex surrounded by a four-meter-high wall. One building was for men, the other for women. Within each building, the interior was completely open. Everything the prisoners did was on display for other inmates and staff to see. Whether it be eating, sleeping, showering, or using the toilet, there was no privacy. Large pictures of the residents and descriptions of their crimes were plastered on the prison's exterior walls. Visitors could go right up to the prison walls and see who was incarcerated and for what crimes. Prison wall visitors could be seen taking selfies in front of abuser pictures, yelling and spitting on pictures, or just crying at the pain the abuser caused.

The prison also served as a deterrent to both those entering the ministry and those currently serving. Every Catholic seminary student was required to travel to Rome and experience life as a prisoner for a week. Students endured the same humiliation and shame that prisoners experienced. Students ate, slept and showered with the prisoners, in full view of others in the prison. Pius XIII and his successor XIV wanted to send a clear message to church leadership that abusers would be caught and live out their sentences in shame for their crimes of abuse. It was working, but not fast enough.

Paul instilled fear among the ministry, having the power to send any Catholic minister, man or woman, to the Vatican prison. The

North America Ethnarchy allowed the Vatican to extradite the guilty to Vatican City and impose its own justice, the punishment being far more effective than what the United States could enforce. Paul became well-known for his ability to force confessions from the guilty, and his vigorous defense of those wrongly accused. He acted in a public relations capacity, speaking to Catholics and non-Catholics about how the Vatican was tough on abuse. His message was simple, "We severely punish the guilty and aggressively defend the innocent." Catholics loved the message because it was fair to those wrongly accused; non-Catholics loved it because justice was served on the guilty. Reports of United States abuse cases since the new policy was implemented drastically declined, but the policy also emboldened victims from years earlier to come out with their story of abuse. It didn't matter when the abuse happened, if Paul felt a minister was guilty, he or she went to prison. Paul was judge and jury, power he grew to lust after.

YOUR HOLINESS
2044

In the three years Paul had been working for the Vatican, his exposure to Pius XIV increased from a monthly meeting as part of Carloni's legal team to weekly one-on-one meetings with the pope. Seeing how the charismatic pontiff was able to captivate millions of people around the world with his message was mesmerizing. Paul learned from him, eventually able to attract large crowds on his own due to his work in the United States. He loved the praise, people cheering for him and chanting his name.

Paul and the pope would meet in a small room in the Apostolic Palace. The room was adorned sparsely with a table, four chairs, and a crucifix hanging on the wall. Paul intentionally sat with his back to the crucifix so he didn't have to see it during his meetings. During one of his status meetings with the pope, Paul was giving his typical report--who was to be interrogated, who was found guilty, and who was being defended. Midway through his update, the pope raised his hand slightly.

"Yes, Your Holiness?" Paul knew to stop when the pope signaled he wanted to speak.

"Your work in the U.S. has been very successful. I would like you to expand your work to the rest of the ethnarchies."

Paul knew not to say no to the pope. No one said no to the pope. "Yes, Your Holiness."

Paul finished his update, appearing calm and collected even though he was beyond excited about the pope's directive. "Anything else, Your Holiness?"

"Yes." Paul wasn't expecting that. Every time Paul asked about anything else, the pope would always respond with "No," then Paul would kiss his ring and leave.

"How can I help you, Your Holiness?" Paul asked.

"Tell me about your mother and father."

Paul was surprised at the request. In all the years Paul worked for the pope he had never asked Paul a personal question. Their interactions always revolved around the abusers. Paul took a deep breath.

"Certainly, Your Holiness." Paul told him of the supermarket, how his father adored his mother, their two-for-one coupon dinners, his bedside discussions with his father, his father dying right after Paul graduated from Harvard, walking with his mother to the mausoleum, and his mother dying one month later. He told him of his brother and sister still in Naples, still running the supermarket originally started by his grandfather.

"You lost both of your parents within two months?"

"Yes, Your Holiness."

"God moves in ways we cannot always understand. Take comfort in knowing that he will explain it all when you enter Heaven."

"Thank You, Your Holiness." Paul kept a respectful demeanor with the pope, but on the inside he wanted to puke. His anger at God never subsided after his mother's death. Every time he looked at his mother's dented folding stool that he kept in his office, he was reminded of how God took her so unfairly, and the guilt of not being with her when she was hit. God allowed this to happen, and Paul wasn't about to let God off the hook for it. Paul kept up a good act of being a practicing Catholic, but to him it meant nothing. His work and growing penchant for hearing applause was what mattered now.

"Anything else, Your Holiness?" Paul asked.

The pope put his hand out for Paul to kiss his ring. Paul kissed it.

"Thank You, Your Holiness." Paul left the room and walked down an empty hallway in the Apostolic Palace to his office. The echo of his footsteps reminded him of walking from the front door of the mausoleum to his parents' plot. He imagined the blank plots with names yet to be etched, then seeing the workers etch his mother's death date in his parents' plot stone cover. He got to his office, closed the door and picked up the dented folding stool he kept in his office. The pope's well-intended statement only served to fuel Paul's anger at God. He slumped in his chair, hugging the stool.

Paul sent thousands of abusers to prison over the next nine years, which had to be expanded twice to hold the increasing population. He became well-known among the world ethnarchies because his simple message of severely punishing the guilty and aggressively defending the innocent struck a chord with both Catholics and non-Catholics. He became the worldwide voice of the Vatican's hard stance on abuse, in everything from interviews to stadium-filled speeches. Even with all his success across the ethnarchies in bringing abusers to justice, his personal ambitions were much higher than merely being a Vatican mouthpiece, he just needed the right opportunity to make it happen.

THE DEMO
2037

By age 21, Caleb had had enough of the shipyard. Paul's question about using holograms to cure loneliness became his obsession. He studied the history of Facebook, Twitter, YouTube, and Pinterest. What made them successful? Where did they fail? He read everything he could about hologram technology. His free time became more and more consumed with the answer to that question. It was the first time in his life that he was learning not because he had to, but because he wanted to. And it was a way to avert an imminent *Caleb Todd, Master of Failure* legacy that replayed over and over in his mind.

Caleb began work on a system where people could connect with others through real-time holograms. A subscriber could meet with a hologram friend for coffee, a walk in the park, or a dinner party. It didn't matter if the friend were in the next room or on the other side of the world, his hologram would be sitting right across from them. Caleb spent two years working on the concept with the goal of attracting an investor to help him build out the system. He persuaded his parents to invest some of their retirement savings so he could hire an engineer to help create the hardware and software components.

Three years later, Caleb was able to arrange a 15-minute meeting with a Naples private equity firm to demonstrate his concept. He prepared for hours practicing his pitch, ensuring the technology worked as planned, and enlisting Paul to help with the demonstration. Bucking the casual dress code of the day, he bought a new grey pinstripe suit to wear. The night before the meeting, Caleb hardly slept, as a combination of excitement, nervousness and fear pinned his eyes open. Even though the meeting was at 10 a.m., Caleb got up bed at 5 a.m., showered, put on his new suit and left the apartment before everyone else got up. He went to Villa Comunale to visit with his familiar imaginary friends who helped him rehearse. He arrived at the private equity firm's office at 9:30 and waited in the lobby, still rehearsing his spiel and ensuring Paul was awake and ready given the six-hour time difference between Boston and Naples. The managing partner greeted Caleb in the lobby and escorted him into a luxurious conference room where ten additional investors were already there, having just finished another meeting. The room was imposing, with a large oblong walnut table polished to a mirror sheen, surrounded by 12 dark brown leather chairs. Caleb let the intimidation get to him, with droplets of nervous sweat gathering on his forehead. He quickly set up his equipment while the other investors got coffee and snacks at a bar in the corner of the conference room. The managing partner started in.

"OK, let's get going." He waited while everyone settled into their seats. "Guys, this is Caleb Todd. He sent me a synopsis of some hologram technology he developed. Interesting concept. I agreed to have him give us a 15-minute demo so we can see what it's about." The managing partner turned the floor over to Caleb, who quickly wiped the sweat from his forehead before he was the center of attention.

"Ladies and gentlemen, thank you for the opportunity to demonstrate my hologram friend technology." Caleb's voice cracked with nervousness as he stood at the head of the conference table. He looked out at the stone faces around the table, not a friendly-looking audience. They didn't care about Caleb, they just wanted to see if his baby held financial promise. Caleb took a deep breath and started his pitch.

"For three years I've been working on a system to create a social network using real-time holograms. The system enables two or more people anywhere in the world to interact with each as holograms in one virtual room. Rather than tell you, let me show you using my cousin Paul in Boston."

Caleb put on a pair of specialized glasses, black horn-rimmed with thick lenses. "These glasses do three things. They have sensors along the frame that scan the body head to toe and detect the minutest of movements, each movement being mimicked by the hologram. The lenses have three-dimensional screens that allow the wearer to see hologram friends in a virtual room. The earbuds attached to the frames have a built-in microphone so friends can talk and listen to each other."

"Where does the connection to the platform happen?" one of the investors asked.

"The glasses interact directly with the internet. No other device needed." Caleb paired the glasses to a hologram projector on the conference room table so everyone could see and hear what was happening in the virtual room.

"Paul, good to see you!" the projector turned on showing a hologram of both Caleb and Paul in the center of the conference room table. Caleb continued. "Paul, just to prove that we are in real time I am going to ask someone in the room to ask you to do something. Anyone want to ask Paul to do something?"

"Blow a kiss," one of the investors asked. Paul puckered up and blew a kiss to Caleb, causing at least a few of the stone faces to crack a simple smile.

"Hop on one foot." Paul hopped on one foot, the hologram bouncing up and down with the audio of his foot hitting the ground in perfect unison with the hologram.

"You can see the audio and hologram are perfectly synced. I can interact with Paul just as if he were here in the conference room."

"Can the holograms touch?" one asked.

"They can, but we haven't created the skin-sensing technology to allow us to feel hologram motions. We think it can be done but it's not there yet."

Caleb's poise in front of the group of investors was remarkable for a shipyard worker with no formal education. During one of his many discussions with Paul, Caleb realized that if he were going to make a go at his creation he would need to know how to persuasively present himself to secure investor trust and get them to believe in him. Caleb and Paul went through intense coaching sessions for two years where Paul used his debate skills to help Caleb speak clearly, confidently, and persuasively. Caleb was an eager student and absorbed all that Paul had to offer. The coaching paid off with Caleb's commanding presence in front of the investors.

"What problem are you solving with this?" another investor asked.

"Loneliness." Caleb looked at faces for reactions. Some affirming smiles, a few nods, a couple of downward glances. No one questioned his answer.

"What's your business plan?" one of the investors asked.

"This is one of the areas I need help. The technology basics are there but I need help figuring out the money side and advancing the technology. That's why I'm here. I need your help."

"I'm concerned you don't have a business plan," the managing partner said.

Caleb didn't want to spar on the business plan issue. Not wanting to appear weak, he mustered a confident-sounding, "I understand."

"What do you call it?" One of the investors asked. Caleb played with names for months but never settled on one. Fearing waffling on two questions in a row, he blurted, "HoloMate."

The managing partner reacted, "HoloMate, clever name." He had seen enough and was ready to wrap up the meeting.

"I need to talk with the partners and decide if this is something we want to participate in. I'll call you in a few days after we've chatted."

"OK, thank you again. Say goodbye, Paul!" Paul waved goodbye, converting a few more stone faces to smile.

After the presentation Caleb went back to Villa Comunale. He replayed the entire meeting in his head, agonizing over every word he said, every question asked, every reaction given. He started questioning himself and whether he came across as too overconfident, underconfident, arrogant, submissive, aggressive, passive. He thought about the disappointing looks around the room over the lack of a business plan. He looked at his phone, 2 p.m., shipyard shift would start in two hours. Just then his phone rang. It was the private equity managing partner. Caleb was shocked to see him calling. "Why is he calling so soon? Am I getting a bullet? This can't be good!" These thoughts raced through his mind in the time it took his phone to ring three times, then he picked up.

"Hello?" Caleb's voice shook as he spoke.

"Caleb, this is Vincent Pagnozzi with Pagnozzi Equity. I've got some concerns about HoloMate that I'd like to discuss. Can you come in again tomorrow at three?"

"Sure, I'd be happy to."

"Good, see you tomorrow."

Caleb hung up. "What was that about?" he thought. "He has concerns? Does he want to reject me in person? If he were going to reject me why not just do it over the phone? And he called back so quickly, does that mean it's a no-go?" Caleb went home, changed clothes, and went to his shift at the shipyard.

Caleb arrived at Pagnozzi's office at 3 p.m. the next day. Pagnozzi greeted him in the lobby and escorted him back to the intimidating conference room. This time it was just the two of them in there.

They sat down and Pagnozzi started, "Caleb I didn't want to do this over the phone."

"Here it comes," Caleb thought.

"I'll get to the point. We like the technology and are impressed with your creativity and determination. But you have no idea as to how to monetize or scale the business."

Caleb squeezed the arms of the leather chair, expecting to get rejected.

Pagnozzi continued, "Here's what we're willing to do. We want you to perfect the skin-sensing technology and make the glasses into something people would actually want to wear, not like the clunky prototype. I'm going to put a CEO in place, a CFO who will figure out profitability, and a COO who will figure out how to scale the operation. You will be the chief technology officer and report to the CEO. We want 70 percent of the company and a buyout option in five years. We expect you to be 100 percent dedicated to this, so we'll pay you 150,000 hera a year. No moonlighting for anyone else. I'll put this in writing along with some other particulars for you to review. Do you have any questions?"

With all the scenarios that Caleb imagined he didn't see this one coming. "Not right now."

"Good. You'll get an email from me in the next couple of days. I'll escort you out."

Caleb followed Pagnozzi out of the conference room and into the lobby.

"Thanks for coming in, Caleb."

"Thank you, Mr. Pagnozzi."

During the ten-minute walk to Villa Comunale, his mind bounced between elation, disbelief, and disappointment. "They believe in HoloMate! I can't believe they're going to support me! But they don't trust me enough to make me the boss! I'd be reporting to someone else!" The thought of being accountable to someone else brought back the feelings of insecurity he had had all his life. "Can the CEO fire me? From my own company? And they want 70 percent of the company! It's my idea, why do they get 70 percent?" He needed a voice of reason to talk with, so he called Paul.

"Hey Caleb," Paul immediately picked up when he saw it was Caleb calling. He had just ordered a latte at a new coffee shop near Harvard. It was the new hip place, worn furniture and vintage artwork looking like it came from a garage sale. The place was loud and packed with mostly Harvard-clad students. "Let me pay for my coffee and find a place to sit. Hold on a sec."

Paul got his coffee, sat down on an old fabric chair in the quietest corner of the coffee shop. "I'm back, what's up?"

"They want to work with me, but I'm not the boss and they're going to have other stuffed shirts running the business. I'm only responsible for developing the technology. And they want 70 percent of the company!"

"Are they gonna pay you a salary?"

"Yeah. 150,000 hera." The most Caleb had ever made in a year at the shipyard was 30,000 hera, barely enough to support his partying lifestyle, let alone live on his own.

"And they're gonna surround you with people to help you succeed?"

"Mm hmm."

"What's the downside?"

"I'm not the boss and I lose 70 percent of the company."

Paul took a sip of his latte. "For sure you want to look at the details, but you need help to pull this off. Even if you're not the boss now, you could become the boss after you've proven yourself. And 30 percent of a successful company is better than 100 percent of a failure."

There it was, the failure word again. The image of *Caleb Todd, Master of Failure* headstone flashed in his head.

"Yeah, you might be right. I'll look at the details and keep an open mind."

"Good. It's getting pretty loud in here so I'm gonna go. Take care, Cuz."

Caleb got to his favorite place at Villa Comunale, his imaginary friends waiting there for him. He wrestled with what to do, getting input from each of his friends. Paul was right, he needed to look at the details of the deal and not be so pigheaded about the 70 percent and not being the boss. He decided to keep the arrangement from his family until he knew it was a done deal.

Caleb received Pagnozzi's detailed offer two days later. He immediately sent it to Paul so they could go through all the fine print together. Paul urged him to have an attorney in Naples look at the deal, which he did. Caleb, his attorney, and Pagnozzi agreed on language and signed the deal the following week. The first thing Caleb did was call Paul to let him know it was a go, then went to the shipyard to quit his job. That evening he got home and told his parents the good news. His brothers Frank and Philip were both there. They both listened intently to the details, then Philip asked about salary. "So how much are you going to make?"

"150,000 hera." Both Philip and Frank were astounded. Neither of them had ever made more than 50,000 hera a year at the shipyard.

"Good job, Caleb," Frank said. Caleb couldn't decide if he were more stunned at Frank giving him a compliment or Frank using Caleb's name as opposed to "Squirt," "Little One," "Doofus," or the many other derogatory nicknames he had used over the years. Either way, he would take it.

"Thanks, Frank."

The next day, Caleb met with Pagnozzi and HoloMate's new CEO in Pagnozzi's conference room. Caleb recognized him as one of the investors from the day he pitched HoloMate to Pagnozzi and his partners.

Pagnozzi was all business. "Caleb, this is Vincent Guardino. You may remember him from our meeting. He is one of our private equity partners and is particularly impressed with HoloMate. He approached me after the meeting about being HoloMate's CEO for a few years while we got it off the ground."

"Hello, Caleb. Looking forward to working together."

"Me too."

"I'm not going to mince words," Vincent put his game face on. "If we're going to be successful, it's going to be HoloMate day and night. There's a ton to do and we've got three years to show profitability. I want to make sure you're in it 100 percent. Are you?"

"Yes, Vincent."

"Great. I've got some office space in city center that we'll use to set up shop. Let's go there after we're done and get to work."

Vincent hired a CFO, Janet DeNitto, to manage the money and COO, Liza Martino, to scale the operation. Two years of 18-hour days followed. They honed the skin-sensing technology, a hologram touch was simultaneously felt on the real person. Martino and her team built out the social connection platform and created HoloRooms where HoloMate friends could meet. DeNitto and her team developed the revenue strategy. HoloMate friends could offer to be a friend for free or could set their hourly rate for friendship. The better and more popular a HoloMate friend, the more they could charge. The hourly rate was split 50-50 between the friend and HoloMate Corporate.

The HoloMate platform launched on Caleb's twenty-sixth birthday, August 21, 2042. The HoloMate team gathered in their conference room for the big moment. They watched as HoloMate came online and the glasses went on sale. As cheers erupted, Caleb closed his eyes and pressed his hands together in front of his mouth as if praying. "I hope this works," he thought.

THREE, TWO, ONE
2066

The HoloMate reporter pulled out his mirror, checked his teeth for stuck food, and slicked down the few wayward hairs on his head. "Ten seconds," he heard his producer say in his earpiece. He put on his HoloMate glasses, took a deep breath, then heard "three, two, one."

"This is Aaron Moskowitz from HoloMate News. I'm on location at the Europe Ethnarchy Embassy in Jerusalem. We have reports that Paul Ambrosi, Salvatore Carlotta, and Caleb Todd, all 50 years old, have been shot."

The scene behind Aaron was one of chaos. It was still raining, but the wind had calmed to a more gentle breeze. It wasn't known whether it was just one or more shooters, or where they were when they fired. Israeli Defense Force soldiers were standing shoulder-to-shoulder at the embassy entrance, with IDF sharpshooters positioned on its roof.

A witness was standing by, ready to be interviewed. Aaron handed her a pair of HoloMate glasses so she could appear as a hologram in the broadcast.

"Tell me what happened," Aaron asked the witness.

"The three were walking into the embassy, then there was a *thump thump thump*." She punched her fist with each thump.

"What direction did the shots come from?" Aaron asked.

"I dunno, I just heard the thumps then I turned around and saw the three on the ground. Their security immediately swarmed them and everyone just started running."

"Where were you when you heard the thumps?"

The already-rattled witness started to cry.

"I was inside the embassy gates, it happened about ten meters behind me. I'm sorry." She apologized as she lifted her HoloMate glasses to wipe her eyes, interrupting the hologram transmission.

"It's OK, thank you for your time." Aaron took her glasses from her, her hologram disappearing. Aaron held his earpiece to his ear so he could hear his producer's voice over the chaos behind him.

"My producer is telling me that Ambrosi and Carlotta were shot in the head and Todd in the arm. They're all en route to Jerusalem Health. As we know more we'll let you know. Stay tuned to HoloMate News for the latest."

Aaron waited for the "And we're off" in his earpiece. He took off his HoloSpecs, looked around at the pandemonium, and just shook his head. "This is going to be bad for Israel," he thought.

GENE THE LAB RAT
2041

S al decided to return to Italy after graduating from Columbia. He didn't even attend graduation, why bother? There was no one he wanted to invite anyway. His father, perhaps feeling a bit of guilt, had tried to reach out to Sal several times over the past few years, each attempt ignored. Sal's anger toward his father continued to simmer, particularly when he thought about his mother, how Gene emotionally abused her through the years, and left Sal to tend to his mother when she was dying. Trying to make amends, Gene offered to arrange an introduction to a Rome-based private equity firm that specialized in biomedical engineering. Sal may have been bitter, but he wasn't one to pass up on a great opportunity. It was the first time he responded to his father in years, and he only did it because he was getting something he wanted. It would be the last time he talked to his father.

Sal met with Louisa Testa, the private equity firm founder and managing partner on October 24, 2041 at Testa's offices in the Monti ward in Rome. Sal showed up with Gene, his lab rat.

"Thanks for meeting with me, Ms. Testa." Sal said.

"Pleasure is mine. What's in the tub?" Sal was holding a small white plastic tub with a carrying handle and holes punched in the top.

"My lab rat, Gene."

Louisa smirked. She picked up on Sal naming the rat after his father.

"Ms. Testa, I'd . . ."

Louisa interrupted. "Call me Lou."

"OK, Lou." Sal took a deep breath, "My research involved creating a microfluidic chip which, when saline-populated with dormant liver cells, regenerated a damaged liver into a healthy liver. I want to use my project to start a company to research cancer eradication through genetically engineered synthetic killer cells."

"Does the company have a name?"

"MD Biometrics."

"MD meaning medical doctor?"

"It's after my mother Marie Desmond."

"Eradicate cancer, pretty ambitious," Lou said. She noticed Sal kept stealing glances at her chest when he thought she wasn't looking. She had done research of her own on Sal and his project. She saw potential but didn't like his wandering eyes. It fit in with what she had already heard about Sal. "We've done our own research on your work, including talking with Dean Andrews at Columbia. You've got quite the reputation as a brilliant, 25-year-old arrogant ass. Why should I invest in you?"

Sal wasn't prepared for her blunt assessment. He could either prove that he was an arrogant ass and give her a flip response or take the high road and tell her why she should invest in him.

"Thank you, Lou." Sal decided on the latter. "Two reasons. First, the dormant cell regeneration through a microfluidic membrane is the first of its kind anywhere. I transformed a damaged liver to a healthy liver and kept it healthy in 27 preclinical experiments. The technology applications are limitless. Second, I have a personal passion for eradicating cancer. My mother died of it and it's my life's ambition to get rid of it forever. My knowledge coupled with passion is what we need to make living in a cancer-free world a reality."

Lou was impressed with Sal's ability to think on his feet and not get rattled by her calling him an arrogant ass. While she still had reservations about Sal's character, she saw the potential in his research.

"Sal, I want you to talk with some of my partners who understand the technology a lot better than I do. I'll get with them, then I'll let you know what we'd be willing to do, if anything."

"Happy to do." Sal continued with his humbled tone. "Let me know who and when, and I'll tell you anything you want to know."

"Perfect, thank you for coming by, Sal." Lou rang her assistant. "Nicholas, would you show Sal out, please?" A few seconds later Nicholas opened the door.

Sal stood up. "Thank you, Lou." He reached out to shake her hand. Staying seated, she extended her arm and gave him a firm I'm-in-charge handshake. "We'll be in contact, Sal." She said.

Nicholas held the door for Sal as he walked out of the office, through the lobby and out of the building. Sal hated being put on the spot like that. She was tough and wasn't going to put up with any nonsense. He had to act humble until he had more investor offers, then he could be tougher when he was in a more powerful negotiating position. That was his plan, nice until more offers came, then be an arrogant ass to try to get the best deal possible.

Over the next four weeks, Sal met with six different partners and experts recommended by Lou. He took Gene the rat to every appointment. Sal explained how Gene's damaged liver was fully repaired using the microfluidic chip and dormant liver cells, and how he had now been healthy for two years with additional saline treatments. He also contacted five other investors to discuss his research and alternatives to fund his work moving forward. He envisioned by end of November having six investor offers to choose from, then turning the screws on his investor of choice to get his most favored terms. Great plan on paper, reality was another thing.

By the end of November, he had heard from five of the six, all rejections. All of them cited that, while the technology was interesting, Sal's desire to focus his work exclusively on curing cancer was too high of a risk for them to take. The only one he'd yet to hear from was Louisa's firm. He considered calling them to find out where they were in their decision, but didn't want to appear too eager or, even worse, desperate. The rejections shook his confidence. "Don't they see the potential here?" he thought over and over again. "I know I can do it, they don't know what they're missing!" As much as Sal didn't want to admit it, he was growing frantic that no one was going to fund his dream. He decided to give it until after the new year, then if he didn't hear from Louisa he would scrap the whole idea and look for a job working for someone else.

On December 17 he got a call. "Sal, this is Lou Testa."

BUONE FESTE
2041

Sal closed his eyes and took a deep breath. "Hi, Lou." He braced himself for rejection number six.

"My partners are pretty impressed with your research and love your cancer passion. We've been running some numbers and have a proposal to present. Can you come in tomorrow and talk with me and a few of my partners?"

He had already set his expectations that come January he would be looking at other jobs. Now there was a glimmer of hope that he could pursue his dream. Wanting to play it cool, Sal responded as if he'd have to fit them in, even though his calendar was wide open. "I've got from two to three available tomorrow. Will that work?"

"I can do from one to two."

"OK, I'll be at your office at one."

"Good. See you tomorrow." Sal heard the beep of Lou hanging up. "A proposal!" Sal thought. "Are they going to let me focus on cancer? How much of the company will they want? Will I have to report to someone else? Anyone but Lou!" There were very few women who intimidated Sal. He was so used to knowing how to manipulate women to get what he wanted. Lou was different. She wasn't charmed by Sal. She wasn't afraid to tell him exactly what she thought. And she'd kick his butt if he got out of line. She reminded him of the counselor at Columbia who told him he could never get his Ph.D. in seven years. The counselor didn't have authority over him, but Lou would. And the thought of a woman holding him accountable drove him nuts.

Sal showed up at Lou's office the next day at one. Lou's assistant Nicholas escorted Sal into a stark conference room next to Lou's office. The conference room had a round folding table surrounded by eight metal folding chairs. The ceiling and walls were white with a projector hanging from the middle of the ceiling. A single whiteboard was on one wall, stained with old markings that wouldn't completely erase and a scribbling where someone used black permanent marker on the board. "They'll be here in a couple minutes," Nicholas told Sal, then shut the door as he left Sal alone in the conference room.

Sal stood in the room for five minutes, too nervous to sit. He went to the whiteboard, looking at the black permanent marker. He remembered a trick at Columbia where you could color over permanent marker with a dry erase marker then erase it, removing the permanent marker. Sal scribbled over the black with a red marker, then erased the scribble. Black mark gone. He put the eraser down just as Lou and four of her partners came in.

"How did you do that?" she asked after seeing the board where the black squiggle used to be.

"Color over the permanent marker with whiteboard marker, then erase it. *Voila!*"

"Industrious, been staring at that for years. Thanks."

"No problem."

"Sal, you may remember Linda Quaranta, Natasha Anosov, Uwe Lutz, and Carmine Galluzzi."

"Certainly." Sal shook hands with each. Then they all sat down.

Linda was first to speak. "Sal, your research is brilliant."

"Thank you, Linda."

Linda continued. "We love your cancer passion and know how important this is to you, having lost your mother to cancer. Our deepest condolences on your mother's passing."

Sal gave Linda a gracious smile. "Thank you."

"We believe you have what it takes to find the cure to cancer and want to partner with you. We're willing to fund your research for two years. After that if there's no viable cure, we refocus the work on broad-scale organ regeneration. You can be CEO and chief scientist and we will supply a CFO and COO. You will also be accountable to a board of directors comprised of the five of us with Lou as the chairman. You keep 40 percent ownership in the company and we retain 60."

Sal was busy taking notes on Linda's points when he heard Lou speak. "Sal, I want to make sure you understand how we do things. As you can see by the no-frills conference room, we run very lean here. We're a no-nonsense operation, watch our expenses like a hawk, and don't put up with BS. We have a strict code-of-conduct policy, adopted by all our companies. As part of your employment contract you will sign a code-of-conduct agreement which we expect you to follow to the letter. Any violation, and we immediately terminate you and buy out your 40 percent. You toe the line and there will be no problems. I wanted to tell you about it before you saw your employment agreement, so you knew it was coming. Understood?"

Lou made sure Sal knew who was boss. She knew of his past at Columbia and thought he was a pompous jerk. She didn't like that he was checking her out during their first meeting. She was concerned Sal was going do something and give Lou and her partners legal headaches.

"I understand, Lou." Sal managed a courteous response even though on the inside he was smoldering. It didn't matter that he earned his jackass reputation and that Lou was just protecting the interests of her investor group.

"Good. We'll have everything put in writing and Linda will get it to you in a few days. Take the holidays to look it over, then let's talk after the new year, sound good?" Lou started getting up, signaling to the rest that the meeting was over.

"Thanks all, I'll wait to see the terms. Thank you for having confidence in me." Sal was doing all he could to keep things positive and not step on anyone's toes.

Lou opened the door to leave and yelled to Nicholas, "Can you show Sal out?"

Nicholas greeted Sal at the conference room door, then escorted him through the lobby and out the front door. "*Buone Feste,* Nicholas," Sal said as he walked out.

"Same to you, Sal."

Sal got the written terms the following week. He would have plenty of time to review the terms over the holidays since he was spending it alone in his apartment near the Pantheon. Christmas would be like his days at Columbia, looking to add women's pictures to his phone, then crashing down to the reality of being alone. The hologram of his mother at his birthday party giving him only a little comfort from his loneliness.

Sal went through the terms, including the strict code-of-conduct policy. He saw clearly that he was on a tight leash. Any accusations of harassment, public disparagement of Lou and her partners, or insubordination were cause for termination and forfeiture of ownership. MD Biometrics may have existed because of his research and brilliance, but it wouldn't be his company. He would be its CEO and chief scientist but would be under Lou's thumb. While he hated the terms, he was getting the opportunity to create a cure for cancer. After he had an attorney review the terms, he signed the deal on January 3, 2042. MD Biometrics was born.

JASMINE AT 20

2042

Sal wasted no time getting MD up and running. Despite how he felt about the arrangement, he was driven to making MD a success. Two years of intense research followed, with over 320 preclinical experiments on rats. Lou agreed to fund a small team of bio- and nanoengineers, but they had to do it in a makeshift lab in rented office space. Not optimal scientific conditions, but that was all Lou was willing to do, so Sal went with it. The lab had one wall lined with cage after cage of rats, all in different stages of testing. Sal painstakingly reviewed each rat's progress every day. Even back at Columbia, Sal had been very comfortable around rats, treating them as if they were his friends. Whenever a rat died, it felt like losing a loved one. He named each rat and memorized which trials went with each rat. Sal kept Gene, his rat from Columbia, in his cubicle, caring for it like a well-loved pet.

It was one particular rat—Jasmine--that provided the breakthrough Sal was looking for. Jasmine, or trial HM-260 as she was technically known, had a microfluidic chip surgically implanted into her right atrium. It was powered by the heart's sinoatrial node, giving the chip a constant source of power that would only cease when the heart stopped beating. After the chip was in place, Jasmine was injected with a saline solution which contained dormant synthetic killer cells. The SK cells could be programmed to search and eradicate any number of diseases in the body. The saline solution with the dormant SK cells passed through the microfluidic chip, activating the dormant SK cells. The now-active SK cells were like natural killer cells but much more effective at finding and killing foreign bodies. Unlike natural killer cells, SK cells couldn't be tricked by some cancers. They were able to recognize gene fragments that were found in every type of known cancer. Once a cancer cell was detected, SK cells went to work breaking down the cancer cells through chromosome fragmentation, where the SK cell disrupted the genetic mapping of the cancer chromosomes.

Jasmine was injected with melanoma cells from a human subject. The cancer cells began to grow, evidenced by a fingernail-sized tumor on her back. The tumor size was recorded at start of the trial and each morning at 6:00. On day 20 of the trial, a lesion measuring 20 millimeters formed on Jasmine's spine. With the microfluidic chip already attached to her right atrium, Sal injected the saline containing the dormant SK cells. Days two and three after injection the lesion showed no changes in tumor size. On day four, Mario, one of Sal's bioengineers, was recording morning MRI measurements.

"Sal, you gotta see this!" Mario called from the wall of lab rats to Sal in his cubicle. Sal bounced out of his chair and came to the wall. "Jasmine is at 14 millimeters."

Sal knew the intimate details of each of the trials. He knew Jasmine was at 20 millimeters just yesterday. "Are you sure?" Sal asked.

"Check it out." Mario showed Sal the MRI results.

"Six-millimeter reduction, it was 20 yesterday, right?" Sal could hardly believe what he was seeing.

"Yup," Mario responded.

"How are her vitals?"

"All normal. She looks perfectly healthy."

"OK, watch her vitals, let me know if anything changes." Sal went back to his cubicle, sat down, gave Gene a grape, and leaned back in his chair with his hands over his eyes. "Don't get ahead of yourself," he thought.

Each day thereafter was Jasmine-watch day. Sal came in at 6:00 each morning to evaluate Jasmine's progress. On day five, Jasmine's tumor was eleven millimeters. Day six: seven millimeters. Day seven:

four millimeters. Day eight: no discernible tumor. Vitals all normal. Jasmine was eating, drinking, and responding to stimulus. On day nine, Sal decided to make an incision to inspect the tumor site. No trace of tumor, it was as if she never had one to start with. Realizing that a sample size of one hardly indicated success, Sal put ten more rats through the same procedures over the next two months, varying the size, location, and types of cancer. All ten yielded the same result--tumor gone, healthy rat. During the extended trial, though, Mario noticed abnormal behavior in Jasmine.

"Sal, Jasmine's not doing well." Mario said.

"Is the tumor back?"

"No, she is lethargic, not eating or drinking, vitals abnormal."

Sal was perplexed by Jasmine's sudden decline. "Let's draw blood and get an SK count."

Mario drew some blood from Jasmine and prepped it for the flow cytometer to detect SK activity. "Her SK count is at zero, but so is her natural killer cell count. Her natural immune system was destroyed by the SK cells."

"Destroyed?" Sal asked.

"Yes, destroyed."

"OK, let's inject more SK saline and see what happens." Could it be that SK cells kill not only cancer cells but natural killer cells too? If so, the body would become wholly dependent on the new SK cells, without them even a minor infection was deadly.

Mario injected SK saline into Jasmine. Within a day, her vitals were back to normal, she was eating and drinking. With continued SK saline treatments, Jasmine's body could fight off cancer, without them she would most certainly die. Wanting to see if this was a trend, Sal observed the behavior of the additional ten rats. Four weeks after the initial SK saline injection, all ten displayed the same symptoms as Jasmine--lethargic, not eating or drinking, abnormal vitals. No SK or natural killer cells present. Five received an additional SK saline treatment, five didn't. The five who did were back to normal by the next day, the five who didn't were dead within a week. Sal did another 20 experiments, same result. Once SK cells die, no immune system, then death.

Excited but cautious, Sal gave an update to Lou and the rest of the board. He invited them to the makeshift lab so they could meet Jasmine and he could tell her story. The day before the meeting, Sal set up a folding table with six mismatched chairs around it, keeping with Lou's frugal tone. The next morning Lou and board members Linda, Natasha, Uwe, and Carmine came to the lab, each taking a seat around the folding table after getting coffee at an espresso machine Sal purchased with Lou's money.

Lou took a sip of coffee. "Mmm, this is really good coffee Sal, what kind is it?"

"Kopi luwak," Sal said. "The beans are harvested from the feces of the civet cat."

"Huh, kind of redefines crappy coffee." Lou's expressionless response followed by silence was met with groans from the rest.

"So she does have a sense of humor," Sal thought to himself. She'd lose it in a hurry if she knew how expensive kopi luwak was. And that she was paying for it.

"OK, on that note, let me get into the Jasmine trial. Mario, go get Jasmine," Sal said.

"Thanks, Mario. Everyone, meet HM-260, or who I call Jasmine. She's a healthy rat who just nine weeks ago had a 20-millimeter cancerous lesion on her back. We began treatment, then eight days later it was gone. Her vitals all remained in the normal range throughout the eight-day period; she ate, drank, and eliminated like a normal healthy rat. We then replicated the test on ten additional rats, all with the same results."

Sal definitely got the attention of the board. Lou was the first to speak up.

"That's incredible, Sal!" This is the first time Sal heard Lou express any type of excitement. "What's the formula?"

Sal had his elevator pitch ready. "We implanted a microfluidic chip into her right atrium powered by the sinoatrial node, then injected her with a saline solution with dormant synthetic killer cells that were more potent and efficient than the body's natural killer cells. After three days we saw no change in tumor size, but then on day four there was a six-millimeter reduction. By day eight the tumor was gone."

"And no side effects during treatment?" Carmine asked.

"None during treatment. Vitals and bodily functions all in normal range."

"Can we see the other ten rats?" Natasha asked.

"You can only see five." This is where Sal explained the experiment's downside.

"Why five?" Natasha asked, her disposition instantly changed from near-giddy to completely serious.

"We discovered an after-treatment side effect that we are still working on. The SK cells kill off natural killer cells. The saline solution treatment only lasts about 18 days, then the SK cells die off. The problem is that the natural killer cells are permanently gone too, leaving the body with no immune system."

They all knew what that meant. No immune system meant death within weeks if not days. The room mood changed from elation to cautious optimism. The cancer-killing SK cells were a success, but the immune system issue still needed work.

"The word revolutionary doesn't do this justice." Lou was direct and not one to put up with nonsense, but she was fair. "It's to be expected there are some things to work out. What are your next steps?"

Sal had his punch list ready. "Number one is figuring out the immune system issue. Next is how to non-invasively insert the chip, how to identify it to the wearer so we can track who has what chip, and how to extend the life of SK cells beyond 18 days. After 18 days, the SK cells lose their ability to be activated by the charge supplied by the chip. Just like a rechargeable battery stops charging over time. That's what happens to the SK cells. I expect to take another nine to 12 months to get this locked down, hopefully sooner."

"OK, Sal, keep pushing forward. Do you need anything from us?"

Sal didn't hesitate. "Can you get us into a real lab and out of this hell hole?"

"Let me see what I can do." Lou saw the upside in his research and wanted them to be productive. She was willing to invest in a more suitable lab if it meant better and faster results. "Send me a note with what you want in a lab."

SAL'S TURN
2044

S al put together his lab wish list, padding it with everything he could think of, expecting Lou to push back. He couldn't believe it when she gave him all he asked for. A mere one month later Sal and his team were in his dream lab. They immediately started figuring out the immune system issue and taking on the other issues as time permitted. Sal met with the board at three, six, nine, and 12-month checkpoints. After 12 months and 300 more trials, they made progress on chip insertion, wearer identification, and SK cell life. Sal briefed the board at its 12-month checkpoint in his new lab. The board sat at a permanent conference table with matched, comfortable chairs, much different from the folding table and mismatched chairs at their old lab.

"We've been able to extend SK cell life to six months, a far cry from the 18 days we were at during Jasmine's trial." Sal started listing the issues identified 12 months ago, and noted the progress made. "We can uniquely pair the chip with the subject's unique genetic markers. When inserted, the chip records the markers of the subject and acts like a lock on the chip. As long as the markers paired on the chip match the markers of the subject, the chip functions. If there's no marker match, the chip won't work." Two issues down, two to go. "Regarding chip insertion, we're able to do it through a magnetic tip catheter which contains the chip. We insert the catheter into the subject's groin and navigate the catheter using magnets into the right atrium, where the chip adheres to the atrium wall." Three down, now the tough issue. "On the immune system, we're not able to revert an immune system back to its original state once SK cells have been introduced. Once the subject has SK cells, they're dependent on them for life. Until we're able to find a solution, they will need to continue getting saline SK solution treatments."

Lou's initial reservations about Sal had dissipated since their first meeting. She believed he was doing his best and acting in their collective best interests. "OK, so what's the next step?" Lou asked.

"Human trial."

He looked around the room, amused at seeing the board members cringe. A human trial meant that the subject would be forever dependent on saline SK until a better solution was found.

"Who in their right mind would volunteer for that?" Uwe asked the question the rest were already thinking.

"Me." Sal didn't hesitate in his response. He believed in his research, understood its risks, and needed to prove it was viable. Lou understood Sal's passion and commitment.

"Are you sure about this?" Lou asked.

"100 percent."

"How and when?"

"Mario and I can start tomorrow. We have Burkitt Lymphoma cells ready to go. It's the fastest-growing cancer, doubling in size every 14 hours. After a week, we'll insert the chip and inject the Saline SK fluid."

Linda couldn't contain herself. "Let me get this straight. You're going to infect yourself with the fastest-growing cancer known, then hope the chip and solution kill it? If it doesn't work, you could be dead in months."

"It'll work, I'm willing to bet my life on it."

This was well beyond making money and hitting deadlines. Sal was literally putting his life on the line to prove the viability of his creation. Lou kept the discussion grounded.

"Sal, you know the risks and I trust you. If you think it's ready for human trial, then we go with your assessment. You understand we need to have releases of liability for the board in place in the event the trial goes awry, right?"

"Feckless board," Sal thought. He's signing in blood and they're concerned about liability. It was either that or do it without the board's consent, which could get him fired.

"I understand." Sal said.

"OK then. Before you start, get with Linda to make sure we've got the right protections in place to hold the board harmless for injury. Only after we've got the liability release does the trial start, got it?"

"Yes." Sal said.

The room was silent. Never before had any of them been in a situation where a person was willing to risk his life as part of a business venture. No one said a word as they got up from their new conference room chairs. Sal went to the door leading out of the lab to say his goodbyes to each board member. Lou was first to leave.

"Let me know if you need anything, Sal."

"Will do."

Natasha and Uwe followed, wishing him good luck. As Linda was leaving, Sal asked about the liability paperwork. "When can we sign?"

"I'll come by tomorrow."

"So, we can start the trial right after I sign?"

"Yes. See you tomorrow."

Carmine was the last to leave. He fist-bumped Sal, "You got balls, man."

"Hopefully I'll get to keep them for a good long time." Sal smirked at Carmine, reminded of when the cameraman at Columbia said the same thing.

SCAN ME!
2045

Linda came by the next morning with the liability release paperwork. Sal gave it a cursory look, then signed. He just wanted to get on with the trial. Whatever the board needed to authorize Sal to move forward, so be it. Linda wished him well and underscored Lou's offer to speak up about anything he needed. "What I need is to get the stupid document signed then get the board out of my way," Sal thought to himself. Instead he just said "thank you" to Linda as she left. Sal and Mario already planned to do the Burkitt Lymphoma injection that afternoon. Good to go.

Mario prepared a tray of alcohol wipes, cotton balls, bandages, a tourniquet, and a syringe containing the Burkitt Lymphoma cells. He moved two stools next to a counter, put the tray on the counter between the two stools, and sat down on one.

"OK, we're ready," Mario called to Sal. Sal was sitting in his cubicle with his feet on the desk, Gene and Jasmine eating grapes on Sal's reclined chest. Sal gently put the rats back in their cages, giving each a kiss on the head before closing the cage doors. Sal came over and sat on a stool, facing Mario. Sal saw the anxiety in Mario's eyes, Mario saw the resolve in Sal's. Mario broke his gaze and looked down at the tray, grabbing a rubber tourniquet and tying it around Sal's bicep, deliberately working slowly in the event Sal had second thoughts about the trial. With Sal's swimmer's physique and low body fat he already presented Mario with prominent veins. Mario grabbed an alcohol wipe and slowly rubbed Sal's skin where the target vein was waiting. He gently picked up the syringe and pushed on the plunger flange until a stream of solution dripped from the needle. He looked at Sal, wanting to confirm he was ready for what was about to happen. Sal didn't say a word, that same determined look in his eyes, ready for the injection. Mario steadied his hand, placed the needle on Sal's skin encasing the waiting vein, and lightly pushed the needle into the vein. Once the needle was in, he pushed the top of the syringe, emptying its contents into Sal's arm. Sal closed his eyes as the plunger made its way down the barrel. When the syringe was empty, Mario pulled the needle from the vein, removed the tourniquet, placed a cotton ball over the vein where a slight drop of blood made its way to the surface, and placed a bandage over the cotton ball. He lifted Sal's hand toward his shoulder, putting pressure on the injection site to stop the bleeding.

"All done." Mario quietly cleaned up while Sal went back to his cubicle. He sat in his chair, pulled Jasmine from her cage, kissed her head, leaned back in his chair, and put her on his chest. "Let's hope my result is the same as yours," he said.

Never had anyone been so anxious to see the signs of cancer. Each morning Mario and Sal conducted a barrage of tests and body scans, looking for any signs of Burkitt Lymphoma. Blood tests confirmed abnormal blood levels, but no tumors yet.

Sal laughed at the irony of his situation. "I can't wait to hear the words that millions before me dreaded to hear," he said as Mario confirmed no visible tumors on day ten after the injection. Days 11, 12, and 13, no tumor. On day 14, Sal noticed a small lump on his jaw as he was shaving. "Finally!" Sal finished shaving, being careful not to nick the area where the lump was beginning to grow. He dressed as quickly as he could then made his way to the lab to take a measurement. When he got to the lab Mario was already there. "It's on my jaw!" Sal said as he pointed to the tumor. "How big?"

Mario did an MRI. "Three millimeters," Mario said. "When do you want to start the SK treatment?"

"20 millimeters."

"Twenty?" Mario couldn't believe Sal would want to wait until the tumor got that big. "We can prove the trial with it being much smaller, why risk it at 20?"

"Jasmine was at 20, I'm going to be at 20."

Mario shook his head. "OK, boss."

Each morning Sal and Mario took measurements. Day two, seven millimeters. Day three, 12 millimeters. Day four, 15 millimeters. Then the measurement on day five.

"23 millimeters," Mario said.

"Let's do it."

"Finally." Mario said. Sal just looked at him and smiled.

That afternoon, Mario prepared the lab for chip insertion. He wheeled a stretcher to an open area in the room and prepared a tray holding a sterile magnetic tip catheter with the microfluidic chip already inserted, a Seldinger needle, a syringe with lidocaine, a guide wire, alcohol wipes, a catheter sheath, cotton balls, bandages and a surgical magnet used to guide the catheter. Entry would be at the groin into the femoral artery. Mario shaved and disinfected the entry site. Sal lay down on the stretcher, showing the same determination as he did during the Burkitt injection. Mario was all business, wanting to make sure nothing went wrong with the chip insertion. Mario numbed the site and inserted the Seldinger needle into Sal's groin area, finding the femoral artery. He threaded the guide wire through the needle into the artery, removed the needle and inserted the catheter sheath over the guide wire. He then pulled the guide wire out.

"How you doing?" Mario asked.

"All good."

"Now the catheter." Mario turned on the catheter camera and threaded the catheter through the sheath into Sal's femoral artery. On a screen next to the stretcher, Mario and Sal saw the catheter tip enter the artery. He then grabbed the surgical magnet and turned it on, a red light showed on top of the magnet. The magnet looked like a computer mouse and served two functions. One was to guide the magnetic-tipped catheter from the femoral artery into the right atrium of the heart. The second was to communicate with the chip throughout the procedure and ensure the chip was functioning smoothly after it had adhered to the atrium wall. When the light was red, the magnet was on but not communicating with the chip. Yellow meant communication was established with the chip, and green meant the chip was successfully adhered and functioning.

"Let's start the journey," Mario said as he started moving the surgical magnet from Sal's groin, up into his midsection on its way to the heart, the light still red. So far so good.

"It looks great!" Sal said as he watched the screen. The catheter followed the surgical magnet's every move as it made its way up Sal's chest.

"Yup, very responsive." Mario now had the magnet in the center of Sal's chest, right above the right atrium. The catheter made its way into the right atrium, positioning its tip along the atrium wall. Mario then slid his finger across the magnet which moved the chip out of the catheter along the wall. The light on the magnet changed from red to yellow, indicating the magnet and chip were now talking to each other. Mario swiped his finger side to side telling the chip to unroll to its full size of a man's pinky nail. Mario moved his finger forward on the magnet to push the chip flat against the heart wall. Once in place, eight small rigid surgical wires grabbed onto the wall which both held the chip in place and powered the chip. The light continued to burn yellow.

"Come on, green!" Mario said, watching the magnet with intensity. Five seconds, then ten, then 15, the light was still yellow.

"Come on, green." Mario whispered, not wanting Sal to hear. Sal didn't need to hear it from Mario, he knew what the yellow light meant.

Finally, after 30 seconds, the light turned green.

"It's in and powered." Mario took a deep breath, continuing to stare at the light to ensure it stayed green.

Sal took a deep sigh of relief and gazed at the green light. Both watched it for a minute to see if it was still green, periodically looking at the screen to make sure the chip was stable.

"Catheter's coming out." Mario put the magnet back on the tray then pulled the catheter and sheath out and dressed the entry site.

"How do you feel?" Mario asked.

"I feel alright, just let me lie here for a minute." Sal was fine, he was just overcome by the fact that this microfluidic chip that he'd been working on since his days at Columbia was now powered up in his heart.

"When you're ready, we'll do the saline." Mario was anxious to get the solution in him, knowing the tumor could double in size every 14 hours. To him every hour counted.

Sal lay there for five minutes while Mario prepared the solution injection. "Sal, you ready?"

"Yup." Sal sat up on the stretcher, put out his right arm, and Mario gave him the SK injection.

"Now we wait." Sal patted Mario on the back, knowing how stressful this was for him. Mario went to his cubicle and slumped in his chair, exhausted from the procedure. Sal went back to his cubicle, sat in his chair, and pulled Jasmine from her cage.

"You and I have a lot in common, Jasmine." Sal kissed her on the head and held her as he closed his eyes and rubbed the tumor on his jaw. "Hope it's gone as quick as hers," he thought.

Each morning after the procedure, Sal had Mario MRI the tumor. Day one wasn't good.

"27 millimeters. Bigger by four." Sal had hoped to at least stop the growth. Day two, 29 millimeters. Still growing, but slower. Sal hoped that was a good sign. Day three, 30 millimeters. On day four, Mario MRI'd the tumor.

"27 millimeters. Down by three." Mario said. Right direction, but they weren't out of the woods.

Day five, 21. Day six, 18. Day seven, 14. Day eight, nine. Day nine, five. Day ten, no visual sign.

"Scan me!" Sal said, wanting Mario to do a PET scan to confirm the cancer was completely gone.

"OK, boss."

The two went to the PET scanner in the lab where Mario prepped Sal for the scan. Sal lay down, then the table with Sal on it moved slowly into the machine. Mario observed the procedure.

"Gone." Mario said.

Sal leapt up from the table, hitting his head on the scanner. "YES!" He hugged Mario, who was just as excited as Sal.

Sal lay back on the table, overcome with emotion. He flashed back to his room full of trophies, and how this achievement was the biggest trophy of all. He thought of his mother, how this could have saved her life. Tears came as he imagined how this could change the world, how *he* was going to change the world. But a human trial of one was just the start. He'd need more trials. A lot more.

CUSTOMERS FOR LIFE
2046

Each week over the next year, Sal had himself injected with a different type of cancer. For the first six months, each injection of the SK cells from the initial saline SK solution treatment eradicated the cancer cells before they had a chance to grow. After six months, Sal noticed sluggishness and growing tumors, which confirmed the saline SK solution treatment life of six months. Mario immediately injected a booster solution treatment. A week after the booster Sal felt normal and the tumors reduced in size. He continued the weekly cancer injections for another six months, 52 cancer injections gone in one year with no side effects.

At Sal's one-year anniversary of starting the weekly cancer injections, he and Mario were sitting alone in the lab sipping kopi luwak and reviewing trial results. Mario decided to ask Sal the question he'd been wanting to ask for months.

"Are you gonna tell the board?" Mario asked Sal.

"About what?"

"The immune system issue."

"Nope. And neither are you. You and your bank account will be very happy."

"Sworn to secrecy," Mario said. Sal had solved the immune system issue months ago, but that meant a person could stop saline SK solution treatments anytime they wanted. Once a person started on the treatments, they would become a customer for life, generating a consistent and huge revenue stream for MD Biometrics. Solve the immune issue and solution sales would be drastically impacted. Sal took his cue from printer manufacturers 50 years earlier that would sell printers for next to nothing and make their money on ink. It was the perfect business model, with certain death being at stake. Mario was the only other person who knew, and Sal promised to reward him well for his silence.

"Once the board sees hera gushing in they'll forget about the issue." Sal said.

The board was delighted with the results. Fifty-two different cancer types, all eradicated. No side effects. Only the immune system issue, which was solved by solution booster injections. The board authorized one year of expanded human trials across gender, race, age, body type, and income class. Each participant was paid 10,000 hera. Among the trial participants was Lou, the only board member to volunteer. The trials continued for another year, all with similar results to Sal's. Sal and the board now had enough data to submit the chip and solution invention to the Europe Ethnarchy's drug administration for approval. One year later they got the approval they were looking for.

Recognizing that chip insertion and solution injection needed to be accessible to anyone, Sal designed two automated appliances to insert the chip and inject the fluid. The chip insertion appliance looked like a tanning bed. A naked patient would lay in the appliance and close the clamshell top over his body. In the top was a robotic arm that shaved, sterilized and numbed the groin area, then inserted the magnetic-tip catheter containing the chip into the femoral artery. Magnets above and below the patient guided the catheter to the right atrium where the chip was inserted and confirmed operational. The catheter would then exit the body and the robotic arm bandaged the area. The procedure took about 15 minutes and was monitored by a certified MD Biometrics technician in the event of a malfunction.

The solution injection appliance looked like a pharmacy blood pressure machine. The patient sat in a seat and a cuff gently wrapped around his neck. Injection in the neck was required in case the patient did not have an arm or leg to accommodate an injection. Once the cuff was in place, a robotic arm sterilized the skin above the jugular vein then a needle injected the saline SK solution into the vein. The procedure took about five minutes and was monitored by a technician. Both appliances bore the MD Biometrics logo, a black circle with the block letters *MD* in bright orange.

Over the next five years, the appliances were installed in pharmacies throughout the Europe Ethnarchy, with the logo prominently displayed in store windows to attract customers. Pharmacists and nurses became certified MD Biometrics technicians by attending a one-month HoloMate certification class. Insurance companies covered the cost of chip insertions and solution injections, it was cheaper than having to pay for cancer treatments. The rest of the world ethnarchies took notice of the treatment and began ordering appliances. MD Biometrics certified as many appliance manufacturers as they could to keep up with demand. Chip and solution production remained in-house, with thousands of MD Biometrics employees manufacturing and certifying chips and fluid. A crucial organization of MD Biometrics not known to the public was its information technology organization, called MDCentral. MDCentral was responsible for recording and tracking every chip manufactured and implanted, and every solution treatment received. They knew who had each and every chip and could control its operation. The general public didn't know about MD's ability to control the chips implanted in their hearts, and even if they did, the benefit of being cancer-free would have outweighed any fear of MD's control. While only those in MDCentral knew of chip control, only Sal and Mario knew what it was really capable of doing.

CLUNKY GLASSES
2043

The first year after HoloMate's launch in August 2042 saw only 3,000 subscribers, well below HoloMate management's expectations of 100,000. The glasses were the problem. They were heavy, the lenses thick, round and nerdy. The ear buds were clumsy and non-functional for hearing aid wearers. The skin-sensing technology was unreliable, frequently confusing body pressure points. A handshake between HoloMate friends could either be felt by the wearer as a handshake, a slap on the arm or a punch on the thigh. The glasses served just one function, communication through HoloMate. If a wearer already wore prescription lenses or wanted to wear sunglasses, they needed to carry around extra glasses. If HoloMate glasses were to be accepted, they needed to ensure the glasses did everything a wearer needed. Caleb's boss, Vincent Guardino, was getting intense pressure from HoloMate's investors to get the glasses right, and he gave Caleb a blank check to make it happen. Caleb hired engineers who specialized in electrochromic glass, bone conduction assistive hearing, and somatosensory systems. He hired a fashion designer to help design eyewear that someone would enjoy wearing as a fashion accessory, not just as must-need glasses. HoloMate's fate hung on the glasses, and Caleb knew he had to get it right.

While Caleb worked on next-generation glasses, Vincent decided to disable skin-sensing, as that was the technology that was the most unstable. With no skin-sensing, wearers could see and hear their HoloFriends but could not feel any touching sensations. Wearers weren't happy, but it was better than shutting down the HoloMate platform completely. With skin sensing disabled, Caleb first worked on lens functionality and fashion. His engineering team created slim electrochromic lenses with three modes. The first mode was a clear-glass mode that scanned the eye and digitally adjusted the prescription of the lens to enable the wearer to see with 20/20 vision. The second mode was a sunglass mode, where the lens digitally darkened or lightened based on sun conditions. The third mode was HoloMode, which enabled the wearer to enter a HoloRoom and meet with other HoloFriends. Rather than see what was physically around him, he would now see a HoloRoom and HoloFriends in the room. It was easy to see if glasses were in HoloMode, the lenses were frosted instead of clear. When the wearer left the HoloRoom, the lenses changed from frosted to clear. The next generation of glasses also came in ten different frame styles, giving wearers more fashion choices. The glasses still included earbuds and did not include skin-sensing, those features would be in future versions. Wanting to divorce itself of the negative image of clunky glasses, HoloMate dubbed the new glasses HoloSpecs I, with a release date of August 1, 2044. HoloSpecs II and III would eliminate ear buds and include skin-sensing, respectively, and were slated for release in 2045.

Caleb didn't mind the challenge of figuring out the technology, or even the long hours. He was passionate about HoloMate and wanted to see its success. It was the annoying status reports and frequent updates he had to give to Vincent and the investors that frustrated him. Every week, it seemed there was yet another request from Vincent to prepare some special update on progress, issues, or budget. He *hated* having to answer to someone else about *his* baby. With each request for information to placate Vincent and the investors, he bristled with disdain at having to pacify stakeholders. He longed for the day when he could change his 30 percent ownership to 100, with no one to answer to and no one to appease; just him at the helm doing things the way he wanted.

HoloSpecs I glasses were available for sale as planned on August 1. HoloMate management viewed the glasses as a loss-leader to getting and keeping customers onto the HoloMate network. They offered to exchange the old, clunky glasses for the new and improved HoloSpecs I for free. For HoloSpecs II and III, the same offer would be made to minimize losing customers. It was all about HoloFriends for life, which HoloMate management adopted as the company's vision.

HoloSpecs I was a huge success. The number of subscribers jumped, with two million subscribers by the end of 2044. Even with the huge subscriber bump, HoloMate wasn't profitable.

And its investors were still nervous.

Caleb went to work on HoloSpecs II. Engineers who specialized in bone conduction technology designed electromechanical transducers that fit into the temples of the HoloSpecs, which converted the sounds in the HoloRooms to mechanical vibrations which were sent directly to the wearer's cochlea. Rather than having to put ear buds in each time a wearer entered a HoloRoom, the wearer simply activated HoloSpecs hearing by rapidly sticking out his tongue three times. While this looked peculiar to some, the HoloSpecs engineers decided that any gestures which controlled the HoloSpecs must be done solely through the head. That way, someone without the use of arms or legs could still operate the HoloSpecs.

HoloSpecs II released on February 1, 2045 along with 20 new fashion choices. As with HoloSpecs I, HoloMate management offered a free exchange program for old glasses. Subscriber growth was now at 200,000 users per month, but the company had yet to show a profitable quarter, creating more angst between the investors, Vincent, the management team, and Caleb. The investor's ceaseless requests for status on HoloSpecs progress, questions on how much Caleb was spending on new features, and second-guessing who was working on the project continued to grate on his nerves. Caleb wanted the investors out, and some of the investors wanted out as well. Caleb had been working with a wealthy angel investor, introduced by Paul, who believed in HoloMate's future and was willing to finance a buyout of HoloMate's current investors. He just needed to find the right time to get them to exercise their buyout. That time came in the form of a HoloSpecs III demo.

DEMO GREMLINS
2045

HoloSpecs III was slated for release on October 1, 2045. Skin-sensing was the capability which would catapult HoloMate into superstar status. Customers wanted it, and the investors needed it to stay in the game. In September, Vincent asked Caleb to prepare a demo of the skin-sensing capability included in HoloSpecs III. Caleb was more than happy to oblige. One week before the October launch, Caleb went to an investor meeting in the same conference room at Pagnozzi's office where Caleb and Paul had first demonstrated the HoloMate prototype. Caleb entered the room; all the investors and Vincent were already sitting at the table, anxious to see the long-awaited HoloSpecs III. The tension in the room was already high, as evidenced by the quiet demeanor of the investors. Vincent kicked things off.

"Thanks for coming in." Even though Vincent was one of the investors, he rightly felt an accountability to his colleagues for HoloMate. A drop of nervous perspiration ran down the side of his face.

"Caleb is going to demo the skin-sensing capability in HoloSpecs III. As you know, the first attempt didn't go well, and we had to disable the feature. Caleb and team have been working hard to get it right. Caleb, you're up."

"Thanks, Vincent." Caleb displayed an air of confidence as spoke. "I'm happy to show you the progress we've made on skin-sensing and what our subscribers will be able to do using the capability." Caleb took two pairs of HoloSpecs III from his backpack. "Vincent, would you go into the conference room next door, put the specs on, and enter HoloRoom AQT-224?" Vincent didn't realize he was going to be part of the demo, but the show was on and he was now part of it.

"Sure." Vincent said. He took the specs from Caleb and went into the conference room next door. He put the specs on and went into HoloRoom AQT-224 like Caleb asked. Caleb put his specs on and paired them to the conference room projector. Everyone in the conference room was now able to see Caleb's and Vincent's hologram at the center of the conference table.

"Can you see and hear me, Vincent?" Caleb asked.

"Yes. The lenses and conduction are working great!" Vincent talked up capabilities released in HoloSpecs I and II to help reassure the investors those capabilities still worked.

"OK." Caleb continued, "I'm going to do something. Tell me what you feel." Caleb's hologram reached out to Vincent's to rub his arm.

"I feel you rubbing my arm." Vincent said.

"Great!" Caleb looked around the conference room. The stoic looks on the investor's faces was enough for Caleb to know they weren't impressed.

"OK, now I'm going to do something else." Caleb's hologram approached Vincent's and lightly stepped on his foot.

"I don't feel anything." Vincent's voice softened as he gave the disappointing news.

"Let me try a little harder." Caleb stepped with more force.

"Nothing."

"OK, one more time." Caleb lifted his hologram foot and came down hard on Vincent's foot.

"I felt a punch on my left arm." Vincent said as he grabbed his arm.

"The demo gremlins are out today!" Caleb tried to make light of the demo fiasco. "Vincent, reboot the specs and let's try again."

Vincent removed the specs, his hologram disappearing from the middle of the conference room table. Caleb looked around the room to expressionless faces while waiting for Vincent's hologram to reappear. After a minute, Vincent's hologram reappeared, then Caleb went through the same foot-stomping steps again. Same result.

"This worked thousands of times in testing." Caleb said. The shock of the failed demo was evident by the anxious shuffling of some of the investors.

"Vincent, can you come back in the conference room?" Pagnozzi said. Vincent came back in, with a few more drops of perspiration on his forehead.

"Release is in a week, and this piece of crap doesn't work!" Pagnozzi was irate, alternating glares between Vincent and Caleb. "Now what?"

"I'm sorry, Mr. Pagnozzi." Caleb said. "I'll figure it out."

"Yes, you will. Caleb, we need to talk among ourselves. You can leave now." Pagnozzi's blood was boiling over the disastrous demo. Caleb left as quickly as he could, knowing Vincent was going to get his butt kicked.

"Vincent, this is bad," Pagnozzi said after the door closed behind Caleb. "How could you let this happen?"

"He'd demo'd this dozens of times before with no issues. He just practiced it yesterday with me. I don't know what happened."

"I'll tell you what happened, it's an unreliable POS," Pagnozzi said. "We've got to talk about whether we want to stay involved in this or shut it down."

Pagnozzi had already taken the pulse of the investors before the failed demo. Most of them wanted out. They just needed a reasonable offer to recoup losses. Vincent was disappointed, but as an investor, understood the issue. They decided to delay the release and get out either by selling or shutting it down.

After leaving Pagnozzi's office, Caleb walked to Villa Comunale. He sat on a park bench next to the Enrico Pessina statue. "I think it worked," he said to himself.

Caleb knew his investors were already nervous about HoloMate. They just needed a catastrophic event to prompt them to action. Caleb rigged Vincent's HoloSpecs III glasses to register faulty skin-sensing signals for the demo, knowing it would panic the investors. Now he could approach Vincent and Pagnozzi with an offer to buy their 70 percent. Caleb sent Vincent a message asking if he could meet with him and Pagnozzi. They met the next morning in Pagnozzi's conference room.

"Mr. Pagnozzi, I feel horrible about the failed demo. I just don't know what happened." Caleb was convincing in his lying.

"Caleb, we already have jittery investors, and your performance yesterday only made things worse."

"I know," Caleb continued. "I still believe in HoloMate and understand I let you down. I own the problems here and I need to fix them. I want to keep going, even if that means buying out your 70 percent."

"How would you do that, Caleb?"

"My cousin introduced me to someone who'd loan me the money to buy you out."

"How much would he loan you?" Pagnozzi asked.

"30 million hera."

Pagnozzi pursed his lips and slightly nodded his head. He and his partners had invested 15 million hera, but because they were so skeptical of the skin-sensing technology, they didn't see enough upside to continue. "Let me talk to the partners." Pagnozzi said.

It didn't take long for Pagnozzi and his partners to take the deal. Caleb secured the 30 million hera loan and paid the investors. After the deal closed, Caleb announced to the rest of the management team that he now owned 100 percent of the company, that he would now be CEO, and Vincent and Pagnozzi were gone. He offered each of the management team members a stake in the company, provided they would stay for four years, which they all accepted. Caleb then miraculously "fixed" the skin-sensing technology and released

HoloSpecs III three months later than planned to feed the illusion there was actually a problem with the specs.

HoloSpecs III ushered in subscriber growth of over a billion subscribers per year. As fashion trends emerged, new HoloSpecs appeared to complement wearers' fashion choices. Caleb knew the real profit wasn't in the glasses, it was in the HoloFriend fees. The glasses were the gateway drug to getting people hooked on the service, so he did all he could to get HoloSpecs in the hands of everyone, everywhere. HoloRooms changed how people socialized. Weddings, birthday parties, and company meetings were popular HoloRoom events. Some subscribers became professional HoloFriends, renting out their friendship by the hour to lonely subscribers looking for someone to talk to. HoloFriends had ratings and reviews for how good of a "friend" they were. Those with higher ratings and positive reviews commanded more hera per hour. VIPs could rent themselves out to show up in a HoloRoom and entertain, speak, or just socialize with invited guests. Once their paid time was up, the VIP would turn off his HoloSpecs then disappear from the HoloRoom. A VIP could visit any number of HoloRooms, all from the comfort of his own home. They loved it and didn't mind forking over half of their fee to HoloMate.

The skin-sensing capability created new opportunities for service providers to reach customers. Doctors used HoloRooms for routine examinations. Dance studios held lessons in HoloRooms. Subscribers went on HoloDates together as a safe means of getting to know someone before meeting face-to-face. The innovation also had a darker side. Pornography, prostitution, and pedophilia all found their way into HoloRooms, dubbed DarkRooms by subscribers. Caleb hid behind the cloak of protecting privacy to absolve HoloMate of any DarkRoom responsibility. Besides, they were making a ton of money from DarkRooms, so why cut off a huge revenue generator? Even if they did try to police activity, how could they do so across ethnarchies? Each ethnarchy had its own laws, with some very permissive and others much more restrictive. HoloFriends could be from anywhere in the world, meeting up as computer-generated holograms, so it wasn't actual people who were engaging in activity, even though sight, sound and touch was experienced by the HoloFriends. Because of filthy activity and HoloMate's turning a blind eye, many spoke out against DarkRooms, one of its most vocal being Bert Winn.

JAMES TREVOR
2045

After they married, Bert and Laura lived in a one-bedroom apartment for three years, diligently saving down-payment money each month from Bert's professor salary and Laura's primary school math teacher salary. The home-buying process was one of the most stressful things either had experienced. Deciding on a home, where to live, what they needed, and what they were willing to concede was all so overwhelming. Making things worse, their real estate agent was not aware of how to work with people on the autism spectrum. His method of rapid-fire questions was well-intended but to Bert and Laura it was difficult to handle. Then there was the agent's lack of organization. He would call Bert and Laura telling them they needed to go look at an apartment immediately, wreaking havoc on their well-planned daily schedule. To neurotypicals, his behavior would have been tolerable; but to people on the spectrum, it was paralyzing. Bert and Laura were recounting their experience with Bert's parents while there for a Sunday dinner.

"How's the apartment search going?" Bert's mother asked.

Laura let Bert give his assessment while she twisted her spaghetti around her fork, using her tablespoon to keep the spaghetti from slipping off the tines.

"Frustrating!" Bert blurted. He knew Laura felt the same way. "He asks so many questions so quickly we don't have time to process what he's asking. He springs things on us. He's not organized. He wants us to make decisions too fast. We're overwhelmed."

Laura balanced the feedback. "He's a nice guy and he wants to please us, it's just difficult for us to work with him."

Bert nodded his head in agreement as he stabbed a link of mild sausage in the serving dish and put it on his plate.

Hayley totally got it. She had helped Bert countless times with feeling overwhelmed and understood their feelings about the real estate agent. Hayley knew just how to talk with Bert to help him cope. It typically started with affirming his feelings.

"Bert, I can see why you feel overwhelmed with all of the randomness. It can be very frustrating. I get overwhelmed with randomness too."

Bert accepted being affirmed, "Yes, it is." He said.

Laura nodded, feeling affirmed as well by Hayley's ability to relate to how she was feeling.

"What do you think would help?" Hayley asked.

"If he wrote out his questions, then we could discuss them and respond back without the pressure of having to answer him on the spot."

"Yep, and how about him springing things on you?"

"I think if we set time aside in our schedule each day just to work with the agent and let him know we would be available at those times, it wouldn't disrupt our routine."

Laura liked where the discussion was going. "If we could get him to work with us on writing down questions and blocking out time in our schedule, that would help a lot. I'm still feeling overwhelmed with how we make the decision on what to buy."

Bert had an idea. "Let's make a chart with the things that are important to us, then for each apartment we see, let's write out how it meets our needs. We can then look at the chart and see what we like and don't like about each apartment."

Hayley picked up her fork, twirled some spaghetti, and put it in her mouth. Ryan gave Hayley a warm smile, acknowledging her job well done. He never connected with Bert like Hayley did, something he regretted.

Things got much better with the real estate agent after Bert and Laura put their strategies in place. They ended up buying a flat north of Villa Comunale and moved in July 2045. It was perfect for them. They wanted something small and easy to maintain, but with separate spaces where each could go to be alone. It was big enough to let them start a family. They painstakingly planned out the move from their current apartment, even sketching out for every room where each piece of furniture would go. They both took a week off from their teaching jobs after the apartment closed so they could take their time moving everything over. Both Bert's and Laura's parents helped them with their move when asked, otherwise Bert and Laura did it all on their own.

Bert and Laura lived in their apartment three years before their son was born. While Laura was pregnant, they used a coach who specialized in helping people with autism become parents. Their coach helped them adapt to their new routine, which would be filled with randomness for the foreseeable future. This was a massive leap for Bert and Laura. Since birth, both of their parents worked hard to achieve and sustain structure in their lives. Now, a miniature version of them was going to ensure their life was anything but structured. Bert and Laura's coach worked with them on what to expect as new parents and to work together to give each some structured down time they both so badly needed. As with everything else in Bert and Laura's life, they had to work together to ensure expectations were clear of each other.

On June 24, 2048, James Trevor Winn was born. Bert was in the birthing room with Laura, and the proud grandparents were right outside the room in the hallway, anxiously awaiting the new arrival. At 2:44 p.m. Bert opened the birthing room door with his brand-new son in his hands. Hayley and Ryan looked at James' reddish skin, dark hair, and dark brown eyes that opened and closed ever so slightly as if fighting sleep. There were happy tears as they celebrated yet another milestone that they wondered if they would ever see, their 32-year-old son becoming a father.

JT, the nickname Bert gave him during a 2 a.m. feeding, was a typical newborn. Awake at all hours of the evening, with bouts of fussiness and slivers of peace and quiet. Bert and Laura decided that Laura would quit her job to be JT's primary caretaker, and Bert would stop teaching night courses so he could take over some of the evening duties. The Winns adjusted every bit as well as neurotypical parents to their new normal.

By JT's first birthday, he was showing some early signs that he was on the spectrum. He wasn't smiling, there was no back-and-forth sharing of sounds, no babbling, no mimicking gestures. Bert and Laura were concerned, not because of JT's being on the spectrum, but of how others would treat him. They both had experienced difficult childhoods. Neither of them was ever invited to play with other kids or go to birthday parties. Neither had been to a school dance. Both were teased by other kids because they were different. Both were bullied. Bert had Paul as his only friend, Laura didn't have any friends. Bert and Laura talked a lot through their courtship and marriage about how difficult it was growing up with autism. Their greatest concern was having a child on the spectrum who would be treated the same way they were when growing up.

At 18 months, JT only said "Ma" and "Da," avoided eye contact, and didn't like to be hugged. He, like his father, loved puzzles and would sit for hours doing the same puzzle over and over again. He had a limited menu, his favorites being spaghetti with butter, mozzarella string cheese, and peanut butter on ciabatta bread cut into triangles. His was tested and their suspicions confirmed, JT was on the spectrum. Bert and Laura feared their son would be treated like they were growing up. They wanted not only JT, but other people on the spectrum, to be accepted and embraced for their uniqueness. They would dedicate the rest of their lives to making that happen.

HoloBlogs
2050

Naples University, where Bert was now a full professor, had started using HoloMate to hold classes in HoloRooms. Bert was asked to be part of a pilot program with three other professors to evaluate HoloMate and its effectiveness in teaching college classes via hologram. While the adjustment was difficult at first, Bert adapted to new way of teaching and actually enjoyed it. He could teach a class from his classroom, his office at NU, or his alone room at home. He loved that he could turn off skin-sensing on his HoloSpecs, which meant that his hologram could touch and be touched by other HoloFriends, but he wouldn't feel the touch sensation. If the noise was too loud in the HoloRoom, he could adjust the volume on his HoloSpecs to a comfortable level. HoloSpecs were sensory-friendly, purely by accident.

This thing called HoloBlogs captured Bert's intrigue. A subscriber created a hologram blog that could be replayed on demand, viewable by either the public or specific subscribers. HoloBlogs were offered as a free or paid service. If a subscriber chose the free service, advertisements, called HoloAds, would appear intermittently throughout the HoloBlog broadcast. If a subscriber chose the paid HoloBlog service, then it would be broadcast ad-free. Bert was interested enough in HoloBlogs that he decided to try it out using one of his history lectures as a test. He thought he'd test the free service to see how the ads worked and if they would take away from the HoloBlog's quality. He recorded a ten-minute HoloBlog, then played it back. Three minutes into the HoloBlog, a ten-second hologram of a man washing clothes advertising laundry soap appeared. "OK, not too bad," Bert thought. After another three minutes, a ten-second hologram of a woman smiling and drinking an energy drink appeared. "I don't like the drink, but still OK," Bert said to himself. Another three minutes went by and the third and final ad showed, nude woman advertising what she could and would do for anyone willing to visit HoloRoom SCT-450. "DarkRooms, I hate DarkRooms," he said as he took off the HoloSpecs, disgusted that something so vile would show up in his HoloBlog.

During their courtship, Bert and Laura made a pledge to each other that they would not partake in what had become a rampant pornography industry across the ethnarchies. It was everywhere, and HoloMate made its accessibility even more convenient. He did some research on controlling the ads in HoloBlogs. While a HoloBlog creator could specify a range of ad topics that could be displayed during the HoloBlog broadcast, there was no assurance that ads outside of those specified topics, including DarkRoom ads, would not be shown. If Bert were to use HoloBlogs and ensure no DarkRoom ads he'd have to pay for it.

Bert made it a point to keep in contact with his only true friend, Paul. Their weekly conversations while they were both in college had given way to monthly Sunday afternoon HoloRoom meet-ups at 2 p.m. Bert was particularly interested in talking with Paul this week about his HoloBlog experience. Bert went into his alone room, customary bottle of water in hand, sat down in the now-tattered beanbag chair that he had used since college, put on his HoloSpecs and went to room PGP-902. Paul's hologram was already in there, waiting for Bert.

"Hey Bert!" Paul said.

"Hey." Bert took a swig of water.

"How's JT?"

"Doing great. You should see him do puzzles."

"And Laura?"

"She's good. I want to talk to you about something." Bert wasted no time getting to what was on his mind.

"Shoot." Paul said.

"I've been trying out HoloBlogs, thinking I could use them in teaching."

"Pretty cool technology." Paul said as he took a bite of an apple. The sudden crunch of Paul's apple bite startled Bert. He turned down the volume on his HoloSpecs.

"Sorry about that." Paul saw Bert's reaction to the apple sound. "I'll chew quietly. So, you have been playing with HoloBlogs."

"Yes HoloBlogs." Bert continued. "I like the idea of recording my hologram for on-demand playback and think I could use it for lectures. There are free and paid options. The free option has ads that play every three minutes. One of the ads that played on my test was a DarkRoom ad."

Paul knew Bert's feelings on DarkRooms, having discussed it before. "Ugh." Paul said.

"I really like HoloBlogs and would like to use it, but I don't know that I want to pay for it, and I'm not sure how many people would be interested in on-demand history lectures if I did do it. And I definitely don't want to risk a DarkRoom ad popping up."

Paul took a muffled small bite of his apple and gently chewed to keep the noise down. "After we talked last month, I started thinking, you and Laura are passionate about helping others understand autism and helping JT be more accepted. Could you and Laura use HoloBlogs to help with autism awareness?"

"I haven't thought of that. What would we do?" Bert's curiosity was piqued.

"Just thinking off the top of my head but you and Laura could do HoloBlogs together to talk about issues people with autism face and give some tips on how neurotypicals can be more inclusive."

"I never thought about that. Me and Laura doing a HoloBlog together. But I don't want to risk DarkRoom ads popping up, I'd have to use the paid service."

"There might be some things you can do to offset the cost." Paul looked down at his apple that had started turning brown. He hated brown apples. Into the trash, making a *thud* as it hit the garbage can. "Perhaps you can do some paid coaching for parents and others who want to talk with you about specific problems. That might be a way to help recoup the cost of the paid service."

Bert got quiet, focused on absorbing Paul's advice. Paul could see Bert's hologram sitting in his beanbag chair, staring downward intently. "How about I type out some ideas and send them to you?" Paul asked, knowing Bert would better comprehend written thoughts.

"That'd be great." Bert said.

"OK, I'll send them to you tonight."

"Thanks, Paul."

They chattered on for another ten minutes about nothing in particular. Bert looked at the clock on the HoloRoom wall and saw 2:15. They always ended their meet-ups after 15 minutes.

"OK, talk to you next month." Bert said. "I'll look for your HoloBlog thoughts tonight."

"Yup, I'll do it tonight. Take care and give Laura and JT my love."

Bert's hologram disappeared from the room. Paul removed his HoloSpecs, happy for his friend but deep down jealous of what he had. Bert had Laura and JT. Paul had his brother and sister but just couldn't seem to connect with anyone romantically. He even visited an upscale gay bar and almost got to making out with a handsome young doctor but it repulsed him just as much as kissing a woman.

Paul sent Bert some written notes just as he said he would. Bert read it while sitting in his alone room, then went into the living room where Laura was reading a book. JT was playing with blocks on the floor next to her.

"Paul and I were talking about HoloBlogs this afternoon. He sent me some ideas that I want you to look at." Bert handed Laura his phone with the message on screen. She started reading.

"Bert and Laura, as promised, here are a few notes on HoloBlogs and how you might be able to help others affected by autism. With the birth rate climbing from one in 68 in 2017 to one in 20 in 2050, it's clear that autism is here to stay and something we need to address across the ethnarchies. People with autism need and deserve to be included and not bullied, mocked, or discriminated against. You both, along with JT, are in a unique position to make a difference. I believe starting a HoloBlog which demonstrates the real-world challenges and strengths someone with autism possesses and how the challenges can be managed, and the strengths leveraged, could be powerful. Call the blog something like *Growing Up Autistic with the Winns* and provide simple, ten-minute HoloBlog posts where you both discuss a specific aspect of growing up with autism. I know Bert is concerned about having to pay for the HoloBlog posts versus risking obscene ads in the free version. I would say pay for HoloBlog but also offer 'for-fee' coaching for HoloFriends wanting autism advice. I'm confident there will be enough interest in your services to pay the HoloBlog fee. None of us want JT to experience the same struggles you both did throughout your life. This is an opportunity to help change perceptions and hopefully make things easier on JT. I am happy to help you as much as you like in this endeavor, just let me know. Your friend, Paul."

"So, what do you think?" Bert asked Laura.

Laura handed the phone back to Bert. "I need to digest more, it's a lot coming at me at once. Can you send that to me?"

"Sure." Bert forwarded the message to Laura.

Laura and Bert both thought about it and discussed it over the next week. They created a chart with pros and cons, the biggest con being the cost of HoloBlog. Even if they didn't do consulting, they decided they could still afford the paid version of HoloBlog versus risking smutty HoloAds in the free version. On May 22, 2050 Bert and Laura launched *Growing Up Autistic with the Winns* and released their first ten-minute HoloBlog post on creating "alone spaces" in your home. They committed to creating at least one HoloBlog post every week for a year. If it did well they'd continue, if not, they'd stop.

It did well, in fact, far better than they expected. By its five-year anniversary, *Growing Up Autistic with the Winns* had 100 million HoloFriends. Bert and Laura talked about a wide range of topics, including autistic parents raising autistic children, going through puberty, achieving intimacy when touch-sensitive, setting expectations on schedules, and varying eating habits. The topics were an honest and unvarnished lens into people on the spectrum. Their HoloBlog led to multiple coaching opportunities with people affected by autism or those who just wanted to learn more. They easily made enough HoloFriends coaching revenue to pay the HoloBlog fee, save for college and retirement, and donate to programs that promoted autism awareness and inclusion. For HoloMate corporate, the HoloBlog fee was peanuts compared to the 50 percent HoloFriend coaching revenue. Bert and Laura's blog was their top HoloBlog site and inspired thousands of new paid HoloBlog sites.

While the HoloBlog and HoloFriend consulting was going great, Bert and Laura were increasingly conflicted by the pervasiveness of DarkRooms. They decided they would need to do something about it, and it was going to tick Caleb off.

KEEP IT QUICK
2066

The HoloMate reporter continued reports of the Jerusalem shooting through the day and into the evening, interviewing witnesses, firearms experts, law enforcement, and anyone who could help piece together what happened. The sideways rain had let up, with only occasional sprinkles. The reporter saw the head of embassy security, Ira Greenbaum, walking out of the embassy entrance and approached him to ask about the shooting.

"Sir, I'm Aaron Moskowitz with HoloMate. May I ask you some questions about the shooting?"

"Keep it quick."

"OK, go to LFTP-939," Moskowitz said. Greenbaum flipped his glasses to HoloMode and tuned in. The two stood there with frosted specs, Greenbaum already getting impatient with Moskowitz. "I'm ready," Moskowitz told his producer. He quickly pulled a mirror from his pocket, checked his hair and teeth, and waited for his producer's voice in his earpiece.

"Three, two, one."

"This is Aaron Moskowitz from HoloMate News on location at the Europe Ethnarchy Embassy in Jerusalem. I'm with embassy security chief Ira Greenbaum. Thank you for making the time, Sir."

Greenbaum didn't respond. He just wanted to answer the questions and get back to work.

"Mr. Greenbaum do you have any information about the shooter?"

"No."

"Do you know where the shots came from?"

"Shots came from an elevated position to the east."

Moskowitz saw he wasn't going to get much from Greenbaum. "Any information on the firearm?"

"Based on recovered bullets looked like a long-range firearm capable of hitting a target up to three kilometers away."

"Any information on the victims?"

"You'll have to ask Jerusalem Health. I need to go." Greenbaum turned off HoloMode, the frosted lenses turning clear, his hologram disappearing from the HoloRoom. Moskowitz heard Greenbaum's footsteps as he walked to a waiting car.

"Thank you, Mr. Greenbaum. This is Aaron Moskowitz with HoloMate News. Stay in room LFTP-939 for continued updates."

"We're out," the producer said in Moskowitz's earpiece.

"Anything from Jerusalem Health?" Moskowitz asked his producer.

A strange voice came through Moskowitz' earpiece, "I've got something, Aaron."

"Who is this?"

"Aliza Breiner." Breiner was a Jerusalem-based HoloMate reporter who went to Jerusalem Health right after the shooting. "I just talked with Caleb Todd. He'll be in LFTP-939 in ten after he's stitched up."

FOUR BILLION SUBSCRIBERS
2060

In the 14 years following HoloSpecs III's debut, HoloMate had grown to over four billion subscribers. There were hundreds of different HoloSpec styles, with many owning three or four pairs for different looks. Special-purpose HoloSpecs worn by athletes and musicians enabled subscribers to view venues like concerts and sporting events in large HoloRooms. There were hundreds of thousands of HoloRooms in use at any one time. The hologram technology continued to improve, with increased image fidelity and realism, allowing wearers to see things like individual eyelash hairs with perfect clarity. Celebrities, politicians, sports figures, musicians and authors were special guests at HoloParties where they agreed to attend for a fixed fee for a negotiated time limit. Once the time was up, the special guest sometimes would say goodbye to other guests before leaving, sometimes abruptly causing their hologram to suddenly disappear from the HoloRoom. HoloMate usage became an addiction for many, some psychologists dubbing it HoloDiction. Insurance companies created specific policy exclusions for any type of accident caused by a distracted HoloMate subscriber. HoloMate was how people interacted, received news, and were entertained.

HoloMate was insanely profitable, thanks in large part to DarkRooms. At any point in time, 50 percent of HoloRooms were being used for pornography, pedophilia, or prostitution. With HoloMate collecting 50 percent of the seller's rate, DarkRoom revenue was one that Caleb wanted to foster, regardless of what went on inside the rooms. HoloMate made the obligatory "we keep your information private" statement but never guaranteed privacy. If the general public knew who visited DarkRooms and what was done in them, reputations could be destroyed, marriages shattered, relationships forever lost. The extreme popularity of DarkRooms spoke for itself; subscribers put fleshly pleasures above the anonymity risk. Subscriber identity was stored in HoloMate's subscriber activity database, with HoloMate storing a recording of every activity committed in each HoloRoom. HoloMate's privacy policy stated that activity would be recorded only with a subscriber's express consent. No consent, no recording.

So the policy said.

In reality everything was recorded regardless of subscriber consent. Caleb had the goods on some of the most famous people on earth, although he had yet to use the recordings against anyone. A few of Caleb's employees knew, but they were paid to keep silent. If subscribers found out about his secret recordings, the very existence of HoloMate would be at risk. He was content to use the recordings for his own viewing pleasure, knowing he could exert extreme pressure by outing any DarkRoom subscriber he chose.

Anything Else?
2058

By age 42, Paul had become one of the most powerful people in the Catholic church. His success at cleaning up the abusers in the church gained him worldwide notoriety. Nine ethnarchies gave him full power to question abusers and, if found guilty, extradite the guilty to the Vatican-run prison. Russia did not allow Paul entry; they chose to take care of abuse cases in-house, meaning abusers were either able to bribe their way out of prosecution or they were interred at Petak Island Prison at Ognenny Ostrov. Paul appealed with Pius XIV's help to the Russia Ethnarchy, his appeal going all the way to Chairperson Popov, only to be denied. Popov's rejection was distressing to Paul as there was no reason provided other than "thank you but no thank you." Both he and the pontiff were angry with Popov but were powerless to do anything about it.

During one of Paul's weekly one-on-ones with the pontiff, Paul provided his typical status, with the pope not saying much. Paul ended every update the same way.

"Anything else, Your Holiness?" Paul asked.

"Yes." This was only the second time Pius XIV said yes to his question, the first time being when he tried to comfort Paul about losing both his parents.

"What can I do, Your Holiness?"

"I have to remove Senator Marino from the senate."

Vatican City was given one senate seat, even though its population was only 300 people. The pope controlled the executive, legislative and judicial branches of Vatican City government, so he had sole authority over all laws, including assignment and removal of senators. There was no vote by the citizens, it was all done through executive order.

Pius XIV continued, "I won't go into the reasons. I need to appoint someone new and I would like you to become my senator. You will represent Vatican City on all ethnarchy issues and do as I direct."

Paul was flattered but didn't like the "do as I direct" qualification. Being chosen as Vatican City senator was a deep honor demonstrating the high degree of trust the pope had in him. On the other hand, he would now be the pope's puppet, having to do whatever the pontiff ordered in this new position.

"Thank you, Your Holiness. I'm honored you consider me worthy. What would you expect of me?" Paul asked.

"I want you to meet with me before every senate session, tell me what you are planning to say, then meet again after every session to tell me what happened." Paul's micromanagement suspicion was confirmed. He would be the papal mouthpiece, directed to say and act only what and when the pope authorized. He'd be Paul the puppet-senator, and the rest of the senate would know it. Pius XIV didn't have to go into the reasons why he was removing Senator Marino, everyone knew it was because Marino couldn't be trusted to vote the pope's bidding. The pope demanded unconditional loyalty, and Marino wouldn't do it. Paul was among the pope's most inner circle, someone who Pius XIV believed would follow directions without question. Paul hated the thought of being a yes-man, but he also saw being senator as a stepping stone to becoming chairperson. If he could just bide his until the next election it would be worth it.

"When do you need me, Your Holiness?"

"I will tell Marino and notify Chairperson Dalca today. You will start tomorrow." Pius XIV was speaking as if it were a done deal, no one said no to him.

"I would be honored, Your Holiness." Paul had become very good at putting on a positive face with the pontiff. "Anything else, Your Holiness?"

The pope put his hand out for Paul to kiss his ring which Paul always did.

"Thank You, Your Holiness." Paul left the room and walked down the empty hallway in the Apostolic Palace to his office. Being a puppet-senator repulsed Paul, he hoped it would be sooner than later before he got his shot at chairpersonship. His opportunity much sooner than he expected.

GREATER AMBITIONS
2057

The black circle with "MD" in block orange letters was recognized worldwide with over six billion MDChip wearers. Every newborn got the chip implanted within their first year. If a chip malfunctioned, MDCentral got a warning which immediately sent a message to the wearer to go to an MD-certified pharmacy for chip replacement. Each time a wearer received an MDSolution treatment, the activity was recorded by MDCentral. MDChip and MDSolution manufacturing had been running three shifts, seven days a week, for the last eight years to keep up with demand. MD Biometrics now had certified manufacturing partners in every ethnarchy charged with producing chip insertion and solution injection appliances and training pharmacists and nurses on their use.

The cure for cancer brought unintended consequences. People were living longer, with the average life expectancy rising by ten years. Longer life expectancies meant more people to feed, putting a strain on an already limited food supply. Sal was well aware of the food shortage but decided it wasn't his problem to solve. His job was all about cancer eradication; someone else needed to worry about the food supply issue. As much as he didn't want to get involved in solving the food shortage issue, he'd find himself front and center of it later.

By 2057 Sal was bored with MD Biometrics. He resigned as CEO, retained a board position, and ran for the Europe Ethnarchy Senate representing Italy. The Europe Ethnarchy included all countries in continental Europe with two exceptions: Russia, which was its own ethnarchy, and Israel, which was a territory to the

Europe Ethnarchy despite being located in the Asia region. This was done exclusively to ensure the protection of Israel from its hostile Palestinian neighbors. Each of the 49-member countries sent two senators to serve on the Europe Ethnarchy Senate. Each country could decide whether the senators were elected by the country's citizens or appointed by the country's leader, with Italy retaining a popular vote structure for electing its two senators. Vatican City, while technically in Italy, was treated as its own country, but due to its smaller size was only allowed one senator. Thus, the senate was comprised of 99 senators plus one chairperson. The chairperson was elected from among the sitting senators through a majority vote of at least 50 senators.

Sal's success as CEO of MD Biometrics yielded him a rock-star-like HoloMate following of over a billion subscribers. His name became synonymous with curing cancer like Bill Gates and Steve Jobs were with technology. He was in high demand at HoloMate events, commanding into the millions of hera for appearances. When he decided to run for senator, he leveraged his popularity in his senate campaign and was easily elected to a ten-year term in September 2058. After his election, Sal spent the next two years learning the ropes of the senate, assessing who was inside the power circle, judging who could help him achieve his ultimate ambition, which was to be the Europe Ethnarchy Chairperson. The existing chairperson, Grigore Dalca from Romania, was elected by the senate in 2057 for a ten-year term. Unless he died or resigned, Sal's first shot at the Europe Ethnarchy Chairpersonship wouldn't be until 2067. There was no way Sal was going to wait that long. He needed to manufacture his opportunity. He'd pay his old friend Mario a visit.

VENTRICULAR FIBRILLATION
2060

When Sal left MD Biometrics he lobbied the board of directors for Mario to succeed him. Mario was not only a brilliant scientist like Sal, he was well-known for his integrity and honesty. It was an easy choice for the board.

"Hey Sal, how you doing?" Mario kissed him on each cheek.

"I like what you did with the place." Mario now sat in Sal's old office in the sprawling MD Biometrics complex. Mario was very loyal to Sal, grateful for the opportunity to work with him and appreciative of how Sal supported Mario as his CEO replacement with the rest of the board. The office was furnished with an ornate walnut desk, a mahogany and inlaid olive wood scrolled conference table from Sorrento, with 12 chairs around the table. Pictures of Gene and Jasmine the lab rats were on the wall, alongside pictures of Mario and Sal early in their career in the makeshift lab, meeting with heads of state, and Sal's mandible tumor from his first human trial. Their friendship ran deep, and Mario would do anything for his old friend.

"How's life as a senator?" Mario asked.

"Good, lots of meetings, administrivia, boring stuff, part of the job."

"Do you miss MD?"

Sal went over to the fridge and helped himself to a sparkling water, opened it, and took a swig. "Sometimes. Much more exciting at MD than the senate."

"I bet." Mario sensed this was more than just a courtesy call. "What can I do for you?"

"I need your help, Mario." Sal struck a serious tone.

"Anything."

Sal got up and made sure the office door was locked.

"Chairperson Dalca is incompetent. He gives in to the other chairpersons, even Solveig from frigging Antarctica. At this rate Europe will be the laughingstock of the world."

"How much longer in his term?" Mario asked.

"Seven years, enough to kill us."

"What do you want me to do?"

Sal didn't hesitate. "I need you to VF Dalca."

Mario knew this day would come. MDCentral not only was able to receive information from the MDChip, but could manipulate the chip, including inducing ventricular fibrillation, which would kill the wearer if not given immediate medical attention. Only the two of them knew of the capability and had yet to use it.

"VF?"

"Yes."

"Can it be traced back to us?"

"Don't worry about it."

Mario was a scientist turned CEO. He loved the science behind what he and Sal created and how MD Biometrics helped people live longer and avoid the pain of cancer. Sal was asking Mario to not save a life, but to knowingly and deliberately take a life, for nothing more than political gain.

"I can't do it," Mario said.

"Mario, this is for the good of the ethnarchy. If Dalca stays, Europe will be nothing more than a puppet for the rest of the ethnarchies, and Popov will run roughshod over us."

When the world agreed on ethnarchy consolidation, Russia was originally included in the Europe Ethnarchy. As the Europe Ethnarchy agreement was negotiated by country leaders, Russia was unhappy with the "equality for all" position the leaders were taking. Russia's population was 17 percent of all of Europe's population, yet they would have the same two-senator representation as miniscule countries like Monaco and Liechtenstein. Russia, led by a young and brash President Anton Popov, pulled out of the agreement last-minute and became their own ethnarchy, with Popov as its chairperson. There was bitterness over the split, neither the Russia or Europe Ethnarchies trusted each other, and Europe held a heightened concern of Russia taking military action against Europe to annex parts of the Europe Ethnarchy into Russia. Popov was brilliant and crazy enough to do it--a weak leader like Dalca was no match against Popov.

"I hate Popov," Mario said. Years earlier his brother was killed while visiting Russia by a drunk teenage driver. The driver was a member of a wealthy and prominent Russian family and was able to bribe officials to have charges dismissed. Mario's brother died, the killer got off with not even a slap on the wrist, and there was nothing Mario or his family could do about it.

Sal saw Mario was softening. "Popov is a wild man, he would love nothing more than to take over Europe. Dalca can't win against Popov. Dalca has to go."

Mario put his head in his hands, agonized over the choices. He hated using MD to take a life, but he hated the Russians even more. Mario lifted his head, his hands pressed together in front of his mouth. "OK."

"Excellent," Sal put his hand on Mario's shoulder, affirming his decision.

"When do we do it?" Mario asked.

"Give me a month to create tension in the senate about the Russia threat, and Dalca's unwillingness to do anything about it. I want the senate to see the problem and for them to see me as being hard on Russia. Then we do it."

Mario nodded his head, not saying a word.

"Thank you, Mario, you're doing a great service for the ethnarchy." Sal and Mario got up, Sal kissed him on each cheek and left the office. After Sal left, Mario dropped to his chair, distressed by what he just signed up for.

Over the next month Sal railed on Popov within the senate, looking for an opportunity to seize control of Europe, and harshly criticized Dalca for his unwillingness to do anything about it. Each day in the senate he beat the same drum--Russia is a threat, Popov is crazy, and Dalca is incompetent. He was successful at whipping many senators into a frenzy, questioning Dalca about his plan for keeping Europe safe from Russia. Sal then took to HoloMate to reach Europeans directly with his message of fear. Given his vast following as the founder of MD, he was able to convince millions across Europe that Russia was a clear threat. Russia, having its own safety concerns, saw the ratcheting rhetoric as a threat to its ethnarchy, and started a propaganda campaign of its own against Europe.

Seeing heightened anxiety in the Senate over the strained relations, Sal called Mario. "Do it."

The MDCentral application which logged chip and solution activity didn't have the VF capability. Sal and Mario didn't want MDCentral's staff to know of the "feature." Sal had a customized application, only on his phone, that accessed the MDCentral database and controlled the secret chip capabilities. Mario and Sal designed the application with strict security features, only recognizing Mario's iris and voice before activating. Once Mario was authenticated, Mario spoke, "Search Dalca, Grigore, Romania." A few seconds later, 220 listings, along with pictures, showed on his phone. He found the chairperson and pressed on his picture. He then saw the entire history of Dalca's MDChip and MDSolution treatments.

"Hmm, just got the chip nine months ago," Mario noticed the insertion and solution treatment dates, the chip serial number, and where the chip was installed. Below the statistics was a button labeled "Special." He pressed the button, the app then requested iris and voice re-verification. Once he was verified, a screen displayed that he hadn't seen since they developed and tested the app on their lab rats. It had two buttons, "VF" and "STOP." VF induced ventricular fibrillation, and STOP stopped the chip from functioning. VF would kill someone immediately by stopping the heart from beating. STOP would terminate chip function and suppress notification of MDCentral of a chip malfunction. As far as the wearer and MDCentral was concerned, the chip was doing its job. Reality was another thing. The non-functioning chip would no longer wake dormant synthetic killer cells and, with the body's inability to create natural killer cells, left the wearer with no immune system. Death was imminent but slower than VF. Mario stared at the screen, horrified as to what he was about to do.

Dalca was playing with his daughters, two and three years old, in the courtyard at the chairperson's residence in Bucharest. It was a beautiful sunny afternoon, the three of them laughing as he pushed them on their swings. His wife was coming out from the residence when she saw her husband grab his chest and drop to the ground. The swings slowly stopped swinging, the girls looked behind them as swings gently rocked, their father on the ground. His wife ran over to him, where he was clutching his chest and moaning in pain. Seeing their mother's panic and hearing their father's moans, the girls started crying. His wife called out to his security detail in the residence, who ran to him, and seeing his condition, called for the house doctor. The doctor ran to Dalca's now lifeless body. He worked to revive Dalca but pronounced him dead, while his crying wife held his head, their two little girls still crying in their now-still swings.

Senator Izydor Janus from Poland was not only the leader of the chairperson nominating committee but was Dalca's close friend. Karoly Lamos, Dalca's security chief, called him.

"Senator Janus?"

"Speaking."

"It's Karoly Lamos."

"Hello, Karoly." Janus knew Karoly as a no-nonsense guy who didn't fill the air with unnecessary conversation. If he was calling, then Janus knew something serious was going on.

"There's no easy way to say this. The chairperson is dead."

Janus was braced for bad news but wasn't prepared to hear that his good friend was gone.

"What?"

"The chairperson is dead," he repeated.

"How?"

"Looks like a heart attack. Was out playing with his kids and just collapsed."

"When?"

"About five minutes ago."

"Was his wife there?"

"He died in her arms."

"How about the girls?"

"Scared."

The line went quiet. Janus just couldn't grasp that Dalca had so suddenly passed. Karoly broke the silence.

"Senator, are you OK?"

Karoly's words jarred Janus. "I'm here. Thank you Karoly."

"Let me know if there's something I can do, sir."

"Thank you." Janus hung up the phone, still not believing Dalca was dead. They had just talked a day earlier about how Dalca was looking forward to spending a day with his wife and daughters. Dalca was a devoted husband and father, something Janus admired. He felt the pain of losing his friend, but also knew, in his position, that he had a responsibility to ensure stability in the ethnarchy. He called his assistant. "Assemble the senate immediately."

The senate assembled in its private HoloRoom within the hour. Janus started, "I just received a message that Chairperson Dalca has died from an apparent heart attack. We need to ensure stability in the ethnarchy while we elect a new chairperson. Per constitution, I, as nominating committee leader, will serve as interim chairperson until we choose a new one. I'll let you know more as I know more."

While the rest of the senate was jolted by the announcement, Sal removed his HoloSpecs. "Good job Mario," he said to himself.

THE ELECTION
2060

With Dalca's death in May 2060, Janus moved swiftly to get a new chairperson elected. Each ethnarchy had the latitude to name its chairperson as it saw fit, with Africa, Asia, Caribbean, Central America, North America, Oceania, and South America holding popular votes among its citizens. Russia and China chairpersons were appointed by each current chairperson. The Europe Ethnarchy chose its chairperson by a vote of the entire senate. The voting was done in rounds. In the first round, senators wishing to be chairperson submitted their names to the nominating committee leader. The entire senate voted for their person of choice from the list, with the top five moving to the second round. Those five then each gave a two-minute speech to the entire senate as to why he or she should be chairperson. After the speeches, the senate voted, with the top two advancing to the final round, and any ties being broken by drawing names from a bag. The top two then each gave a five-minute speech to the entire senate, which was also broadcast on the senate's HoloMate channel to Europe Ethnarchy citizens. The broadcast had no bearing on the voting, it was merely symbolic. With the vote coming up on June 29, 2060, senators interested in running had four weeks to lobby other senators for their votes.

Seven senators expressed intent to run for chairperson, including Paul from Vatican City and Sal from Italy. Each of them worked their network, wining and dining fellow senators, lobbying to secure their votes. Promises were plentiful--plum committee positions, favors to benefit constituents, support of senators' pet projects. Whatever needed to be said to secure votes.

On election day, the senators convened in the senate building in Brussels. While many senate meetings were conducted via its HoloRoom, Janus wanted to hold the vote in person. All 99 senators were present, including the two from the annexed country of Israel. This vote was crucial for Israel, as there were a number of senators who believed Israel's annexation should be voided and the territory returned to the Asia Ethnarchy.

Janus approached the podium and opened the session. "Europe Ethnarchy Senate, I now call this special election session to order. We gather here today to select the Europe Ethnarchy Chairperson who will serve the remainder of the late Grigore Dalca's term which ends December 31, 2067." Janus continued with the rules regarding three rounds of voting, reminding the senate that he had the latitude to alter the process if he saw fit.

Janus announced the names of each of the seven senators who had submitted their names and had them stand. The senators applauded the candidates, who shook hands with each other, wishing all good luck. Janus grabbed the pre-printed ballots with the seven names from the podium and had them passed out to each senator.

"Senators," Janus continued, "please vote for one name only from the list and do not make any other marks on the ballot. The voting must be kept anonymous. I will collect the ballots after one minute." Janus did not want anyone else handling the completed ballots to avoid any possibility of vote tampering. After one minute, Janus walked row by row, collecting ballots from each senator, adding them to his own ballot. After collecting all 99 ballots, he walked back to the podium.

"I will now announce each ballot name and tally the votes." The seven names were listed on a whiteboard next to the podium. As he announced a name, the senate caretaker put a hash mark next to the name. As hash marks filled the whiteboard, there were whispers among the senate about who was winning, who was losing, who would be voted for on the next round. After all 99 votes were counted, Janus announced the results, putting the ballots in his coat pocket.

"Senator Kask, 11. Senator Kuzma 12. Senator Carlotta, 12. Senator Kivi, 12. Senator Ambrosi, 20, Senator Jordanopolous, 16. Senator Backus, 16."

Janus walked to the whiteboard, placing a red check mark next to Ambrosi, Backus and Jordanopolous, they advanced to round two. He put a line through Kask. He circled Kuzma, Carlotta, and Kivi, who tied. Only two of the three would advance.

"We have a three-way tie for the last two slots, so we'll follow senate rules and draw two names from a bag."

Sal couldn't believe it. The person who beat him in number one ranking at Academy was safe to the next round. There was a two-in-three chance he would advance, all determined by a piece of paper that some bureaucrat would pull from a bag. He gazed at Paul, who was looking at the whiteboard, a slight smile on his face as he looked at the 20 and the check mark next to his name. Janus wrote names on three identical small pieces of paper, folded each, and put them in a bag.

"Senator Ambrosi, because you received the most votes, I would like you to draw two names from the bag." More insult to injury for Sal. Not only was his future being determined by a drawing of names, but his main competition in life would be drawing them.

"Yes, Senator Janus." Paul walked up to the podium, turned his head away from the bag to avoid seeing the names, reached into the bag, pulled one piece of paper, and handed it to Janus.

"Senator Kivi." Janus announced, putting the bag down behind the podium.

Sal now had a 50-50 chance. Senator Kuzma was sitting next to him, much more relaxed than Sal. She would have been happy to serve as chairperson, but felt she was a longshot to win. She was expecting to lose and was OK with it.

"Good luck, Senator," Kuzma said to Sal.

Sal didn't say anything, still fuming at Paul determining his future as a politician. Kuzma turned away and whispered to Kivi, "What an ass."

Janus picked up the bag from the back of the podium containing the two pieces of paper. Paul reached into the bag, pulled the second piece of paper, and handed it to Janus.

SPEECHES
2060

J anus looked at the piece of paper and announced the name. "Senator Kuzma."

Sal couldn't take it. He burst from his chair and walked out of the room, slamming the door behind him, the entire senate seeing his temper tantrum. Janus put the two pulled names back in the bag and put it in his coat pocket. He gave instructions on the next round. "Senators Ambrosi, Backus, Jordanopolous, Kuzma, and Kivi, you will each deliver a two-minute speech on why you are best qualified to be chairperson. The speech must be on your own merits, not an attempt to discredit others. If I hear any negative comments you'll be immediately disqualified. Senator Ambrosi you're first."

Paul approached the podium, bottle of water in one hand, notes noticeably absent. He would deliver his speech from memory. Kuzma leaned over to Kivi, "Political disaster in the making," she said. Kivi just smiled, thinking the same thing.

Paul looked across the room, noticed Sal's empty seat. Sal had started to make his way back into the room but turned around and left again when he saw Paul at the podium. Paul took a last glance at the clock and began his speech about "peace through strength." He talked of the Europe Ethnarchy being a great military power that would garner the respect of other ethnarchies. He talked of the importance of defending Israel and not letting it fall into the hands of its Palestinian neighbors. As he talked, he confidently panned his gaze across the senators, as if he were talking to each of them individually. His message was of the greatness of the Europe Ethnarchy, and how he would be focused on creating an economy the other ethnarchies would admire. He finished with two seconds to spare, the senators applauding his speech, his competitors recognizing the high bar Paul set. Once Sal heard the applause, he came back into the room and took his seat.

Senators Backus, Kivi, and Kuzma delivered their speeches, all three positive and respectable. Senator Jordanopolous, who had lost to Dalca in the prior election and was still bitter, approached the podium and began his speech.

"Fellow Senators, I believe the Europe Ethnarchy has only begun on its road to greatness." He originally planned to use notes, but after Paul gave his speech without notes he felt the only way to compete was to give his speech extemporaneously. It was to be his undoing.

"In the short time Chairperson Dalca was in office, he did nothing to distinguish Europe from the other ethnarchies."

"Stop!" Janus said.

Startled, Jordanopolous looked at Janus.

"No negative messaging. You went negative on Dalca. Disqualified."

Jordanopolous began to protest, but Janus wasn't having it. "Disqualified," Janus repeated.

It wasn't part of his plan to diss Dalca and he had it nowhere in his notes that he decided not to use. He just couldn't help himself. Jordanopolous walked down from the stage and slowly made his way back to his seat, embarrassed by the disqualification and ticked that Dalca defeated him again, this time from the grave.

Janus then approached the podium, "I have the ballots with the five names. Because Senator Jordanopolous was disqualified, do not cast a vote for him." Each senator voted, Janus collected the ballots, then announced the votes while the caretaker tallied on the whiteboard. Once the tallies were complete, the caretaker counted hash marks and wrote numbers by each name.

Janus announced the results. "Senator Backus, 29. Senator Kuzma, 18. Senator Kivi, 19, Senator Ambrosi, 31, Senator Jordanopolous, 2."

Even though Jordanopolous was disqualified, two senators, Sal and Jordanopolous, voted for him anyway. Janus let it go as it had no bearing on the top two vote-getters.

"Senators Dalia Backus and Paul Ambrosi advance." Janus said. "Let's take a 15-minute break before round three."

Paul and Dalia were close friends. Dalia had been in the senate ten years before Paul joined. She helped Paul understand how the senate worked, who the influencers were, who was a buffoon. Paul told her about his parents' deaths, his experience working with the pontiff, and his internal struggle with not having a desire for women, something he'd never told anyone about. Dalia talked about her children and grandchildren, how her husband adored her, and how she respected him. Dalia reminded Paul of his mother, and she saw Paul as one of her kids.

The senate reconvened, with two chairs now on the stage to the right of the podium for Paul and Dalia. Janus approached the podium.

"Senator Ambrosi, because you had the most votes from round two, you may choose the speaker order." Janus said.

"I would like to go first."

Janus removed his glasses. "As I mentioned at the beginning of the day, the process can be altered if I see fit. A significant skill the chairperson must possess is the ability to adapt to the unexpected. Rather than having five minutes to make your final appeal, you will only get one minute. And Senator Backus will go first."

Both Dalia and Paul had prepared five-minute speeches, neither planning to use notes. Even though they now had only 60 seconds, neither were rattled, and they took the changes in stride. Dalia approached the podium, confident in her message.

"Fellow senators, my intent in running for chairperson was to protect us from some of our colleagues who I felt would be bad for the Europe Ethnarchy. Whether it be corruption, favoritism, bias, or hatred of Israel, I wanted to be a voice of fairness for everyone in the ethnarchy. Fortunately for us all, Senator Ambrosi embodies the leadership and character traits the ethnarchy needs to succeed now and in the future. I know more than Paul the Senator, I know Paul the man. He would be a far better chairperson than I could ever hope to be. Therefore, I concede the contest to Senator Ambrosi, and I would like to be the first to congratulate now Chairperson Ambrosi. Congratulations, Paul!"

Dalia left the podium and walked over to Paul. He stood from his chair and hugged his good friend. The room was silent. Never before had one of the top two candidates for chairperson conceded as part of their final appeal to the senate. Sal was in utter disbelief. "She rolled over without even going to a vote!" he thought. "He won by concession!" This was just more salt in the wound for Sal.

Janus came to the podium. "Senator Backus, I accept your concession. Chairperson Ambrosi, would you still like to use your one minute?"

"Yes." Paul approached the podium. "Dalia, I never saw that coming!" Paul attempted to break the ice with the rest of the senate. Some gave it a chuckle, others were still shocked. "Fellow senators, I am humbled to serve as your chairperson. You have my commitment that I will work tirelessly to continue building on the greatness of the Europe Ethnarchy that Chairperson Dalca and the chairpersons before him have done so diligently. I will be the chairperson for all, not some, and vow to protect Europe's interests over and above all others, including my own. I would like to thank Senator Janus for administering the election with integrity, and also would like to thank my old friend Senator Sal Carlotta for being such an inspiration to me since we were 14 at Naples Academy together. Thank you all very much."

The senators had recovered from the jolt of Dalia's concession and gave Paul a standing ovation. Paul stood behind the podium looking out over the senate, loving the cheers.

Janus approached the podium, grabbed Paul's hand and lifted his hand above their heads. "Fellow senators, please join me in congratulating our new Chairperson, Paolo James Ambrosi!" While most of the senators continued cheering, Sal politely clapped, despising the fact that he not only lost to Paul but came in sixth in a field of seven.

Janus left the senate room, went back to his office and closed the door instructing his assistant he wasn't to be disturbed. He took the snifter of brandy on the credenza and poured himself a glass. He sat at his desk, took a sip, and pulled the bag used in round one from his left coat pocket. He pulled the last piece of paper from the bag, staring at the name, KUZMA. When Janus wrote the three names on the pieces of paper for the first drawing, he wrote KIVI on all three pieces, guaranteeing Kivi would be chosen in the first drawing. After Kivi's name was announced and Janus put the bag behind the podium, he discreetly removed the last two pieces of paper with Kivi's name on them, pulled two pieces of paper with Kuzma's name from his left coat pocket, and put them in the bag. Kuzma's name was guaranteed to be drawn because her name was on both pieces of paper; there was no way Sal was advancing. Ever since Sal hit on his wife at Dalca's election party, Janus couldn't stand the man, and this was his opportunity to get even with him. He took another sip of brandy, got up and walked over to his paper shredder, sliding the pieces of paper through it, destroying them for good. He then pulled the first round of ballots from his right coat pocket.

"Let's see what the vote really was," he said to himself as he tallied the round one votes on a piece of paper. "Huh, the son-of-a-bitch would have made it to round two," he thought as he put the ballots and hand-tally in the shredder. He then opened his credenza and pulled a second set of ballots which matched the fake tallies

Janus gave during the vote. He walked out of the office with the bogus ballots and gave them to his assistant. "I accidentally took these with me, can you give them to the senate caretaker for archival?" He smiled knowing he not only kept Sal from the chairpersonship but humiliated him to boot.

DINNER AT THE PALACE
2060

The palace butler was dressed in a black jacket, white formal shirt, black bow tie, gray vest, and white gloves. His footsteps echoed as he walked down the long hallway to the large foyer to answer the front door. He saw a well-dressed couple standing at the door.

"I'm Caleb Todd, this is Angelique."

"Yes, Mr. Todd. Ma'am," the butler said.

The butler opened the door and stepped aside, and Caleb and Angelique walked into the chairperson's palace, Paul's new home. Paul arranged a dinner to celebrate his election with his three Academy friends.

Caleb's black tuxedo fit perfectly on his frame. He still had an aversion to wearing gray, stemming from his days of fearing guesting at Academy. As the butler helped Angelique off with her coat, he turned his head away in embarrassment, due to her skimpy black cocktail dress which did little to contain her shapely form from bursting forth. She smiled at Caleb as the blushing butler hung up her coat. Angelique was there as a trophy of his success, and she was paid well for it.

As they followed the butler from the front door through the long hallway, Angelique was taken by the magnificence of the palace. A large chandelier with gold arms and crystal prisms hung in the palace entry, the reflection of its light bouncing off the polished white marble floors. The walls were emerald green, the ceiling made of scalloped gold tiles. Ornate tapestries hung on the left wall and portraits of Italy's presidents and the Europe Ethnarchy chairpersons on the right. Henri Matisse's *Crucifix,* on loan from the

Vatican, stood on a platform between two of the tapestries. As they entered the parlor, they saw a portrait of the current Europe Ethnarchy chairperson, which had been hung the day before. Caleb looked at the portrait and said to Angelique, "That's my cousin."

They went into the parlor, seeing another butler serving drinks to the waiting guests. Paul and Angelique sat down on a white Bugatti grain leather sofa where the butler approached them for their drink order.

"Two Campari Spritz," Caleb said.

"Yes, Sir." The butler went to the bar at one corner of the parlor to make the drinks. Caleb and Angelique sat on the couch facing the portrait of Paul. Angelique attempted to make small talk with Caleb, having only met one week earlier in Caleb's private DarkRoom, the only one which couldn't be recorded. Angelique was from Paris, one woman of hundreds vying to meet with him in his DarkRoom. As CEO of HoloMate, he became the person men wanted to be like and women wanted to be with, just as he dreamed as a 14-year-old with his imaginary friends at Villa Comunale. He flew Angelique to Rome in HoloMate's private jet to accompany him to Paul's dinner. She would later spend the night with him at his penthouse, then be flown back to Paris the next day.

"Your Campari Spritz," the butler handed Caleb and Angelique their drinks.

"I can't believe the chairperson is your cousin." Angelique said.

"Yes, one of the only relatives who cared about me when I was a nobody."

"He looks like a nice guy," Angelique said.

"If it weren't for him I wouldn't have started HoloMate. He challenged me to solve the problem of loneliness, and I figured out how to do it and make gobs of money."

"So, he's responsible for HoloMate?" she asked

"For giving me the idea, but I built it." Caleb was grateful to Paul but didn't want to give him too much credit.

Caleb turned toward the picture and saw two more people enter the room. "Hello, Senator," Caleb said as he and Angelique rose to greet them.

"Caleb." Senator Carlotta and his date entered the room. Sal was perfectly put together in his Bottega Veneta tuxedo, royal blue bow tie, and matching pocket square. His date, Zola, was wearing an elegant royal blue dress that matched Sal's tie and pocket square and tastefully accentuated her form. When they first met a year earlier, she showed a curious interest in him, his relationship with his parents, his love of his work. She found him physically attractive but was much more attracted to the vulnerable and sensitive man inside the cocky façade he typically displayed. He tried to add her picture to his phone but she made it clear she wasn't going to sleep with him. She was old-fashioned in that she was saving herself for the man she married. With any other woman, Sal would have quit the pursuit if he knew he wasn't going to get sex. But Zola was like no other woman he'd ever been with, one who seemed to truly be interested in him for who he was on the inside. It wasn't long before they fell in love. He didn't want to mess it up.

Sal shook Caleb's hand and continued, "This is my girlfriend Zola," Sal said as he put his arm on Zola's back. She had porcelain-doll skin, a long neck, with her auburn hair slicked back and twisted into a low bun. Her face was framed by bezel diamond dangle earrings with a matching diamond necklace.

"It's a pleasure, Zola. I'm Caleb Todd," shaking her hand.

"I've heard so much about you, Mr. Todd," Zola said. "Sal says you're the brains behind HoloMate. I use it all the time and love it."

"Thank you." Caleb was so entranced by Zola he completely forgot about Angelique, who nudged his side to get his attention.

"I'm sorry, this is Angelique."

Sal recognized Angelique from an encounter in a DarkRoom a year earlier before he started dating Zola. Little did Sal know that Caleb had been following Sal's DarkRoom meetups. He met

Angelique after seeing her with Sal. It was a weird hologram tryst triangle.

Angelique let on as if she'd never met Sal. "Nice to meet you both."

The butler approached Sal and Zola, "Can I get you a drink?"

"What are you drinking, Caleb?" Sal asked.

"Campari Spritz."

"I'll have the same."

"Acqua Panna please," Zola said.

"Caleb, when was the last time we saw each other?" Sal asked.

"Gosh it's been at least five years. You've really done well."

"And you, too," Sal said. Caleb and Sal were never close growing up, with Sal seeing himself at a higher social and intellectual level than the son of a shipyard worker and Caleb not liking that Sal looked down his nose at him. Through the years they closely watched each other as they grew their businesses into two of the most influential entities in history. Their resentment had changed to mutual respect.

"Hey, guys!" Paul walked into the parlor, dressed in a simple black tuxedo, white shirt, and black tie.

"Chairperson." Caleb and Angelique went over to shake Paul's hand.

"Please, it's Paul, or Cuz, for you." Caleb gave a smile.

"This is Angelique."

"It's an honor, Chairperson," Angelique said, shaking his hand.

"Glad you could join us." He turned to Caleb. "How you doing?"

"All good, HoloMate's humming along. You're one of our best celebrities."

"Just doing a job," Paul said. He then turned to Sal and Zola.

"Senator, thank you for coming. Zola, you are looking particularly beautiful this evening."

"Thank you, Chairperson," Zola said.

"Please, for the rest of the evening, it's Paul. I'm so tired of hearing 'Chairperson' all day!"

Sal seethed at Paul's flip remark. *He* was supposed to be the chairperson.

The doorbell rang, and the butler answered the door. "Hello, I'm Bert Winn this is my wife Laura Winn. Sorry we're late." The Winns received Paul's invitation to the chairperson's palace, deciding to come to Rome from Naples a day early to do some sightseeing. They got caught in some unexpected traffic while traveling from their hotel to the palace and arrived 30 minutes late, which bothered Bert and Laura. They hated being late for anything.

"Not a problem, Mr. Winn, Ma'am," the butler said. As they walked down the hallway to the parlor, images from the tapestries appeared to leap out at Bert. On one tapestry he noticed a scrolling branch which looked like an angry hissing snake. He imagined the angry hissing snake crawling around the tapestry devouring the other scrolls. The snake leapt from tapestry to tapestry continuing its destruction, seemingly following Bert and Laura as they walked. Laura looked at Bert, sensing something in the tapestries had triggered his imagination.

"What do you see?" Laura asked.

"An angry snake eating the tapestries."

"Show me on the way out." Laura and Bert grew to appreciate each other's vivid imaginations and openly shared them with each other. As they approached the end of the hallway, Bert noticed Paul's portrait to his right before turning left into the parlor. Paul was first to greet them.

"Bert, my friend!" Paul shook Bert's hand. "And Laura, you look beautiful as always." Laura indeed looked beautiful. She wore a slightly loose-fitting teal cotton dress which both flattered her and was sensory-friendly. She had gone to a beauty salon earlier in the day to have her hair and make-up done, then to a nail salon for a manicure and pedicure. That was a first for her to pamper herself, and she kind of liked it.

"Thank you," Laura said.

Bert and Laura walked over to the others.

"Bert, how are you?" Sal said, giving him a fist bump. Sal remembered the first time they met how Bert was uncomfortable with being touched. "This is my girlfriend, Zola."

"Hello, Sal, hello, Zola." Bert continued. "This is my wife, Laura. We've been married 18 years and we have a son JT who's 12."

"Hello, Laura," Zola said. "Your hair is beautiful."

"Thank you, I went to the hair salon today. I love it too."

Caleb extended his hand, "Hey, Bert, hey, Laura." Caleb knew Bert and Laura well; their HoloBlog, *Growing Up Autistic with the Winns* was HoloMate's most popular HoloBlog with over a hundred million subscribers. Bert and Laura were making Caleb a lot of money, so he wanted to treat his stars right.

"This is Angelique." Bert was visibly embarrassed by Angelique's skimpy dress, looking at her once then casting his gaze on her face to avoid scanning Angelique's near-naked body.

"Hello, Angelique. This is my wife, Laura." Laura was shocked at her dress and couldn't help herself.

"Hi Angelique, aren't you cold?" she asked.

Sal, Paul and Zola snickered at her comment, after all, she just asked what they all were thinking.

"I'm fine, thank you." Angelique said. Caleb looked to change the topic.

"*Growing Up Autistic* is doing great!" Caleb said, taking the focus off Angelique's outfit. "You're the number one HoloBlog. Great job, you two!" Bert and Laura's HoloBlog had been a huge success since debuting in 2050. They had helped millions across all ten ethnarchies better understand autism and help those on the spectrum live life to their fullest.

"Thank you, Caleb," Bert said. "We hope we're helping others affected by autism."

"Laura, tell me about your HoloBlog," Zola said as she moved next to Laura.

"It's about me, Bert and JT just living our lives," Laura said. Angelique wanted to be part of the conversation, joining the two.

"So, you have autism?" Angelique asked.

"Yes, all three of us do."

"But you're married." Angelique had never been around someone with autism, her only exposure to autism was through movies. "Autistics can marry?"

"Yes, we've been married 18 years."

"And you have a child?"

"JT, he's 12."

"Did you adopt?"

"No."

"Autistic people can have sex?"

Laura looked over at Bert, uncomfortable with Angelique's questions. Zola, who had a sister with autism, saw Laura getting agitated and stepped in.

"Laura, I love your dress." Zola said, trying to change the topic.

"Thank you, I bought it here in Rome."

"I heard autistics can't wear certain types of clothes," Angelique started in again. Zola rolled her eyes at Angelique's obliviousness.

"Some fabrics can be irritating."

"Do you prefer to not wear clothes?"

"Sometimes." Laura continued. "You seem to not like wearing clothes, are you autistic?" Laura asked Angelique as she looked at her barely-there dress. Zola let out a laugh then tried to cover her mouth in vain.

"Do I look autistic?" Angelique was agitated by Laura's question, not because of her dress, but because she would dare be compared to someone with autism. Paul had been watching the back and forth and saw that Laura was getting uncomfortable with Angelique's questions. He decided to rescue Laura.

"Laura, can you come and talk with Bert and me about the blog?" Paul asked.

"Gladly." Laura left her conversation with Zola and Angelique to join Paul and Bert. Angelique looked at Zola as if to get affirmation that Laura insulted Angelique. Zola saw the opportunity to exit the discussion and went with Paul to talk more with Bert and Laura, as she had become interested in learning more from them. Angelique, now standing by herself, took a sip of her drink and started wandering around the parlor, taking in the ornate accessories and beautiful artwork on the walls.

"Dinner is ready," the butler motioned toward an adjoining dining room. The room had the same marble floors with a rectangular cherry dining room table and eight matching chairs. Two large windows were at either end of the far wall with royal blue floor-to-ceiling curtains framing the windows. A massive crystal chandelier hung from the trayed ceiling. On the table were seven formal place settings with gold flatware, gold-rimmed white plates, and already-filled crystal water and wine glasses. Each guest found the name on their place card and sat. The butler then retrieved plates of arugula salad from the kitchen and began serving each guest.

Paul took a sip from his glass of white wine. "Thank you all for coming," Paul started. "Our days at Academy were a special time for me, one where my three best friends played a significant role in my becoming the man I am today." Paul didn't consider Sal a best friend but wanted to include him to try to smooth things over after the chairperson vote. Paul continued. "Bert, you opened my eyes to the world of someone with autism and helped me to understand the importance of inclusiveness. Caleb, you inspired me with your HoloMate vision and how you turned your passion into a successful enterprise. Sal, your undeterred fixation with finding a cure for cancer and making it available to millions changed the world. I wanted to invite you here to simply say thank you, and to Laura, Zola and Angelique, thank you for being the roses to our thorns."

Nods and thank-yous from Paul's guests.

The butler moved from guest to guest, serving salads. Zola looked across the table at Bert and Laura.

"What's next for your HoloBlog?" Zola asked. This wasn't a polite question for her, she was genuinely interested.

"We're going to talk about DarkRooms and their dangers."

That got Caleb's attention. They want to attack his cash cow.

"What does that have to do with autism?" Caleb asked.

"It's not about autism, it's about decency." Laura added, looking over at Angelique. Angelique gave Laura a snide glance.

"Your HoloBlog is supposed to be about autism; that's what people care about." Caleb said.

"Maybe, but we feel very strongly about DarkRooms and want to speak out against them," Bert said.

"You need to stick to autism." Caleb wanted to exert some force to get them to comply.

"There's nothing in our agreement that says we are limited in our topics. Paul reviewed our contract when we first signed it and said we could talk about anything we wanted." Bert said.

Caleb looked over at his cousin, feeling betrayed.

"He's right," Paul said. Caleb knew there was nothing he could legally do about it, so he tried another angle.

"Your followers won't want to hear about DarkRooms, you'll lose your audience and your coaching revenue." Caleb said as he took his first bite of salad.

"Maybe," Laura said. Bert and Laura had been talking about this for months. They had saved up enough hera so they weren't reliant on future HoloBlog or coaching revenue. They could completely shutter the business and still live comfortably for the rest of their lives on what they had saved. "We're willing to take the risk," Laura added.

Paul decided to cut the escalating tension. "Zola, what do you do?"

"I work at a Christian homeless shelter."

"Really! I volunteered at a homeless shelter when I was in college," Paul said. Sal was not happy that Paul and Zola had found a common interest. He imagined Paul beating him in a competition yet again, this time for the first woman other than his mother that he had an emotional connection with. "What do you as Christians do at the shelter?"

"We like to say that we provide both physical and spiritual nourishment."

Paul was expert at faking interest in topics. He thought the spiritual nourishment comment was garbage, but his outward conversation conveyed that there was nothing more fascinating than what she was saying.

"That's so interesting!" Paul said.

"Perhaps the chairperson would like to visit the shelter sometime; you would be an inspiration to so many!"

"I'd love that," Paul had no intention of visiting a Christian homeless shelter, it would be easy to claim he was too busy to do if the topic ever came up again.

The butler brought the main course, a cloud of tension hung over the rest of the meal, despite the benign conversation. Bert and Laura were still staunchly against DarkRooms and were bent on speaking out against them. Caleb didn't want his HoloBlog stars speaking out against his DarkRooms moneymaker. Zola and Paul continued making connections on topics, fueling Sal's jealousy of Paul. Paul knew he was driving Sal crazy by connecting with Zola. Paul had no interest in Zola, he only did it to get under Sal's skin. The evening's banter was all fun and games compared to the two greatest threats keeping Paul awake at night: the famine crisis and project Zeus.

TWO KILOMETERS AWAY
2066

Aliza Breiner, the Jerusalem-based HoloMate reporter, had been at Jerusalem Health for the last hour, trying to find out whatever she could about the shooting, the status of the victims, and whether the shooter was also at the hospital. Caleb had just emerged from getting his left forearm stitched from a bullet that grazed his arm. Other than being shaken by the experience, he was fine.

"Are you ready, Mr. Todd?" Aliza asked.

"Ready."

Aliza and Caleb tuned into LFTP-939, their HoloSpec lenses changing from clear to frosted. The producer spoke into Aliza's earpiece, "We're on in ten." Aliza pulled out her mirror, smiled, rubbed lipstick from her teeth, and handed the mirror to Caleb. He did a quick check and handed it back to Aliza.

"Three, two, one."

"This is Aliza Breiner from HoloMate News at Jerusalem Health. I have with me Caleb Todd, founder of HoloMate and one of the victims. Thank you for joining, Mr. Todd."

"Thank You, Aliza."

"Can you tell me what happened?"

"The chairperson, senator, and I were walking from our car into the embassy. I saw the chairperson and senator go down on the steps, then felt something like hot metal on my forearm. I looked down and saw my arm sliced open. I then looked at the chairperson and senator, both on the steps, hemorrhaging from their heads. There was no sound. I heard the shooter was far away."

"That's right," Aliza confirmed. "We learned the shooter was two kilometers away."

"That makes sense. Didn't hear shots."

"How's your arm?"

"OK, have you heard any more about Sal and Paul?"

"Just one second." Aliza heard her producer's voice in her earpiece. "I'm getting a report on the chairperson and senator. Both the chairperson and senator have been admitted into surgery, the chairperson for a bullet wound above the right ear. Hold on, we're getting more on the senator." Aliza paused, holding her hand to her earpiece, trying to hear her producer. Aliza continued, "The senator has also been admitted to surgery, word we're getting is the senator's jaw is severely damaged. Do we know any more Ira?" Aliza asked her producer for more information. She continued, "That's all we've got right now. Mr. Todd are you alright?"

Aliza turned back to Caleb to see him sitting on a chair nearby, his head in his hands. "My God, Paul, I'm so sorry." Caleb switched off his HoloSpecs, the lenses turning from frosted to clear. As Aliza walked over to Caleb to see how he was doing, two orderlies wheeling a man covered in a sheet from one of the trauma rooms passed by, the disgusting smell of burnt flesh stung her nose. She overheard one talking, "GSW to the head and car fire."

BLACKMAIL
2061

C aleb looked at the name on his phone before he answered.
"Hello, Mr. Chairperson."

"Hey, Cuz."

Caleb was surprised to get an out-of-the-blue call from Paul. Ever since Paul was elected chairperson a year ago, phone calls were planned in advance, with Paul's assistant arranging the call time and duration. "What's up?"

"I need you to come to my office, I need your help."

"Certainly, when?"

"Can you come by this afternoon at three?"

"Sure."

"What's your clearance level?"

"Secret." Because of HoloMate's prevalence across the world, Caleb had collaborated with the Europe Ethnarchy on surveillance operations and was granted secret clearance. The next level of clearance was top-secret, which was reserved for need-to-know on the most serious of ethnarchy security issues.

"You'll need top-secret clearance, I'll fast track it through. See you at three."

Caleb hung up. This didn't sound like a routine surveillance operation, in fact it was anything but.

Caleb got to Paul's office at the Europe Ethnarchy government building where the Italian *Ministero della Difesa* in Rome once stood. Caleb passed through tight security, including a full body scan for contraband, iris recognition to confirm identity, and checking of all electronic devices before visiting the chairperson.

"Your phone, sir." Caleb gave his phone to the armed security guard.

"And your HoloSpecs, sir." Caleb removed his glasses and gave them to the guard, who then handed Caleb a claim ticket for his personal effects. "OK to proceed," the security guard called to a second armed guard who escorted Caleb to Paul's office. He was greeted by Paul's assistant.

"Hello, Mr. Todd, the chairperson will be with you in four minutes. Please take a seat."

"Thank you." Caleb sat across from the assistant in one of two red low-back chairs with a small table between. Behind the chairs on the wall was a large portrait of Paul. "Odd," Caleb thought to himself. Ever since they were kids, Caleb knew Paul as one of the humblest people. He remembered back to the palace, seeing Paul's portrait in the hallway. "Maybe this is just protocol," Caleb reasoned, justifying why his selfless cousin would be displaying portraits of himself.

The door to Paul's office opened. "Caleb! come in!" Paul gave Caleb a kiss on each cheek, then led him into his office. Two walls of the office were floor-to-ceiling windows looking out over Rome, with Paul's deep walnut desk near the windows in the corner. An oval walnut conference table with ten leather chairs was to Caleb's left as he entered the office and a small kitchen with a doorway that led to a private toilet to his right. The walls were painted deep purple with framed pictures of Paul with Pius XIV, chairpersons from other ethnarchies, Paul's degrees from LSE and Harvard, and Paul with notable celebrities and sports figures. On the wall right next to the door hung a framed shadow box with the dented folding stool and a picture of Paul with his parents and siblings inside.

"Can I get you something?" Paul asked as he shut the door and walked toward the kitchen area.

"Just water."

"Grab a seat," Paul pointed to the conference table then reached into the fridge for two bottles of water.

"I need your help with two things," Paul started in as he walked to the conference table, handing Caleb a water. Caleb waited for Paul to continue.

Paul took a sip of water. "Our intel in Russia identified a top-secret program that Chairperson Popov is personally overseeing. He's creating a network of space-based directed-energy weapons capable of pinpoint-accurate strikes from up to 10,000 kilometers. Popov recruited scientists from around the world, including the United States Space Force to design and oversee its development. Intel says they're close to launching the weapons, how close we're not sure. Popov calls the program Zeus."

Caleb listened intently, wondering what Paul could possibly be thinking that Caleb could help with.

Paul continued, "We have a list of key men and women working on the program. I need you to help us dig up information on them that we can use to extract intel on Zeus." Paul wasn't specific with "dig up information," but he didn't need to be. Paul wanted Caleb to see who visited DarkRooms, so Paul could blackmail them in exchange for intel.

"What type of information?" Caleb asked.

"Anything they wouldn't want loved ones, family and friends to see." Paul said. Caleb's suspicion was confirmed. "Can you help me?"

"Yes."

"Good, now for the second ask. I want you to assist our cyberintelligence unit as we get intel, using what you've learned on HoloMate however it can be helpful."

"Assist them with what?"

"Seizing control of the network." Caleb took a sip of water, taking in the second ask. This was far more serious than surveillance work or even digging up dirt. This was about hijacking a space-based weapons network. Paul continued, "First step is for you to meet cyberintel director, Dominic Natalizio. He'll tell you what you'll do. I'll have him contact you."

"OK." Caleb's initial shock was giving way to a bungee-jump type of thrill; excitement, fear, angst, and anticipation. "I'm happy to serve, Mr. Chairperson."

"Good." Paul got up from his chair, signaling the meeting's end. He walked Caleb to the door. "Say hi to your parents for me," Paul said as they walked past the framed dented folding stool on the way out the door. "I wish I could tell you the same," Caleb thought.

The next day Director Natalizio called Caleb, giving him more detail on the program and the list of 37 program personnel Caleb was to research. The list included name, height, weight, eye color, hair color, ethnicity, last known address, picture, spouse, children, passport number, and pictures of unusual body markings. Searching HoloMate by name or picture would most likely be useless, as most DarkRoom patrons used aliases and some kind of mask to hide their face. He would have to rely on unusual body markings as an identifier. He scanned each body marking into HoloMate, hoping for a hit on at least one. Three matches came up, including a 43-year-old man from Bridgeport, Connecticut named Aaron Riccio, also known as Daddy219 in the DarkRooms. Caleb's DarkRoom search for Daddy219 yielded a treasure trove of encounters, mostly with young Asian boys. Caleb called Natalizio. "I think we got a hit," Caleb said. "Aaron Riccio."

"Do you have video?" Natalizio asked.

"Oh yeah."

"Send it over, I'll take it from here."

"On its way."

Natalizio hung up, then accessed information about Riccio from cyberintel's database. He was the father of two young girls, married for 13 years, a deacon in his church, with a sterling reputation as a computer systems engineer. Riccio's employer was listed as MDC

International, based in Moscow. He temporarily moved his family to Moscow to work on what was thought to be a weather satellite project.

Paul watched one of the hologram videos of Riccio that Caleb had sent, repulsed at what he saw, but even more by what he heard--boy after boy wailing in terror while Riccio had his way. He turned off the video. "We've got our man," he said to himself, then went into the bathroom and puked.

Two Europe agents paid Riccio a visit at his Moscow home one evening while his wife and girls were visiting family in Bridgeport. They told him about the DarkRoom videos, which he vehemently denied. The agents then showed him the videos, at which point Riccio began crying uncontrollably. Riccio was the director responsible for Zeus' software that controlled targeting and weapons selection. The agents calmly told him the terms of the deal. Riccio was to provide weekly updates on Zeus' progress as well as weekly code drops of targeting and weapon selection source code to the Europe Ethnarchy cyberintel. In exchange, cyberintel would then run the code on its simulator to ensure authenticity. If the code was proven authentic, cyberintel would pay him 5,000 hera and not make his DarkRoom holograms public. If the code was not deemed authentic, payment would not be made but, more importantly to Riccio, one of his DarkRoom holograms would be sent to his wife and made public. Riccio was just the type of person Natalizio wanted, and he got him.

GOAT MILK SQUARES
2061

D r. Rhona MacLurig, CEO and synthetic biology scientist at SynFoods in Glasgow, Scotland had been experimenting with synthetic biology for 18 years. Sal had heard of their work in creating synthetic food and requested a site visit to better understand their research. He and MacLurig sat in a small taste-testing room next to her lab. "What do you think, Senator?" She asked.

"It tastes like a ham and cheese sandwich," Sal said. What Sal was eating wasn't real ham, cheese, or bread. It was produced in a lab.

"What you're eating is a genetically enhanced product where the DNA sequence of natural foods is replicated in a lab and colored, formed, and texturized to look, feel, smell, and taste like the real thing. It's still experimental but is showing a lot of promise."

"I'm familiar with the technology," Sal said. "What I'm mostly concerned about is whether it can be produced inexpensively and in large enough quantities to feed millions of people."

MacLurig took a sip of tea. "It's a tradeoff of function versus form. The more we try to make something look, feel, smell and taste like the real thing, the more complex and expensive the manufacturing. Producing something that looks, feels, smells and tastes like a chunk of cheese is much more time-consuming and expensive than producing something with the texture and visual appeal of a square of tofu and a slight taste and odor of cheese. The nutrients are there, it just doesn't have the aesthetic qualities."

"How much more expensive and how much longer?"

"Ballpark is about ten times the cost and five times the manufacturing time." MacLurig got the message that Sal was not at all interested in the aesthetics of the food.

"Do you have a sample?" Sal wanted to see if he could choke one down.

"I have one that we engineered from goat milk." MacLurig got up and went into her lab, coming back with a white plate containing two squares of what looked like gelatin. Sal picked up one of the squares. It was cream colored, spongy and jiggled slightly as he picked it up. He brought the square to his nose, picking up a very faint dairy smell. He put the square in his mouth, squeezing it between his tongue and the roof of his mouth. The texture reminded him of tapioca pudding with pearls that popped as he pressed his tongue, the taste like room-temperature milk.

"It's disgusting." Sal spat out what was left in his mouth into a napkin.

"It's function over form," MacLurig reminded him. "It takes some getting used to."

"How about the nutritional value?"

"Three squares supply a day's worth of nutrients. Eat one in the morning, one at noon and one in the evening with plenty of water and you'll feel full like you've eaten three meals."

"What's the shelf life?"

"With the right additives we could get it to an unlimited shelf life."

"Are the additives safe?" Sal asked.

"Nothing that your synthetic killer cells couldn't handle," MacLurig said with a smile, coyly deflecting the question back to Sal and his own work as a scientist. She didn't know how safe the additives were because they hadn't been tested extensively.

Sal looked down at the uneaten second square sitting on the plate. He shook the plate slightly, watching the square wiggle from side to side.

"I need to talk with the chairperson, this could be viable. Can I take this with me?" Sal pointed to the second square, now still on the plate.

"Sure, I'm here to help. When do you go back to Rome?"

"Tomorrow."

"If you're available, maybe we can have dinner about seven, I promise no goat milk squares." MacLurig said.

Sal had been devoted to Zola for over two years. Even though they weren't married, Sal hadn't had a romp with another woman since he had started seeing Zola. He quickly reasoned it was only dinner.

"Sure, you choose the place," Sal said.

"I'll message you the address later this afternoon." MacLurig sent him the address to her apartment in downtown Glasgow, where they had dinner and never made it to dessert. Sal couldn't help himself, but this time he didn't put a picture on his phone.

Sal called Paul's assistant to schedule time with him the morning after he got back from Glasgow. The two met in Paul's office at ten. Sal sat down at the conference table in Paul's office, pulled a plastic container from his backpack, and set it in front of Paul.

"What's this?" Paul asked.

"Taste it."

Paul opened the container, the cream-colored square jiggling as he pulled the top off. Paul grimaced at the sight.

"Why?"

"It might be our answer to famine."

Paul reached in the container, pulled out the square, and smelled it. He could see the pearls in the square. He put it in his mouth, squishing the square in his mouth, breaking the delicate pearls and getting the faint taste of goat's milk.

"It doesn't taste like anything, and it feels gross in my mouth. What is it?"

"Synthetic food."

"How nutritious is it?"

"Three a day with water gives a full day's worth of nutrition."

Paul pondered what he was taking in. A gelatinous square of gooey nothing with goat milk pearls engineered in a lab was supposed to be the answer to famine in the ethnarchy?

"Who makes it?" Paul asked.

"A company called SynFoods in Glasgow."

"Does it come in anything other than goat milk vomit?"

"Possibly, but we need to balance function with form." Sal liked how MacLurig phrased the tradeoff messaging, so he used it with Paul.

"Right. What's the shelf life?"

"Indefinitely." Sal didn't want to tell Paul about the additives required to make it safe.

"You're the scientist, what do you think we should do?" Paul wanted Sal to commit to a plan of action.

"We should do our own trial for three months, consuming only SynFood, then decide if it's effective."

"Three-month trial? Who'd participate?" Paul asked.

Sal thought about it for a moment, then Paul answered his own question.

"If you say it's safe, I know exactly who should participate." Paul did some quick math. "Get 27,000 squares to Brussels in two weeks," Paul said to Sal, not asking even if it was possible to do. Paul got up, opened the door to his office, and yelled to his assistant, "Let's put another item on the senate session agenda."

SynFood Trial
2061

The senate met two weeks later in Brussels. Paul administered the agenda for the day-long meeting, working his way through to the last item--Famine. Paul opened the discussion.

"Our colleague Senator Carlotta had a very interesting meeting with a company called SynFoods in Glasgow. They have an innovative product that can supplement our food supply and still provide the needed dietary nutrients. They claim the product can be taken on its own with only water and no other food source. Senator Carlotta and I both tried the product and he recommends we conduct a three-month trial before we certify its use across the ethnarchy. I am asking the senate to affirm conducting a three-month trial of the product, then we will evaluate the results before proceeding."

Paul then motioned to the senate caretaker, who wheeled out a cart with 100 SynFood squares. He and three helpers then passed out the squares to Paul and each senator.

"This is what we're talking about," Paul said as the jiggly squares were given to each senator on a napkin. Paul was the first to eat his cube.

"Come on, it's not going to kill you," Paul said.

The senators started eating their squares, some swallowing without issue, others grimacing while they ate, a couple spitting them out, grossed at the consistency.

"Reactions?" Paul asked.

"Does it come in other flavors?" one senator asked.

"It can, we just need to balance function with form." Paul used Sal's description that he borrowed from MacLurig.

"It's kind of nasty," another said.

"It'll take some getting used to," Paul wasn't sure he could ever get to a point of liking it, but he might just be able to tolerate it.

Discussion and debate continued for an hour. To the general population, the fear of famine was the single most important issue affecting their daily lives. Food shortages were becoming a nearly daily occurrence, and senators were under intense pressure from their constituents to do something about it. When Paul saw the discussion waning, he decided to close the topic and put it to a vote. Paul had voting ballots ready for the senate caretaker to distribute. The senate, including Paul, voted 90 to ten to conduct the three-month trial.

"The motion passes," Paul said. "Before we adjourn, we have one more piece of business. We've already chosen 100 people for the three-month trial. Every senator, myself included, will participate in the trial. As you exit, you'll be given a box with a 90-day supply of SynFood squares."

Collective groans. Paul snapped back.

"Senators, you just voted to proceed with the trial, so what's good for others should be good enough for you. I am expecting full participation. If you don't participate, I'll tell your constituents that you thought you were too good to take part. That won't play well for you."

The senators left the session, picked up their boxes, and left amidst grumbles, not looking forward to the next 90 days.

Three months later, the senate reconvened in Brussels, focusing solely on the topic of SynFood. The senators and Paul held to their word and ate only SynFood and water for 90 days. Dr. MacLurig also attended the session to hear the feedback, expecting to fend off complaints about the product. The feedback astonished her. Senators reported feeling stronger, more alert, having greater energy levels and clearer thinking. Any texture and flavor issues went away after a few days, and some even seasoned their squares with favorite spices to counter the blandness. Even though during the trial they only ate SynFood, all of them agreed the best alternative was a hybrid SynFood/traditional food diet. The senate asked MacLurig to create a manufacturing and distribution plan for the Europe Ethnarchy, as well as an agreement that MacLurig would ensure the Europe Ethnarchy's needs would be met before considering supplying to any other ethnarchy.

SynFood ramped up its production to 100 million SynFood squares a month, not nearly enough to accommodate the Europe Ethnarchy's population of 700 million citizens. Paul looked to Sal and his experience running MD Biometrics to work with SynFood to grow its production ecosystem. The senate knew Sal was the one making SynFood a success, but the general public saw Paul as its famine savior. And it made Sal furious that Paul was getting the credit for his work, something he didn't want to be involved with in the first place.

THE DEDICATION
2066

Caleb switched on his HoloSpecs and started his report. "This is Caleb Todd, CEO of HoloMate, reporting on day 15 following the assassination attempt of Chairperson Ambrosi and Senator Carlotta." Caleb personally took over the reporting of the shooting of his friends Paul and Sal, reporting status from the hospital each morning, noon and evening. Billions around the world tuned into Caleb's HoloMate channel to hear about the beloved chairperson. "I just spoke with the doctors treating the chairperson and senator. The chairperson has been declared brain-dead. The senate has requested he be kept on life support for seven more days. If he shows no signs of recovery he'll be removed from life support. I should caution you that the likelihood of recovery from brain death is extremely rare. We can only hope and send good thoughts, but it doesn't look good." Even though the senate requested keeping Paul alive for seven more days, Caleb didn't hold much hope he'd survive. He talked with the doctors enough to know that recovery from brain death was virtually impossible.

Caleb continued, "At four today I will be at the Jerusalem Capitol Complex where Israeli President Dichter will commence the Peace Monument dedication."

After the peace treaty was reached between Israel and Palestine, Dichter commissioned a monument to be built honoring the Europe Ethnarchy for its role in brokering the agreement. Paul, Sal and Caleb were to attend the ceremony on the day they were shot. Dichter wanted to hold the ceremony while Paul was still alive, even if he was brain-dead, rather than after his death.

Caleb continued with a brief update on Sal. "Senator Carlotta is awake and aware, able to communicate through writing on a whiteboard." Sal's jaw was unrecoverable; what remained after the shooting was completely removed. "He's being fed through a nasogastric tube through his nose into his stomach. This is Caleb Todd, see you at four." Caleb turned off his HoloSpecs, his hologram disappearing from the channel.

Caleb arrived at the Jerusalem Capitol Complex, his arm still bandaged from his bullet graze. The complex was erected in 2049 just north of the Dome of the Rock where some historians believe the Temple of Solomon once stood. The complex replicated some elements of Solomon's Temple, with an outer court, inner court and capitol building. The dedication was to occur in the outer court, with the monument standing at the outer court entrance for everyone entering and exiting the complex to see. Caleb made his way through the gates of the outer court with its six-meter-high limestone walls surrounding the complex. Next to the outer court entry was a three-meter structure draped in deep purple fabric surrounded by a red rope barrier. Members of the Europe Ethnarchy Senate and other world dignitaries filed into the outer court, filling it to capacity. President Dichter and members of his cabinet entered the outer court. Dichter took his place next to the structure draped in purple. Caleb switched on his HoloSpecs, entered HoloRoom LFTP-939, and switched on the portable camera on his HoloSpecs so others in the HoloRoom could see the dedication.

"This is Caleb Todd at the Jerusalem Capitol Complex, where Israeli President Ari Dichter will unveil the Peace Monument celebrating peace between Israel and its neighbors. He's about to speak."

President Dichter switched on his HoloSpecs. "Distinguished guests and people around the world, three-and-a-half years ago, Israel entered into a peace agreement with our neighboring countries, allowing the citizens of Israel to live their lives without a constant fear of military strikes. What was once a society steeped in terror is now one of love and hope. Israel owes its freedom to the Europe Ethnarchy and the tireless efforts of Chairperson Paul Ambrosi. I am pleased to dedicate this Peace Monument in hope that peace will be maintained not just for the next three and half years, but for generations to come." The peace treaty was signed on September 1, 2062 between Israel and its neighbors Egypt Sinai, Jordan, Syria and Lebanon. The peace treaty mandated seven years of cease-fire between Israel and its neighbors. The Europe Ethnarchy established military bases in Israel as a "peace through strength" move to remind Israel's neighbors what would happen should they break the treaty. Due to the high degree of mistrust between Israel and its neighbors, the agreement would be only for seven years, with future negotiations to begin at the beginning of year six. The peace treaty only existed because the Europe Ethnarchy threatened military intervention against Israel's neighbors.

Dichter pulled the purple fabric from the structure, revealing a polished gold statue that glistened in the sunlight, almost as if the statue was illuminated. There were oohs and aahs from those in the outer court followed by rousing applause. Caleb marveled at the attention to detail and its god-like grandeur. He looked at it from head to toe, struck with its lifelikeness, it was almost as if it was alive, as if it could talk if it wanted to. He then looked at the base and the etching, *Paolo James Ambrosi, Europe Ethnarchy Chairperson, Dedicated March 1, 2066.* Caleb smiled at the distinction bestowed on his cousin who helped him so much through his life. He considered it an honor to pay for its commissioning.

THREE NOWS
2062

September 1, 2062 marked the 1,000th HoloBlog episode of *Growing Up Autistic with the Winns*. Through the years they had covered a wide range of topics--autism, parenting, faith. Millions had watched JT, now 14, grow up with autism, cheering his strengths, grieving his challenges. The last few years saw Bert and Laura increasingly critical of DarkRooms, with their ruinous effects on relationships, and their seductive addiction claiming hormone-raging teenagers. They had psychologists, pastors, and other experts as guests speaking about DarkRoom HoloDiction and its detrimental effects. Talking out against DarkRooms became an obsession for Bert and Laura, just as puzzles were an obsession for Bert when he was a toddler. Bert and Laura didn't care if they repelled followers because of their crusade, they felt it was more important to be evangelists against DarkRooms. Their following increased, while DarkRoom visitor instances declined by ten percent. Caleb was livid over Bert and Laura's campaign against HoloMate's meal ticket but feared any action against them would hurt their business even more.

Bert introduced the day's episode, "Today we have as a special guest, Dr. William Ellison from the University of Arizona in the United States. Dr. Ellison is the executive director of the Autism Alliance of Southern Arizona and has done extensive research on DarkRooms and their effect on the autism community. Thank you for joining us from Arizona, Dr. Ellison."

Ellison was sitting with a cherry cola in his office in Tucson, having already switched on his HoloSpecs. Ellison, Laura, Bert, and

JT's hologram images were sitting at a table in their HoloRoom, a beautiful picture of the Tucson desert at sunrise in the background.

"Thank you for having me, Winn family."

"Dr. Ellison tell us about your DarkRoom research," Laura said.

Ellison sipped his soda, preparing for a long explanation. "Happy to. For five years we've conducted hundreds of experiments," Ellison was interrupted mid-sentence by a deep bass voice. The voice was slow and deliberate, loud but not piercing to the ears. The voice said *Now* three times, then Ellison heard a perfectly-pitched Middle C trumpet sound, starting soft, gradually growing louder. The trumpet, like the voice, was loud but not annoying. Ellison, Bert, Laura, and JT were confused as the trumpet sound overtook every other sound. After five seconds of the trumpet crescendo the sound turned into a loud screech, hurting Ellison's ears. At that same moment Bert, Laura, and JT disappeared from the HoloRoom, leaving only Ellison in the room. Ellison looked at the three empty spots where the Winns sat just moments ago.

"Bert, are you there?" Ellison asked. "Laura? Bert?" Total silence. "Bert, are you there?" No response. "Must be a technical problem," Ellison thought to himself. He stayed in the room with his HoloSpecs on for another minute, then started to hear screaming outside his office. He removed his HoloSpecs, got up from his desk, and opened the door. He looked across the room filled with cubicles, his colleagues running from cubicle to cubicle, wondering where their colleagues who had been working there just seconds earlier had gone. He walked over to his assistant's desk and looked at her empty chair, only seeing a dress draped over the chair, her jewelry and HoloSpecs where she sat just moments ago.

Bert's parents, Ryan and Hayley, had been watching the HoloBlog from their home in Naples when the voice and trumpet sound commenced. Ryan removed his HoloSpecs and looked at Hayley. He watched her facial expression as the trumpet sound built. She had a glow about her, with the most peaceful look he had ever seen on her face. She removed her HoloSpecs and looked at Ryan, still looking radiant with the lovely smile. As the screech began he watched Hayley's glow turn into a bright light, then she disappeared, the bright light sucking into itself as her clothes, jewelry, and HoloSpecs fell to the chair and ground, her simple gold wedding ring rolling to Ryan's foot. Confused, Ryan went to Hayley's chair, seeing only what was left of her personal effects. Her bra, necklace, and earrings and fell to the floor as he picked up her blouse. He saw a surgical screw from when she had shoulder surgery years before still in the chair next to a ceramic dental crown.

Nothing left of her--skin, hair, nails--all gone.

He called out to her, still in disbelief. "Hayley, where are you? Hayley? Hayley?" He looked around the apartment, calling out to her, his voice becoming more frantic with each word. "Hayley? Hayley? Sweetheart? HAYLEY!"

Nothing.

He went back to his chair and put on his HoloSpecs. The HoloRoom where Bert, Laura, and JT were interviewing Dr. Ellison was empty except for Dr. Ellison, who was sitting there for a moment, then disappeared. Ryan picked up his phone and called Bert. No answer. He left a message, "Bert are you there? Something's happened to Mom. Call me back." He called Laura and JT, no answer. "What's going on?" He said as he put down the phone.

Sal and Zola were honeymooning in Mykonos, Greece. They had split up a year earlier after Sal confessed of his one-night-stand with MacLurig. Sal recognized he messed up when he cheated on Zola, his intense guilt forcing him to confess. Sal had never loved a woman like he did Zola, and he almost lost her because of an evening of indiscretion. She eventually forgave him, and when he asked her to marry him six months later, she said yes.

Sal and Zola sat on the balcony of their beachfront villa, enjoying some wine before heading off to dinner. The sun was setting just above the Aegean Sea horizon, tips of orange reflecting off the water.

The two sat with their feet on the balcony railing, enjoying the warmth of the setting sun. Until Zola, Sal had never understood what it was like to unconditionally, romantically love a woman. Before Zola, women were objects of physical love, but his love for Zola was far beyond sexual expression. He looked at her enjoying the sunset, eyes closed, smile on her face, completely at peace. As he watched her, he was startled by hearing *Now* three times, then the trumpet sound. He looked over at her as she opened her eyes and looked at him. Keeping her peaceful look, she smiled at him, then he heard the screech. She didn't appear to hear the screech, she just kept smiling as she began to glow. The screech stopped just as he saw her clothes and jewelry drop to the chair. It was completely quiet for about ten seconds while he attempted to digest what had happened.

He heard screaming from the beach below, peering over the railing at a woman frantically looking around an empty stroller that just held her one-year-old daughter. He looked at Zola's chair, her dress dangling from where she sat, jewelry on the ground, MDChip nestled in her clothes. As he looked around, it all started making sense to him. Zola had become Christian when they first started dating and was doing a Bible study on the end times. He remembered her reading about the rapture in First Thessalonians and talking with Sal about what would happen--a shout, then a trumpet, then believers being caught up in the air to meet the Lord. She had talked with him a number of times about becoming Christian. He thought it an interesting fairy tale but never believed it was true. Now the love of his life was gone, and he was still there.

Left alone again.

SEKARANG
2062

It was a long evening. Reports of disappearances began coming in around 5:30 p.m. the day before. Paul was preparing for an upcoming meeting with the chairperson from Asia when he heard the low-bass voice, trumpet, screech, silence, then people screaming. He left his office and saw his assistant. "What was that?" he asked. His assistant just sat there horrified, staring at the empty chair of one of Paul's staffers, his clothes crumpled on the chair. Paul walked down the hallway toward the door outside the Europe Ethnarchy government building, his security detail running behind him. As he was walking, he peered into offices, seeing some people confused by the strange sounds, not knowing what happened, others stunned at the sight of coworkers' clothes left where they had stood just moments before.

Paul walked out the front door to the street, aghast at what he saw. There was a gridlock of cars and trucks on the street, with drivers honking horns at driverless cars, and passengers horrified as they stared at empty driver seats. Paul slowly walked down the street, seeing some people crying, some just wandering and looking downward at crumpled clothes, a prosthetic arm, porcelain teeth, surgical screws and plates, saline breast implants, rings, necklaces, watches, wallets, phones, HoloSpecs. He watched a man numbly pick up his wife's wedding ring. He went back into his office, his security detail still in tow. As he got to his office he saw his assistant, still dazed from the event.

"What happened, sir?" his assistant asked.

"I don't know."

Paul went into his office and closed his door. He put on his HoloSpecs and tuned into HoloMate News. A special channel, FFF-29a, was immediately set up to provide continued coverage of the disappearance. He sat there through the night watching the reports around the world. Witnesses talked of the deep-bassed *now*, the trumpet, then the screech. As people recounted what happened he noticed that the voice spoke in each person's native language. A witness in China reported hearing "xiàn zài," one from Indonesia heard "sekarang," and an Estonian heard "nüüd." Even though the spoken word was different, the sounds and events were identical. HoloMate News then broadcast a Catholic cardinal from Chicago whom he remembered from his days working for the Vatican. He was being interviewed by a reporter.

"Cardinal Bala, can you describe what happened?" the reporter asked.

"The rapture, the rapture happened." Cardinal Bala was distressed not only about the events which occurred, but that he was still here to talk about them.

"Can you explain it?"

"In First Thessalonians chapter four, verses 16 and 17, the apostle Paul wrote about the Lord coming down from heaven with a loud command followed by a trumpet sound, then the dead believers of Christ rise to meet him in the air, followed by the living believers, who also caught up with him in the air. Those who are gone were believers who made the decision to accept Christ as Lord and Savior. Those who remain didn't."

"What about the babies and young children?" the reporter asked.

"He took them too; they were too young to make that decision, so he took them."

The reporter only knew of the rapture through joking banter, that a rapture was a way of escaping bad things about to happen. He was intrigued with the cardinal's account. "What happens after the rapture?"

Cardinal Bala lifted his HoloSpecs to wipe his eyes, his hologram figure momentarily blurred. "Some theologians believe the rapture marks the beginning of a seven-year tribulation period where the Antichrist rises to world prominence. Scripture refers to him with various names, The Son of Perdition, The Beast, The Man of Sin, The Lawless One. He, along with another individual called The False Prophet, will captivate the world with their wisdom and charisma, then will ultimately bring about the end of the world as we know it. According to the book of Revelation, there will be 21 judgments during the seven-year period. The first seven are called seal judgments, the next seven, trumpet, then the final seven, bowl judgments. It's literally going to be Hell on earth, then the end of the world as we know it will happen."

"So we've got seven years left before the world is done with?"

"If you believe what the Bible has to say." Cardinal Bala grew more distraught as he explained what was to come.

"Do you know who the Antichrist is?" The reporter asked.

"It's not clear yet, but he will make himself known."

"How?"

"According to the Book of Daniel, he will negotiate a peace agreement with Israel and Palestine. That'll be the first sign."

"Who was the other person you mentioned?" The reporter asked.

"The False Prophet. He'll be the Antichrist's right-hand man, providing a path for people to worship the Antichrist. The two, along with Satan, comprise what's called the unholy trinity."

"So, Satan's involved too?" The reporter gave a sarcastic smile, not buying what the Cardinal had to say.

"He's the one behind it all."

Cardinal Bala's account of what happened and what was to come sounded like an interesting science fiction fantasy. His skepticism showed with his next question.

"Cardinal Bala, you're a man of the cloth, you've dedicated your life to your religion. If only believers were raptured, why are you still here?"

The cardinal knew the question was coming. Through tears, he gave the best answer he could, "I didn't believe in Jesus as Savior, I thought doing good deeds was enough." With that, Cardinal Bala turned off his HoloSpecs and left the interview, his hologram disappearing from the HoloRoom.

Paul stayed at his office the entire evening, watching events and occasionally dozing off for only minutes at a time. At five in the morning, he showered in his private bathroom, got dressed, and laid out his plan. First and foremost, he needed to assemble the senate, or whatever was left of them. At seven, he gave the order to his assistant to assemble the senate in one hour on the Europe Ethnarchy's secure HoloMate channel. Thirty minutes later, his assistant knocked on his door.

"All 99 senators are confirmed to attend at eight, sir."

Paul laughed to himself, "No Senators raptured."

At eight, Paul put on his HoloSpecs and tuned into the ethnarchy HoloMate channel. He asked the senate caretaker to take roll, but the caretaker wasn't on the meeting. Paul continued without the him.

"Senators, I've been up all night watching the world recount the event which happened yesterday afternoon at 5:30. I watched the same story over and over being described by people of every race. The deep bass voice, the trumpet, the screech. People hearing the same voice and word in their native languages. Crumpled clothes, MDChips, prosthetics, jewelry, surgical screws and plates, other personal effects everywhere. Mothers and fathers weeping over empty buggies. Mass gridlock due to abandoned cars. Pilotless planes having to be auto-landed with petrified passengers sitting amid empty clothes. A Chicago cardinal talking about how the Bible foresaw the events, how those of us still here are somehow second-rate citizens in God's eyes. Whether the Bible reference is true or not, the fact remains that we have a worldwide crisis that not only impacts those in the Europe Ethnarchy, but across all ethnarchies. Our most important job is to reassure our Europe citizens that we plan to care and protect them, to restore and keep order. As leaders, our job is to remain calm and in control. If our citizens see us getting nervous, it will only make them more agitated. Any questions so far?"

Paul took a sip of cappuccino and waited for reactions. All 99 senators were silent, waiting for Paul to continue.

"Here's what we're going to do. I'm asking Caleb Todd to keep HoloMate channel FFF-29a open 24/7 for government use to provide information to citizens and reassure them that we are getting things cleaned up. I don't want rogue fake news reports creating even more panic. I'm also dispatching the ethnarchy military, first to major cities across Europe, then to smaller cities. They will gather personal effects, take headcounts of who is gone and who remains, and keep order. There will be people who will see this as an opportunity to loot and commit other crimes. Strict curfews will be implemented between nine at night and six in the morning. Military commanders will be authorized to use whatever force necessary to keep order, including execution. I will coordinate with core service organizations, power, water, and communications to maintain service delivery. Sal, I will need you to get with SynFood and assess production capability."

No answer.

"Senator Carlotta?"

"Sorry, yes I'll do," Sal said. He was on the senator meeting from Mykonos, still on the balcony where Zola was raptured hours earlier.

Paul continued, "After I'm done here I'll talk with the other chairpersons around the world to understand their status and inform them of our plans."

Paul took another sip and changed his tone from directive to reassuring. "Look, I know you all are probably very scared right now,

I'm scared too. We need to channel the fear into action, the nervousness into focus. No one will want to follow someone who looks like he or she is falling apart. If you feel like you need a few minutes to vent, do it with me. Let's show the citizens we are taking care of things. Use your networks to reach out to your constituents and tell them it will be alright. Let's plan on reconvening each day at eight in the morning and five in the evening to debrief. Any questions?"

Nothing.

"Good. Let's get to work." Senators rapidly disappeared from the HoloRoom.

Paul shifted into gear, doing all he said he would do. He talked with the military commanders who still remained, deploying them to the Europe Ethnarchy's largest cities. By the time they reached the cities, many citizens had already picked through abandoned property and had started looting deserted businesses. The military picked up truckloads of garbage, personal effects, MDChips. They set up massive sorting operations, salvaging those things which were usable, and burning the rest. Martial law was instituted with strict curfews. Violators were dealt with swiftly, with the military authorized to use force to keep peace. Sal talked with MacLurig at SynFood to assess food production. About half of its staff was gone.

"You're still here," Sal said to MacLurig.

"And you too," she said.

Paul spoke with the nine other chairpersons, none of whom was as composed and deliberate as Paul. His actions in Europe became the blueprint for how the rest of the ethnarchies would execute. He kept to twice-a-day communication with the senate, maintained the HoloMate FFF-29a government channel to keep citizens informed, and demonstrated crisis leadership qualities like no leader in history. The world followed Paul's leadership, but one region saw the chaotic situation as an opportunity to act.

SEVEN YEARS
2062

I T had been a week since millions around the world were raptured. For Ryan, it was a roller-coaster of sadness, disillusionment, anger, fear, loneliness. Hayley's clothes still lay on the chair in the living room where she sat right before disappearing. He went to Bert's apartment each day, seeing the piles of clothes, HoloSpecs, and jewelry still in the chairs where Bert, Laura, and JT sat when they were raptured during their HoloBlog broadcast. He walked down the narrow streets in Naples, his favorite *gelateria* ransacked by looters, melted gelato in the showcase, dripping onto the floor. All through the streets, clothes were still on the ground, soaking wet from a rainstorm the prior day. He wore Hayley's gold wedding ring on a chain around his neck. His daughter in Germany hadn't answered her phone since it happened.

He was the only one in his family still here.

Through his mourning, Ryan took comfort in watching Bert, Laura, and JT on their *Growing Up Autistic with the Winns* HoloBlogs. He decided to start from episode one and work his way through all one-thousand. He sat in his chair with his HoloSpecs, sometimes laughing, sometimes crying at things his son and his young family did and said. It was one episode, though, that brought a clarity to what was happening around him.

The episode started with Bert's introduction. "Welcome to *Growing Up Autistic with the Winns*. Today we are going to talk about a spiritual topic called the end times." In the past week, Ryan had heard the term as HoloMate pundits talked about how the Bible and current events intersected. He didn't know Bert dedicated a

HoloBlog episode to the topic. He turned up the volume on his HoloSpecs.

Bert continued. "Laura and I attended a sermon on what will happened during the end times and it caused us to do more study on the topic. We want to talk with you about what we learned." Bert's hologram took a sip of water then continued. "Without warning, those who believe that Jesus is their Lord and Savior will leave this earth and be taken to Heaven. That event is called the rapture. To those who aren't raptured, it will look like people simply disappeared, but all their earthly effects like clothes and jewelry will stay on earth." Laura interrupted. "When we are raptured, we'll shed our earthly bodies and be given new bodies, bodies that have no blemishes, no aches and pains, and no fabric sensitivities."

"That'll be great won't it, Laura?" Bert said. "It will be great to not have an aversion to certain types of clothing."

"Yes it will." Laura had dealt with clothing sensitivities her entire life due to her autism.

Bert went on. "In conjunction with the rapture, there is a seven-year period called the tribulation. There are different points of view on when the rapture happens during the tribulation period. Some believe that people will be raptured prior to the seven-year period, some halfway through, and some at the end of the seven-years. The points of view are called pre-tribulation, mid-tribulation, and post-tribulation. Laura and I believe that the rapture will happen at the beginning of the seven-year period so that's how we'll explain it."

Laura took over. "Like Bert was saying, the rapture starts a seven-year tribulation period. At the beginning of the tribulation, a very charismatic world leader beloved by many will broker a seven-year peace agreement between Israel and its neighbors. This world leader will be highly intelligent, a great speaker, will understand economics and politics, and will persuade millions to love him. During the first half of the tribulation period, there will also be increased strife in the world including war, famine, disease, and natural disasters. These events are known as the seal judgments. There are a total of seven that happen in the first half of the tribulation."

Bert chimed in. "The first half of the tribulation sounds bad but believe it or not, the worst is yet to come. At the midpoint of the tribulation, this great leader will suffer a head wound and is expected to die, only to miraculously come back to life. His sidekick, called the False Prophet, will commission the erection of a statue of the Antichrist in Jerusalem. Satan himself will indwell in this leader who then becomes known as the Antichrist. It's at this point that the second half of the tribulation, or what is known as the Great Tribulation, begins. The first thing the Antichrist will do is break the peace agreement with Israel and its neighbors, effectively disbanding Israel and its people. He will then deem himself as God, and with the help of the False Prophet, force people to worship him or pay the consequence of refusing. Scripture says that anyone worshiping the 'beast,' another name for the Antichrist, will have a 666 mark on his or her forehead or right hand. Those that don't have the mark won't be able to buy or sell."

Ryan paused the HoloBlog and took off his HoloSpecs. This was a lot to take in. He went to the kitchen and poured a glass of wine, and went back into the living room, thinking about what Bert and Laura had described, and wondering how it could possibly get worse.

Bert continued. "During the Great Tribulation period, there will be an additional 14 judgments, known as the trumpet and bowl judgments. This three-and-a-half-year period will see devastation never seen in history. Millions will suffer and die through man-made and natural disasters. The Antichrist and False Prophet will continue their control over the entire world, with three leaders ultimately rising up to challenge the Antichrist. The challenge will happen at the end of the Great Tribulation and is known as Armageddon. It's at this point that Jesus comes down from Heaven, swoops up the Antichrist and False Prophet, and throws them into the Lake of Fire.

Satan, the one behind it all, is also bound and thrown into something called the Abyss for a thousand years." Bert stopped to get a drink and let Laura tell the rest of the story.

"After Satan is bound, Jesus will establish heaven on earth in Jerusalem, also known as Holy City, which will come down out of Heaven. Jesus will then live on earth, where there will be no more death, mourning, crying or pain. Those who have accepted Jesus will live with him on earth, those who haven't will be cast into the Lake of Fire. The events are described in the book of Revelation, chapters six through 22."

Bert closed out the blog. "Laura and I realize some of this may sound hard to believe. Some of you may laugh at it or get angry at us. Others may choose to ignore it. As for Laura and me, this is what we believe, and everyone needs to make their own choice."

Ryan took off his HoloSpecs, grieving over what Bert and Laura had to day. What he once thought was a fairy tale was starting to play itself out in real life. If the rest were true, he feared for the world for what it was about to experience but was happy the rest of his family wasn't there to see it.

ZAID RAHN
2062

Zaid Rahn had a long history of creating havoc in the Palestine region. Raised in Amman, Jordan, Rahn was bred to resist Israel's statehood. He came from a long line of resisters, beginning with his great-grandfather, who resisted the formation of Israel as a state in 1948. The ethnarchy formation in 2025 particularly roiled Rahn for two reasons. The Palestine region was now governed by Chairperson Chiyo Ikeda from Japan. Ikeda was a very competent leader who diligently worked to ensure all countries in the Asia Ethnarchy were well represented, but in Rahn's mind she wasn't Palestinian and couldn't possibly understand their issues. The second reason was even more bothersome to Rahn. When the ethnarchies were formed, Israel was included under Europe's Ethnarchy, where it enjoyed its protection from Israel's neighbors Jordan, Syria, Lebanon, and Egypt Sinai. Europe's army was the most powerful on earth, and any military action in the Palestine region could easily be squashed by Europe. Despite being included in the Asia Ethnarchy, the four formed the Palestine Coalition to increase their bargaining power in the ethnarchy and ensure their interests were represented. Rahn was the coalition's leader, with his singular focus on the liberation of the Palestine Coalition from the Asia Ethnarchy and the annexation of Israel.

Rahn was meeting with his coalition lieutenants at his sparsely appointed headquarters in Amman. "Now is the time to act. Europe is in turmoil and won't be able to defend Israel. We need to move." With the rapture happening a week earlier, the Europe Ethnarchy's military had been focused on restoring and keeping order. Looting, rape, murder, vandalism, and assault were rampant across Europe.

Even with an active military, there weren't enough resources to control the throngs of citizens taking advantage of the situation. Rahn continued, "Their military is so preoccupied they'll never be able to devote resources to defending Israel against us."

"What about Ikeda?" one of Rahn's lieutenants asked.

"What about her? She's got the same problem." Ikeda was a close ally of Paul and had been a dedicated follower of his playbook to restore order. The Asia Ethnarchy military was working to restore order in its own cities, they couldn't dedicate resources to an Israeli/Palestine conflict.

"If we do this we'll lose any leverage we've got with Ikeda," another of his lieutenants said. If the Palestine Coalition attacked Israel, they'd be the scourge of the Asia Ethnarchy.

Rahn paused to think, taking a sip of his Arabic coffee. The brew must have sparked something in his mind. He smiled. "I'll call Popov."

Rahn had met Russia Chairperson Popov several times over the years. They were acquaintances at best, aware of each other but not good friends. Popov, like Rahn, was not happy with the ethnarchy formation and wanted an opportunity to get back at Europe for the perceived injustice.

"Chairperson Popov, I have a Zaid Rahn who is insistent he talk with you. What shall I do?" Popov's assistant poked his head into Popov's office to get Popov's direction. Popov was a burly, balding man with an ever-present cigar and gruff voice, almost a reincarnation of Winston Churchill. He took a puff of his cigar as he tried to recall the name, remembering him from a summit they both attended years back. He recalled being impressed with Rahn, seeing him as a brilliant but unpredictable leader. He was intrigued.

"Put him through," Popov said as he put his cigar in the ashtray on his desk.

His assistant pulled his head from the door and closed it, then Popov's phone rang.

"Yes," Popov said as he picked up his phone.

"Chairperson Popov this is Zaid Rahn. Thank you for taking my call. We've met several times. I've always been impressed with your leadership."

"What do you want, Rahn?" Popov was a no-nonsense guy who didn't take well to being buttered up.

Rahn was undeterred by Popov's surliness. "Chairperson, I'm the leader of the Palestine Coalition which includes Jordan, Syria, Lebanon, and Egypt Sinai. Since the ethnarchy formation, we've been irate with Europe because they annexed Israel, our deserved land. Israel is and should be ours, and we want it back. With the chaos in Europe right now, this is an opportune time for us to act. If we do it, we'll lose Ikeda's support and have no leverage with her. I want the Palestine Coalition to secede from Asia and join the Russia Ethnarchy after we take control of Israel."

Popov was intrigued but also a shrewd negotiator. "Why would I do that?" Popov asked.

Rahn was ready for the question. "I know how much Russia hates Europe for what they so wrongly did to you back in 2025. Putting Israel in the Russia Ethnarchy would be a crowning jewel for you and a slap in the face to Europe."

Popov would love nothing more than to take something from Europe and declare it as his own. The proposal had appeal, but, being the clever politician he was, he wouldn't appear eager to act. "I need to think. Call me in three days."

This was the best response Rahn could have hoped for. "Thank you, Mr. Chairperson."

Popov hung up, picked up his cigar and took a puff, blowing smoke rings as he exhaled. He watched the rings dissipate and smiled at the thought of humiliating Paul's Europe Ethnarchy on the world stage.

Three days later, Rahn called Popov, who laid out his non-negotiable terms. Popov would not overtly support Rahn's military action nor would he provide military personnel. Popov didn't want to be viewed as openly supporting the rogue action. He would, however, help with supplies and hera. Should Rahn be successful, he would then accept the Palestine Coalition and the conquered Israel into the Russia Ethnarchy. If Rahn were not successful, then the Palestine Coalition would remain as a powerless entity in the Asia Ethnarchy with the Europe Ethnarchy breathing down its neck. Failure to reannex Israel was the worst possible outcome, and Popov wanted Rahn to be positive about the actions he was about to take.

"Do you understand the terms?" Popov asked.

"I need to talk with my lieutenants, I will call you in three days." Rahn said.

"Call me in two days."

"Very good." Rahn hung up. He met with his lieutenants the next day and discussed the proposal. It was a risky venture, but they concluded Europe was in no way able to defend Israel. They decided to accept the proposal and got to work on their supplies and funding ask. The next day, Rahn called Popov. "We accept, I'll send you our list of our needs tomorrow."

"Send it today, then I'll tell you if we accept after we see your list." Popov loved keeping those he negotiated with off balance, even if they were to become allies.

"Yes, Chairperson." Rahn said. He knew he was being toyed with, but he needed Russia too much to protest. Rahn sent the list to Popov, and Popov agreed to supply only half of what Rahn requested. That was fine with Rahn, because he doubled what he really wanted, knowing Popov would negotiate him down. Rahn and his lieutenants met, they would strike Israel in two weeks on September 22, 2062.

Four Targets
2062

It was midnight on September 22, a warm and dry evening in Amman, Jordan. Rahn and his lieutenants knew the risks of moving forward. Failure meant no food rations, no economic support, and no voice in government. The Palestine Coalition would be a wasteland of forgotten countries left to rot.

But the reward was great.

"Are we a go?" Rahn went around the table asking each of the eight to confirm. One after another each gave their "go." They would launch their attack on the Jerusalem, Tel Aviv, Haifa, and Center districts in two hours via air strikes and surface-to-surface missiles. Their strategy was to ambush with force and speed before Israel and the Europe Ethnarchy could respond, seizing control within 24 hours of first strike. Rahn and his lieutenants were confident in their strategy. They didn't anticipate what was waiting for them.

In the two years since being elected chairperson, Paul had built a vast and powerful intelligence network. Under cyberintel director Dominic Natalizio, the Europe Ethnarchy had agents working in all ten ethnarchies, building relationships, paying bribes, and threatening extortion. Paul taught interrogation techniques he honed while prosecuting Catholic ministry abusers. He had dirt on every chairperson, only using it if absolutely necessary to get what he wanted. Rahn had been on Natalizio's watch list for the past year, with one of his agents secretly serving in Rahn's inner circle of lieutenants. Natalizio knew of Rahn's discussions with Popov, including their plan to strike Israel, and where and when they would strike. Paul readied for the conflict, activating battleships and aircraft carriers already in the Mediterranean. To ensure it looked like the

Palestine Coalition was firing first strike, Paul would wait until the first plane or missile was in the air before launching his sea-based strikes. He could then claim that the Europe Ethnarchy was merely defending itself from the Palestine Coalition. He also knew that Chairperson Ikeda would denounce the Palestine Coalition strike, which would allow him to annex the coalition countries into the Europe Ethnarchy. Because he himself was concerned about those in the senate who might leak information, he kept the military plan on a strict need-to-know basis.

At 12:30 in the morning, Paul, Natalizio and a small group of military and communications personnel sat in the ethnarchy situation room in Rome, eyes fixed on satellite camera images of each of the Palestine Coalition launch locations. Each screen showed an image, Rome time, Israel time, and the Europe Ethnarchy general accountable for taking out the location. The room was quiet, with Paul relaxed in his chair as if this was just another day at the office. At 12:48 there was movement on screen three, a missile launcher in Tyre, Lebanon positioned to strike Haifa. Paul gave strict orders not to strike until a missile was in the air. He looked up at the screen, watched the launcher get into position and continue its ignition sequence. Missiles targeting the Jerusalem, Tel Aviv, and Center districts readied on the other screens. Two minutes later, the first missile from Tyre launched.

"Execute!" Paul gave the order to his ships in the Mediterranean. In three seconds, they began their massive attack on the missile already deployed, then on the Palestine Coalition airbases and missile launch locations.

"Get me Chairperson Ikeda," Paul said to his communications director.

Chairperson Ikeda was just arriving at her office in Tokyo when her assistant transferred Paul's call to her. They'd been friends, and she was happy to get his call, but wondered why he would be calling in the middle of the night Rome time.

"Hello, Paul," Ikeda said.

"What are you trying to do, Chairperson?" Paul knew that Ikeda had no idea about the Palestine Coalition attack, but he needed to feign outrage toward her to catch her off guard and gain her support in denouncing the attack.

"What do you mean, Paul?" she asked.

"The strike against Israel! Asia is attacking Israel!" The act was working. Paul gave the room a smile and waited for Ikeda's response.

"What attack?" Ikeda said.

"We detected missile activity along the Israel border targeting the Jerusalem, Tel Aviv, Haifa, and Center districts. We've had to scramble our own defenses to protect Israel. With all the turmoil in the world I can't believe you would do this to me, Chiyo!"

Ikeda just didn't know what to say. Paul kept silent, putting more pressure on Ikeda to come up with an explanation. She had none.

"Paul, I had no idea," she said. She was visibly nervous, signaling to her assistant just outside her office to come in. "I need to find out what's going on."

"Chiyo, I'm going to defend Israel, and if that means the loss of lives in the Asia Ethnarchy, then so be it."

"Paul, let me get into this, I'll call you back in 30 minutes."

"This may all be over by then," Paul said. He watched his screens as he saw Palestine Coalition military sites obliterated by Europe Ethnarchy missiles.

Rahn was right about one thing, the action would be swift and decisive. He just wasn't expecting to be on the losing end. It ended with not one plane or missile reaching Israel, the Palestine Coalition being badly damaged, Ikeda denouncing the rogue action, and Paul playing the innocent victim defending one of its territories. Ikeda wanted nothing to do with the Palestine Coalition and was more than willing to transfer control of the coalition countries over to the Europe Ethnarchy. Paul accepted the countries and instilled a seven-year peace-through-strength military enforcement treaty in the region. He installed military bases in Lebanon, Syria, Jordan and Egypt Sinai and commissioned the creation of the Europe Ethnarchy Embassy in Jerusalem to reinforce Europe's presence in the region. Paul would spend much of his time there, ensuring that peace was kept between Israel and its neighbors. Rahn and his lieutenants managed to escape the counteroffensive, eventually making their way to the Jordanian Highlands with plans to regroup, still unaware that one of them was a covert Europe Ethnarchy agent.

While the treaty garnered strong support from six of the chairpersons, three of them saw his actions as threatening to their ethnarchies. They weren't going to let Paul's conduct go unchecked.

TRIPOLI, LIBYA
2063

The Africa Chairperson Khaled Maghur greeted Chairpersons Anton Popov from Russia and Bo Zhao from China at the entrance to his palace in Tripoli, Libya. Ever since the annexation of Lebanon, Syria, Jordan and Egypt Sinai into the Europe Ethnarchy six months earlier, the three Chairpersons had been concerned about Paul's continued influence and power in Europe. They all knew of his electric personality, how the other chairpersons fawned over him, how multitudes across the ethnarchies viewed him as god-like. This latest move, sold by Paul as necessary to keep peace between Israel and its neighbors, looked like the first of many territory grabs to Maghur, Popov and Zhao. They didn't trust Paul and were determined to stop him.

The three walked into the palace, a small entryway leading into a large parlor. The parlor was adorned with colorful African art from the day's most popular artists, including ebony and tamboti wood carvings, and portraits of past and current Africa Ethnarchy chairpersons. A butler approached the three with a tray of green tea and fritters in syrup. Each helped themselves to the food and drink, then followed Maghur to a round ironwood table with three ornately carved chairs. As the three sat, Maghur sipped his tea then started the discussion.

"Chairpersons, I think we all know of the actions by Ambrosi and agree on the seriousness of the annexation."

Popov took a cigar from his pocket and lit it. Maghur despised cigar smoke but decided not to make an issue of it. Popov knew he hated cigar smoke, which was precisely why he lit up. Zhao smirked when he saw Popov light up, also knowing Maghur hated the smoke.

Maghur continued, "Africa never liked the Egypt Sinai deal at ethnarchy formation, but our chairperson at the time was weak." When the ethnarchies were formed in 2025, there was a dispute over whether Egypt's Sinai Peninsula should be part of the Asia or Africa Ethnarchy. Sinai was a peninsula in Egypt but was considered part of the Asia continent. The chairpersons at that time agreed that the Sinai Peninsula would be named Egypt Sinai and be included in the Asia Ethnarchy. Maghur was Egyptian, grew up in Cairo, and despised that his home country was split between ethnarchies. With Paul now holding Egypt Sinai, any likelihood of reunifying Egypt would be ever more difficult.

"You should have done like we did," Popov said. Russia was in a similar situation in that much of Russia was in Asia. When Russia broke with Europe to form its own ethnarchy, it threatened military action on both Asia and Europe if they didn't agree to Russia annexing its entire territory into its own ethnarchy. The Asia and Europe Ethnarchy chairpersons at that time agreed, allowing Russia to remain whole. Popov, being raised in Irkutsk, a Russian city, but part of the Asia continent, was pleased his home city wasn't under rule of the Asia Ethnarchy.

Not having said a word yet, Zhao took a bite of his fritter, enjoying the sparring between Popov and Maghur.

Maghur bristled at Popov's jab but tried to play it cool. Maghur continued, "Ambrosi's built a strong military and intel network, just look at what he did to the Palestine Coalition. Defeated without landing one missile. What's to stop him from continuing his march? He's more dangerous than Hitler ever was."

"What's your plan?" Popov wanted Maghur to show his cards.

Maghur was ready. "Ambrosi is building strong coalitions with the other six ethnarchies, and each would come to his rescue if he were attacked. We need to take them out, then keep them out when we attack Europe."

Zhao stayed quiet, not because he wasn't capable of participating. He was a brilliant military strategist who had built formidable sea and air forces capable of annihilating entire cities thousands of miles away. His mind was already working on China's role in the alliance. He was also embarrassed by his poor English skills, limiting what he said to avoid looking weak to his peers.

"I'm worried about North America," Popov said. The North America Ethnarchy, led by the United States, had strong sea, land, air, and space forces with installations not only in North America but in the Central America, Caribbean, Oceania, and South America ethnarchies. The protection came at a price--food rations. North America's citizens looked as if there was no worldwide food shortage, with obesity continuing to be one of its biggest health issues.

Popov took another puff of his cigar, intentionally blowing smoke in Maghur's direction. "We need to take out the North America installations," he said.

"Between the three of us, we've got the nukes to do it," Maghur said.

Time for Zhao to speak up, "No nukes." Popov and Maghur both looked at Zhao, surprised not only by his comment but that he actually joined the conversation. Zhao continued in his broken English "Once one fires nuke, everyone fires nuke, end of world. No nuke if we to survive as human race." Zhao had a point. They couldn't do something that would trigger nuclear war, they needed to do it with conventional weapons.

The three continued their discussion on attack strategy throughout the day. They agreed that Africa would take out Central and South America and Caribbean installations, China would take out those in Oceania, Asia and Western North America, and Russia would take out the Eastern North America sites. The coordinated attack would then be followed by air and sea attacks on Europe by Africa and Russia, with China utilizing its long-range capability to keep crippled installations at bay. The attack was to commence April 23, 2063. Popov would have loved to use Zeus, but it was nowhere near ready for deployment.

Cyberintel Director Natalizio met with Paul in his office a week after the three chairpersons met in Tripoli. "We've got intel that Africa, Russia and China are planning strikes." Natalizio's intelligence network was working like a well-oiled machine, utilizing its embedded agents to give critical intel to Paul and Natalizio.

"On who?" Paul asked.

"First on Central, South, North America, Caribbean, Oceania, and Asia military installations. Then on Europe."

"When?"

"April 23rd."

Paul leaned back in his chair. "They want to take everyone else out and make Europe fend for ourselves, right?"

"That's how it looks," Natalizio said.

"What's our Zeus mole say?"

"It's not anywhere near ready."

"OK, keep me posted on intel. Good job Director," Paul said.

"Thank you, Mr. Chairperson." Natalizio got up and left Paul's office.

Paul sat in his chair, reflecting on the state of events. He knew Popov was bitter about the ethnarchy split; he also knew Popov had a grand vision to revive the former USSR under Russian rule. He knew Maghur was worried about the Palestine Coalition annexation and hated that Egypt Sinai was under Europe. He presumed China's involvement because his relationship had been frosty with Zhao due to Paul's alliance with the Asia Ethnarchy and Chairperson Ikeda, and Zhao's strong relationship with Popov. Paul was confident he could ward off attacks on Europe from the three. His question was, should he warn the other chairpersons?

THE THREE FOOLS
2064

Director Natalizio prepared a daily morning status of military, cyberintel and communications activity for Chairperson Ambrosi, outlining actions from the last 24 hours and those which would occur in the next 24. Because Natalizio had been invaluable in gathering intel and thwarting actions against the Europe Ethnarchy and the degree of trust Paul had in him, Natalizio had acquired significant power over the operations of the Ethnarchy. Natalizio was all business in his execution and was deeply loyal to Paul, two traits that Paul not only admired, but demanded in his followers.

Paul read through the morning status as he sat at his office conference table drinking his morning Americano. Natalizio had made an espresso in Paul's kitchen and brought it to the conference table, waiting as Paul read the report.

"One thousand Europe casualties yesterday," Paul said as he sipped his coffee. Ever since Chairpersons Zhao, Popov, and Maghur waged war on Europe a year ago, over 500 million lives were lost worldwide. The world referred to the three as the Compact, but Paul called them the Three Fools. The Compact launched their attack on United States installations across the Central America, South America, Caribbean, Oceania, Asia and North America ethnarchies. Paul had ample opportunity to give the other ethnarchies warning of the Compact's attack plans but chose to keep the information from his supposed allies. Publicly he denounced the Compact and expressed support for the other six ethnarchies. Privately he wanted to see all nine ethnarchies weakened by war. The weaker they were, the stronger the Europe Ethnarchy appeared. Paul invested all his military might in defending Europe and ensuring the strength of his ethnarchy. The Three Fools pissed off the rest of the world and Paul looked like the unprovoked casualty just wanting to keep peace. If Paul's allies only knew he could have warned them of the strikes from the Compact, they might have seen him not as the innocent victim but as a backstabbing war monger.

Paul continued reading the report. Natalizio did as he always did, sitting there quietly waiting for Paul to respond to something. In the many occasions he had been in Paul's office, he never asked Paul about the framed shadow box with the dented folding stool and a picture of Paul with his parents and siblings inside. "Isn't essential to business," he thought. "If the chairperson wanted to tell me about it, he would."

Paul read through the report then saw at the bottom, "Items for Discussion" followed by three bullets--SynFood, Stigma, and Zeus.

"Let's go through the discussion items," Paul said.

"Mr. Chairperson, SynFood production has dropped 25 percent in the past month due to ground strikes in Glasgow and across the distribution network." SynFood had become the primary nutrition source in Europe, due to rice, wheat, corn and soy production dropping when the Compact commenced military action. With SynFood production and distribution slowed, more and more Europe citizens were dying of starvation. Even though it was bad in Europe, it was worse in other ethnarchies. They had no SynFood-like capability.

"Get Senator Carlotta on it, keep it on my radar." Paul said.

"Yes, Sir."

"What about Stigma?" Paul asked.

Natalizio took a quick sip of his espresso and pulled some notes from a folder to ensure he was accurate in his description. "We're getting reports of a strange cancer which appears impervious to the MDChip. MD Biometrics has been diagnosing the cancer and is calling it . . .," Natalizio shuffled the papers in front of him to find the term. "They call it Stigma Cutaneous T-Cell Lymphoma. It's a blood cancer which shows up on the body as stigma-shaped lesions."

"What's stigma-shaped mean," Paul asked.

Natalizio took out his pen and drew on the back of one of his note pages. "The sore looks like this," drawing an S-shaped symbol with the top half about three times the size of the bottom half. "The sores can show up anywhere on the body and are excruciatingly painful."

"What does Carlotta have to say about his brilliant invention?" Paul asked.

"He's working with MD's team, it's his highest priority."

"Any idea of casualties?" Paul asked.

"No, with all the war and famine casualties, it's difficult to tell."

Paul took another sip of coffee, two topics down, both bad news. "What about Zeus?" he asked, hoping for a bit of good news.

"Missile strikes have slowed development of Popov's baby. Riccio doesn't know by how much, just that it's slow and Popov is furious."

For Paul, this wasn't great news, but at least it wasn't horrible. He wanted to press Riccio for more information. "Get a date from Riccio, remind him what will happen if he doesn't come through." Paul didn't care how compliant he'd been since the blackmail threat, he just wanted more.

"Yes, Mr. Chairperson, anything else?"

"No. Thank you, Director." Paul said. Natalizio finished his espresso, got up from his chair, and left the office, taking a quick glance at the shadow box on the way out.

Paul leaned back in his chair, coffee cup still in his hand, thinking about the discussion with Natalizio. He stared down at the paper that Natalizio had drawn of the strange Stigma shape. Billions around the world had received the MDChip and were getting twice-yearly MDSolution treatments. Up until now there were no known side effects or cancer recurrences. "What's changed?" he thought. He called out to his assistant. "Get me Senator Carlotta."

Five minutes later, Paul's assistant came into Paul's office, "I've got the senator."

Paul picked up his phone. "Natalizio told me about Stigma, what's going on?" Paul skipped the pleasantries with Sal, no time for it.

"We're not sure yet what causes it or how to kill it."

"When will you know?" Paul knew it was difficult for Sal to answer the when question, he just wanted to turn the screws on him.

"I don't know," Sal said.

"Not good enough. When will you know?" Paul asked the same question again.

"We're working on it as fast as we can, Chairperson." Sal said, gritting his teeth as he tried to keep his composure with Paul.

"Make sure Natalizio gets daily updates."

"I'll do my best, Mr. Chairperson." Sal just wanted to be off the phone and stop the verbal onslaught.

Paul hung up the phone without saying anything more, leaned back in his chair and took another sip of coffee.

Sal got off the phone, still smoldering from the conversation. He'd been working with Mario night and day to try to find a root cause and cure for Stigma. They were both perplexed by the strange cancer type and why the MDChip/MDSolution protocol was ineffective in its eradication. Not having an answer was driving him crazy but Paul's treating him like an imbecile outraged him even more. He had enough, time to call Mario.

"Mario, I need you to VF Ambrosi." Sal said.

Mario hated that they ever created the VF capability and resented that he let Sal talk him into killing Chairperson Dalca.

"Sal, I can't." Mario said.

"Why?"

"I just can't."

"Mario, I need you to do this, Ambrosi is a mad man and he's going to get the ethnarchy blown off the face of the earth. We need to stop him."

Mario was still loyal to Sal but was deeply conflicted by the ask.

Sal was unrelenting. "Mario, for the sake of the ethnarchy you need to do this!"

"Let me pull him up in MDCentral." Mario tried to stall, hoping Sal would calm down and rethink his request.

"OK," Sal said.

Mario logged into MDCentral and did a search on Paul.

"He's not in here," Mario said.

"Are you sure?"

"I'm sure. He doesn't have a chip."

"Seriously?" Sal couldn't believe it. Of the billions who had gotten the chip, the one person he wanted to VF the most didn't have it.

"He's not there." Mario said with relief.

Sal backed down. "OK, I'll be there later to work on Stigma."

"Bye." Mario hung up, upset that Sal would put him in a situation of murdering again. Despite his loyalty, Mario's resentment towards Sal grew, something that Sal would ultimately regret.

CTP-74
2065

MacLurig had been working with Sal and Mario on root causes for the Stigma blood cancer. Over the past year, they researched environmental, chemical, genetic, and nutritive possibilities for why Stigma decided to rear its ugly head and why the MDChip/MDSolution protocol was ineffective in fighting it. Reported Stigma cases had been growing exponentially, with the vast majority occurring in Europe. Looking at SynFood as a possible source, Sal contacted MacLurig to find out if something in SynFood was the culprit. The three were meeting via HoloRoom, MacLurig in Glasgow, Sal and Mario in Rome.

"It's CTP-74." MacLurig said. "It's the integral preservative which gives SynFood its unlimited shelf life. Without it, SynFood would only have a shelf life of a few days and would need refrigeration. Without CTP-74 there is no way we could manufacture and distribute SynFood in the volumes you need."

This was the last thing Sal wanted to hear. He was the hero of the senate for solving the famine issue in the Europe Ethnarchy. Now the very thing that Sal championed to feed its citizens was killing them. While facing the senate with this information was bad, he dreaded telling Paul how Sal's MDChip/MDSolution baby was defeated by SynFood and its CTP-74 preservative.

"Is there a replacement?" Sal asked.

"Nothing anywhere near the shelf life you're used to. We could possibly get to a few weeks of shelf life but that's it." For months Sal had been putting intense pressure on MacLurig to decompose SynFood to see if there was something in it causing the cancer. She'd been working day and night to understand if SynFood was causing

Stigma but was also frustrated with Mario and Sal for not doing enough to fix the MDChip/MDSolution protocol.

MacLurig continued, "What about on your end? Anything to upgrade the chip and fluid?" What MacLurig didn't know was that Sal and Mario had been working on an upgrade to the MDChip/MDSolution protocol that would reprogram the synthetic killer cells to eradicate the Stigma blood cancer. They successfully created an upgrade to the chip, but it would require every chip wearer to have the old chip removed and replaced with a new one. Manufacturing billions of new chips, then getting them into the distribution network would take at least a year just to get new chips into pharmacies. Then there were the billions of people who would have to go through the procedure.

"We can do a chip upgrade, but the logistics is not only cost-prohibitive but takes too long. We do have another idea which might be more feasible." Sal and Mario had been testing a new concept whereby a new clear chip placed on the wearer's body interacted with the MDChip in the wearer's heart, taking over the firmware functions on the MDChip and upgrading the dormant SK cell procedure. As long as the MDChip wearer had the second clear chip on their body, the SK cells in the wearer's body would be able to eradicate Stigma along with all the other cancers it had been killing for years. The clear chip was easy to produce and distribute, and the wearer just had to affix the adhesive-backed chip to his or her body. Once affixed, the newly-programmed SK cells went to work on the Stigma blood cancer. Both Sal and Mario tested the clear chip on themselves and were satisfied enough with the results to move forward.

Sal continued, "We have been testing a secondary chip that's been successful at eradicating the blood cancer. I still need to talk it through with the chairperson."

"What do you want me to do about CTP-74?"

"Keep looking for an alternative preservative but don't stop production. We need the SynFood."

"Will do, talk later." MacLurig turned off her HoloSpecs, her hologram disappearing from the HoloRoom.

"You didn't tell her," Mario said.

"I need to talk to the chairperson first."

The next day Sal visited Paul at his office.

"Sir, Senator Carlotta is here," Paul's assistant said.

Paul was sitting at his desk and motioned Sal in.

"Mr. Chairperson," Sal said.

"Come in." Sal came in to Paul's office and sat in a small wooden chair in front of Paul's desk. Paul used to hold meetings at his conference table to make his visitors more comfortable, but he recently replaced the plush leather chairs in front of his desk with uncomfortable hard wooden chairs. Paul sat in his plush leather high-back chair behind his desk, a reminder to his visitors that he was the boss. Sal hated the wooden chairs that were nothing more than an intimidation tactic for Paul's visitors.

"What do you want?" Paul said.

"We know what's causing Stigma, it's a preservative in SynFood called CTP-74."

"So stop using it."

"It's not that easy, without CTP-74 we don't get the shelf life we need. SynFood would be worthless."

Paul put his head in his hands, running his fingers through his hair.

"So now what?" Paul asked.

"Mario and I created an upgrade to the MDChip, which is a clear chip that affixes to the wearer's skin. We've been testing it on ourselves and it works great. It's simple to manufacture and distribute, and the wearer can put it on without any help."

"What about other cancers?"

"Everything else works as before."

"So, let me get this straight," Paul lifted his head from his hands. "A wearer sticks a clear plastic chip on their body and their MDChip is now able to kill Stigma?"

"Right."

"And it only works on those who have the MDChip?"

"Yes."

"And this would be better than trying to adapt SynFood?"

Sal shuffled in his wooden chair. "Yes, I think so."

Paul leaned back in his chair and put his hands behind his head, his blue shirt showing his underarm sweat stains. "Is this the best you've got?"

Sal knew Paul was exerting his power over him, and it drove him crazy.

"There's one more thing, it's contagious."

Paul leaned forward, staring Sal down. "I thought cancer wasn't contagious."

"This is like nothing we've ever seen, it's transmitted like a common cold, through the respiratory system." Only Sal and Mario knew it was contagious, he didn't tell MacLurig or anyone else. He wanted to discuss it with Paul first. Sal was expecting a volatile response from Paul and was surprised to see a faint smile on Paul's face.

Paul leaned back in his chair and thought for a minute. "Here's what I want you to do." Paul's voice became calm and measured. "Continue full scale SynFood production with CTP-74, begin production of the clear chip and put a certificate of authenticity symbol on it, something like three Stigmas so people know it's a legitimate chip. Put out a HoloMate bulletin telling of the chip and that production will begin as quickly as possible. Don't tell anyone about the CTP-74 link or Stigma being contagious. When can you have StigmaChip ready?" Paul decided to name the clear chip after the Stigma blood cancer, no need to ask Sal what he thought.

Sal sat there for a minute trying to digest the directives Paul gave. "We'll have StigmaChip production and distribution ready in six months."

"Good. Manufacture as much SynFood as possible. I'm going to let other ethnarchies buy it on the open market." Up to this point Paul had made SynFood only available to Europe Ethnarchy citizens. Making it available on the open market was an abrupt shift in strategy.

"Why are you letting other ethnarchies buy it?" Sal asked.

"I'll worry about that, you just focus on StigmaChip and SynFood production."

Once again Sal was reminded of how much he hated being under Paul's authority. He mustered up a "Yes, Mr. Chairperson," got up out of his chair and left Paul's office.

"Shut the door," Paul yelled as Sal was leaving. Sal gave the door a defiant subtle slam on his way out.

Paul sat back in his chair, thinking about the meeting, his faint smile back on his face. "This could work out perfectly," he thought as he closed his eyes.

MAN IN THE FEDORA
2066

The war with the Africa, Asia and Russia Compact had been going on for three years. The Compact's strikes on installations in Central America, South America, Caribbean, Oceania, Asia and North America ethnarchies were met with swift response by the United States. What was supposed to be a war on Europe became a war between the Compact and the United States. New York, Chicago, Los Angeles, San Francisco, Phoenix, Seattle, all war-torn. The vast U.S. military installations across the ethnarchies kept the Compact on its heels, thwarting their full-on assault plans for the Europe Ethnarchy. Paul watched as the other ethnarchies pummeled each other, which was just fine with him.

Ever since the Palestine Coalition became part of the Europe Ethnarchy three years earlier, Paul showed an increased fascination with the region. He learned about its geography, people, customs, religions, and the sources of the conflict that existed for years. He visited the Jerusalem Embassy every month, met with Israeli president Ari Dichter regularly, and ensured the military was keeping peace in the region. He had visions of consolidating the region into a single country with Dichter as its leader. There were occasional reports of shootings and altercations, but nothing that Paul's powerful military couldn't easily squash. It was an odd attraction that even Paul's closest confidants didn't understand, but none questioned Paul and his obsession.

HoloMate became a place of refuge for the world's population. In the 41 months since the rapture, HoloMate usage skyrocketed as people took comfort in reaching out to each other for encouragement, solace, and hope. Those who became believers after the rapture created "HoloChurches" where believers in Jesus could gather to worship and pray for each other. As HoloChurch popularity grew, there were increasing numbers of protests by subscribers who either didn't believe or were angry at God that they weren't raptured. The conflict became so great that HoloMate ultimately banned HoloChurches, shutting down 144,000 of them.

At Paul's edict, SynFood was now being sold on the open market, with embargos in place for the Africa, Russia and China Ethnarchies. SynFood was still being manufactured with the CTP-74 preservative that caused Stigma. None of the other ethnarchies knew of the link between CTP-74 and Stigma or that Stigma was contagious. Because famine was rampant across the world, ethnarchies not restricted by embargo leapt at the opportunity to buy SynFood for its starving citizens. Other than Paul, Mario, Sal and MacLurig, no one else knew that those ingesting SynFood were subject to the deadly blood cancer.

StigmaChip distribution commenced in the Europe Ethnarchy, serving its own citizens first. The clear chip was two centimeters square, etched with three stigma symbols on its face. StigmaChips were made available at the same pharmacies where MDChips and MDSolution was administered. StigmaChip installation was simple, the wearer only had to put a dollop of a specialized surgical glue on the back of the chip then affix the chip to his or her forehead. Once the chip was in place, the wearer had one minute to remove it before it permanently adhered to the skin. The chip would have worked on any part of the head or torso, but Paul was insistent that it be on the forehead. Mario had software embedded in the chip that sensed where the chip was placed on the body. If the chip was on the forehead, it would glow green for three seconds after being affixed. If it was anywhere else on the body, it would continuously blink red until removed and placed correctly on the forehead, where it would begin its function.

Zeus' development over the past six years had been plagued with delays due to the Russia Ethnarchy's war activity against the United States installations. Resources continued to get drained from Zeus to higher-priority initiatives, frustrating Popov. He had learned since forming the Compact with Africa and China that conventional warfare was a no-win situation unless one side gave up. He also knew the consequence of using nuclear weapons and believed the words of China Chairperson Zhao, "Once one fires nuke, everyone fires nuke, end of world." Zeus would give him the power to strike anywhere in the world from the safety of space using a combination of lasers and hypersonic missiles. Despite the development setbacks, it was to a point where Russia could run a test in the vast Siberia region. Wanting to see progress, Popov approved the test. Russia launched what it told the world was a test weather satellite 5,000 kilometers into space with the intent of firing a single laser-shot in the Central Siberian Plateau. Thanks to Riccio, Paul knew all about the test, including when the satellite would launch, and when and where it would fire its laser. The satellite successfully launched, established its orbit, then fired its test shot. To Paul's amusement, the laser shot missed its target by 2500 kilometers, striking in a remote area of the Chersky mountain range on the boundary of the North American and Eurasian tectonic plates. The force of the laser triggered a massive earthquake measuring ten on the Richter scale. Popov was furious that the laser strike missed its target by so much. While the rest of the world thought the earthquake was an act of nature, Paul knew who was responsible, and took comfort in knowing Natalizio was getting regular code drops from Riccio. Paul couldn't wait to see Popov's reaction when he would hijack Zeus.

Israel president Ari Dichter always enjoyed Paul's monthly trips to Jerusalem. The trips were a combination of business and pleasure, with Dichter taking time on each trip to show him more of Israel, talk about its history, enjoy its food, meet its people. Paul was fascinated with every bit of it, from Abraham's wife Sarah giving birth to Isaac at 90 years of age, to Jesus' birth from the virgin Mary and the claim that he was God, to Hitler's attempt to annihilate the Jewish race that led to the re-establishment of Israel as a country after World War II. Dichter never understood Paul's obsession with Israel, but as long as Paul paid attention to Israel and protected it, he didn't care. Dichter was so indebted to Paul that he commissioned a peace monument commemorating the treaty to be placed in the Jerusalem Capitol Complex. The monument would be dedicated during Paul's next trip to Jerusalem, March 1, 2066.

Paul and Caleb were sitting in Paul's office planning out the March trip to Jerusalem. Feeling as if he could trust fewer and fewer people, Paul asked Caleb to be his communications director. Caleb's loyalty to Paul, expertise in communications and control over HoloMate meant Paul could establish the narrative he wanted without others diluting or undermining his authority. HoloMate became the sole voice of the Europe Ethnarchy, with Paul-sanctioned propaganda shown through HoloAds.

Paul was sitting at his desk, Caleb in the hard wooden chair opposite Paul. Caleb started running through the Jerusalem visit agenda. "We arrive at nine, have breakfast with President Dichter at his residence, then to the embassy at eleven for SynFood and Stigma updates, lunch at one, peace monument unveiling at two." Caleb was particularly excited about this visit to Jerusalem. When he learned about Dichter's plans for the peace monument, Caleb contacted Dichter to ask him what help he needed in completing the monument. Dichter needed hera as Israel was experiencing a significant budget shortfall, so Caleb reached into his own pocket and agreed to fund its commissioning personally. With all Paul had done for Caleb through the years, it was the least he could do. Caleb was glad to do it, and Dichter was just as happy to accept it.

Caleb continued, "After the unveiling, you and Dichter have free time to do whatever the president has lined up for you, then we fly back to Rome at seven."

"Is Senator Carlotta going? He needs to give a SynFood and Stigma update."

"He's staying in Rome and will participate via HoloRoom."

"Not good enough, tell him he's going with us." Paul no longer asked for things to be done, he just demanded them.

"Yes, Mr. Chairperson." Caleb had already had this discussion with Sal earlier in the day. Sal told him he wasn't going to Jerusalem. Caleb didn't push it with Sal, knowing Paul would demand he go.

"Anything else?" Paul asked.

"No, Sir."

"Bye, Caleb."

Caleb got up from his chair and left the office, taking a quick glance at the shadow box with his aunt's dented folding stool, as he did each time he walked out. Caleb walked past Paul's assistant and dropped off the itinerary. "Can you coordinate schedules with everyone for the Jerusalem visit?" Caleb asked.

"Yes, Sir," the assistant said. As Caleb left, the assistant looked through the itinerary, where Paul was going to be and when. He copied the itinerary and put the copy in his jacket pocket. That evening his assistant left the Europe Ethnarchy government building, walked down the busy street, spotting a man wearing a red fedora walking towards him. As the man in the fedora walked by the assistant, the assistant reached into his jacket pocket, pulled out the itinerary, and held it to his side, where the man in the fedora surreptitiously grabbed the itinerary and handed the assistant an envelope. The man in the fedora continued walking down the street, the assistant never turning back to see where he went. The assistant went into a supermarket, took out the envelope, opened it, and flicked his thumb over the 10,000 hera inside.

The man in the fedora continued walking down the street, arriving at an apartment building about a kilometer away. He went up to apartment 449 where he slipped the itinerary under the door. A short, heavy, balding man wearing only boxer shorts and tank top picked it up off the floor. He looked at it, snapped a picture of the itinerary with his phone, then sent it to his supervisor back at Russia headquarters. His supervisor received the itinerary, printed it, walked from his desk down a hallway and knocked on his boss's door. The supervisor could smell the cigar smoke through the closed door.

"Chairperson Popov?" the supervisor said as he knocked.

"What."

"Ambrosi's Jerusalem itinerary."

"Give it." Popov said.

The supervisor opened the door, put the itinerary on Popov's desk, and left, not saying a word. Popov took the paper and turned his back to the supervisor while he looked at it. He then called out to his assistant, "Get Alexeev in here."

Make it Clean
2066

General Vadim Alexeev was Popov's closest advisor. A crusty, blunt 80-year-old, with thinning gray hair, roadmap face, and booming voice, Alexeev was held in the highest regard among his peers and subordinates. Early in his career, he was a member of the supposed-to-be-disbanded KGB, working special operations across the world for the Russian government. Like Popov, he longed to someday see a revived USSR and saw the formation of the Russia Ethnarchy as a stepping stone to getting there. He was a good soldier, respected the chain of authority. He would take a bullet for Popov, and Popov knew it.

"Chairperson, you wanted to see me?" Alexeev asked.

"Who's your best man in Jerusalem?"

"Maxim Dedov." Dedov was a 35-year-old operative raised in Bethlehem by Russian spy parents who moved to Israel 50 years earlier. Known in Israel as Yaron Schneider, Dedov was married to an Israeli woman and had two young children. His wife only knew him as Yaron Schneider, computer engineer for Jerusalem Health. She had no idea of his Russian alter-ego as an expert marksman.

"I need him to kill Ambrosi," Popov said.

"When?"

Popov looked at the itinerary. "March first at 11 a.m. he will be at the Europe Ethnarchy Embassy."

"Anything else?" Alexeev asked.

"Make it clean." Alexeev knew what Popov meant. He didn't agree with Popov, but always followed orders.

"Yes, Mr. Chairperson," Alexeev said. He turned to leave while Popov reclined back, put his feet on his desk, looked at the itinerary, the ash trail on his lit cigar growing longer.

Alexeev walked back to his office. "Get me Dedov!" he yelled to his assistant.

Alexeev told Dedov about the mission. Dedov lived for moments like this--killing Ambrosi would forever emblazon his name among the heroes of the Russian Ethnarchy KGB. He considered it an honor to be chosen for the assassination. Just as Dedov was about to hang up, he heard Alexeev's voice.

"Dedov," Alexeev said.

"Yes, Sir."

"Take Nestor with you."

"Sir?"

"Take Nestor with you." Nestor was another KGB agent working in Jerusalem. Dedov and Nestor were rivals, neither liking the other. Dedov wasn't happy about having to take Nestor along, but knew better than to question Alexeev.

"Yes, Sir," Dedov said, then hung up.

Alexeev then called agent Nestor and told him about the assassination plan, that Dedov would be the assassin and that Nestor would go with him.

"What is my assignment?" Nestor knew Dedov was more than capable of doing the assassination on his own.

"Make it clean," Alexeev said.

"Yes, Sir."

Nestor heard Alexeev hang up and smiled as he put his phone in his pocket.

BRAHMS LULLABY
2066

The gentle rain that started the morning on the first of March had turned into a heavy downpour. Agents Nestor and Dedov sat in their car at ten in the morning on a bustling street in Jerusalem, two kilometers away from the Europe Ethnarchy Embassy. Neither of them said a word to each other, with only the swiping sound of the windshield wipers breaking the silence. Both had done these types of jobs before, this was just another day for them. At 10:15 Dedov got out of the car and grabbed a backpack from the back seat. He closed the door, looking into the car at Nestor, "You coming?" he asked.

"Alexeev told me to stay down here and wait for you." Nestor said.

That was just fine with Dedov, he didn't want Nestor there anyway. Dedov ran to a tall building across the street, then made his way up to an office used by KGB agents on the top floor. He walked into the office and looked out the window, able to faintly see the embassy in the distance. He sat down on the floor next to the window and opened the backpack, taking out each item and laying it next to him on the floor. He carefully pieced together the stock, action, magazine, barrel, and telescopic sight, slowly rubbing his hand along the barrel as if caressing a lover. He opened the window slightly, pulled binoculars from the backpack and looked out the window at the embassy, marking the spot their car would pull up to the embassy entrance. The distance between the street and the entrance was 15 meters, with ten steps from the base of the sidewalk leading up to the embassy entrance. Earlier in the week he scoped out the area to determine the best spot to shoot. Anticipating crowds, Dedov planned to hit the target three steps from the top of the stairway; it was high enough to avoid hitting someone on the sidewalk. Anyone walking behind would be on lower steps, affording a clearer head shot. Dedov put down his binoculars and readied his sniper rifle capable of hitting targets up to three kilometers away. He'd used the very same rifle for other assassinations and loved the feel of it in his hands. He smirked to himself as he thought about how his wife had no idea he even knew how to fire a rifle, let alone being ranked as one of the best sharpshooters in the Russian military. He looked at his watch--five minutes before they were scheduled to arrive. He moved a small table to the window, took out a rifle tripod, placed it on the table, then set the rifle in the tripod cradle. Strong winds joined the rainfall, creating a sideways-blowing rain. He noted the wind coming from his back, so there'd be no air resistance to his shot. He took out his phone, selecting *Brahms Lullaby* from his music collection. His assassinations were always done to *Lullaby*, it was just his thing he liked to do. He picked up his binoculars and looked along the street for Paul's motorcade, seeing four black cars coming from the north, stopping in front of the embassy. From the third car, three men wearing suits stepped out and began making their way down the 15-meter walkway to the steps that led up to the embassy. They were joined by six agents who arrived earlier, three walked in front and three behind. The three from behind opened umbrellas to protect the men wearing suits from the blowing rain. Dedov could only see from the waist down on each of the three, their upper body hidden behind the umbrellas.

"Which one is he?" Dedov thought as he looked at the three at the base of the stairs. Dedov quickly thought through his options. He could just shoot the one in the middle, assuming Paul was between Sal and Caleb. But what if he were wrong? He knew Popov wouldn't accept anything other than a successful assassination. He couldn't go back to him with an excuse of shooting the wrong person. He also knew Popov wouldn't accept a "didn't want to violate protocol" excuse as to why he didn't shoot. His least-worst alternative was to shoot all three, which he decided to do. As the three walked up the stairs he decided to shoot the man on the right at the fourth step, the man in the middle at the third step, and the man on the left at the second step. The three started up the stairs. With *Lullaby* in the background, Dedov trained his sights on where the man on the right would be at the fourth step. He was cool and emotionless as they climbed the steps. He counted to himself, "seven, six, five," then pulled the trigger to a loud *pop*, then positioning to the man in the center, *pop*, then the man on the left, *pop*. He watched as a clean bullet hole pierced the umbrellas, then saw all three go down, blood splattered on the three agents walking in front of them. He quickly disassembled the rifle, put the parts and binoculars in the backpack, grabbed his phone and silenced the music, closed the window, and left the office. He walked down the building stairway, exited the building, and calmly walked back to the car where Nestor was waiting in the driver's seat. He threw the backpack in the backseat, opened the door and got in.

"Done," Dedov said. As he was putting on his seatbelt, Nestor opened the driver side door, pulled a revolver from his jacket and put a bullet in Dedov's head, blood and flesh splattering on the passenger window. Nestor reached in the back seat, grabbed the backpack, stepped out of the car, calmly opened an umbrella while walking across the street, then pulled a detonator from his pocket and blew up the car with Dedov's body inside. Nestor then called Alexeev. "Done and clean," Nestor said.

Alexeev hung up without saying a word, distressed that Popov ordered the execution of one of his best agents.

BLACK EYES
2066

Paul's brother and sister traveled to Jerusalem from Naples after they heard of the assassination attempt on Paul. They took turns day and night sitting next to their brother, holding his hand, stroking his hair. They talked with him about the amusing things they did growing up, their father's funny quirks, how their father told Paul not to let life get in the way of love. They brought little family heirlooms into his hospital room that they hoped he would recognize if he opened his eyes. In the 24 days since being shot, he had not shown any signs of life, only being kept alive by the life-support system he'd been on for over three weeks. The Europe Ethnarchy constitution clearly established that the senate had power of attorney, making the decision whether a sitting chairperson could be sustained on life support. Alberto and Anna could be with him and comfort him but had no say in Paul's life support decision. The senate had previously voted to keep him on life support until March 25th, then if he was still brain-dead he would be removed. On the evening of March 24th, Anna sat at Paul's bedside, looking at his now graying wavy hair. He still had the same boyish good looks that she admired growing up, even with tubes coming out of his nose and mouth and cotton pads over his eyes to keep them from drying out. Anna learned to drown out the persistent beeping and whooshing sounds of the devices monitoring her brother and keeping him alive. She hated being there but couldn't imagine not being there.

Later that night, Anna had dozed off next to Paul, when she was awoken by what started out as Paul stirring in his bed, then building to violent shaking. She heard the *beep beep beep* of his heart monitor speed up and saw his blood pressure shoot up. This went on for about ten seconds, with his final convulsion the tubes from his nose, mouth, and arm shot like projectiles from his body, completely disconnecting him from the machinery keeping him alive. Then everything went silent. No movement, no beeping. Three nurses and the on-call doctor rushed into the room to see him convulse, the tubes shoot from his body, then silence. Paul's security detail, stationed outside the room day and night, stood in the doorway watching his still body. They all had been expecting that he would be removed from life support and die. It was like nothing they'd ever seen before in a brain-dead patient. The doctor came to Paul's side, putting his fingers to his neck to confirm there was no pulse. As the doctor reached down, Paul's body leapt from the bed, coming back down on the bed with such force that it shook the cotton pads from his eyes. The startled doctor put his hand on Paul's neck.

"He's got a pulse!" the doctor said. Paul opened his eyes, the first time since he was shot over three weeks ago. His normally blue eyes were completely black, looking as if his pupils had been fully dilated.

Anna leaned over him, "Paul, can you hear me?" she asked.

Paul blinked his eyes a couple times. "Anna?" he asked as he looked at his sister.

"Yes, it's me!"

"Are we in Naples?"

"We're in Jerusalem."

"What are you doing in Jerusalem? Is Alberto at the store?" He asked.

Anna laid her head on his chest, starting to cry. The doctor and nurses couldn't believe it, a man brain-dead for over three weeks who had showed absolutely no signs of life was now not only breathing on his own but alert and talking. Paul's security detail stood at the doorway, watching the miracle of their boss seemingly coming back from the dead. His security chief called Senator Dalia Backus, who had assumed chairperson responsibilities since the day of the shooting. "He's alive and talking."

"What?" Dalia couldn't believe her friend and chairperson was seemingly brought back from death's door. "Is he still awake?"

"We're in his room with the doctor, nurses and his sister. He just asked her what she was doing in Jerusalem."

"Can I talk with him?" Dalia asked.

"I'll put you on speaker."

The security chief walked over to Paul and hit the speaker button on his phone. "OK, Senator."

"Paul?" Dalia said.

"Dalia, how you doing?"

"I should be asking you that."

"I'm thirsty." One of the nurses brought Paul a cup of water with a straw. He took a couple of sips then leaned his head back. "I think I need to take a nap, then we can get back to work," Paul said.

"Take all the time you need," Dalia said. "I'll talk to you tomorrow, I love you Paul."

"Love you too Dalia."

Anna still had her head on Paul's chest, still amazed her brother was alive. She called Alberto, then Caleb, to let them know the good news. Caleb rushed to the hospital to give a HoloMate broadcast update.

Caleb got to the hospital then up to Paul's room. He saw Anna sitting next to Paul who was sleeping peacefully in bed, tubes strewn about the floor. He couldn't believe his eyes. "What happened?" he asked Anna.

"He was quiet, then began shaking violently, then the tubes and cotton pads shot from his body, he opened his eyes, and asked me why I was in Jerusalem," she said, laughing through tears. "He talked to Senator Backus, took a couple of sips of water, then said he wanted to take a nap. That's when I called you."

Caleb for sure thought Paul was going to die. Now he was napping and looking as if the past three weeks never happened, the only evidence being the bandage on his head where the bullet pierced his skull. "Let me get on LFTP-939."

Caleb switched on his HoloSpecs on and put a second pair on the napping Paul, tuning both pairs to LFTP-939. He listened for his producer.

"Caleb, you're on in ten."

Anna ran her fingers through Paul's hair to attempt to get him hologram-ready. Caleb was ecstatic to give the news to the world.

"Three, two, one."

"This is Caleb Todd with HoloMate News in Chairperson Paul Ambrosi's hospital room." Followers in LFTP-939 could see Caleb's hologram standing next to Paul's hologram lying in the bed. "Thirty minutes ago, Chairperson Ambrosi awoke from . . ." Caleb was interrupted.

"Caleb?"

"Chairperson?" Caleb said.

"Hey, Cuz," Paul said. Caleb looked at Paul, amazed he was able to breathe on his own, let alone talk to him, noticing his black eyes.

"How you feeling?" Caleb completely forgot he was in the HoloRoom, it was as if it were just Paul and Caleb and not millions of followers watching them.

"Thirsty and tired," Paul said. Caleb gave him a sip of water from the cup on the table next to the bed.

"You look great, Chairperson."

"I talked to Dalia," Paul said.

"I know."

"I just need to take a nap and we'll get back to work."

"Certainly, Chairperson." Caleb took the HoloSpecs off Paul, his hologram disappearing from the HoloRoom.

Caleb was overcome by the moment, never expecting to hear his cousin's voice again. He stood there for a minute, then remembered he was still in the HoloRoom, the millions of followers watching him stand there by himself. He shook his head slightly as if to wake himself from a daydream. "HoloFriends, what you've just seen is nothing less than an absolute miracle. Chairperson Ambrosi is not only no longer brain-dead, but he's talking and wants to get back to work, it's almost as if he weren't human." Caleb started choking up, having to stop for a moment to gain his composure. He continued, "I'll be here day and night monitoring every moment of Paul's, I mean Chairperson Ambrosi's condition and bring you news as it's happening." Caleb turned off his HoloSpecs and rubbed his eyes, trying to take in all that just happened. Alberto had just arrived at the hospital and joined Caleb and Anna in Paul's room, the three of them hugging and crying, just as Paul did with his brother and sister when their mother died. This time, though, it was tears of happiness.

Over the next couple of days Paul managed to stay awake more, ask questions, move his arms and legs. One afternoon while Caleb, Anna and Alberto were in the room with him, he asked about the shooting. They had wanted to tell him what happened but didn't want to do it until he was ready. They told him about the shooter firing three bullets from long range and how he had never been found, how he was hit in the head, Caleb was hit in the arm, then Paul asked about Sal.

"Sal was with us, right?" Paul asked.

"Yes." Caleb said.

"Is he OK?"

"He's in a private room on the fourth floor."

"Can I talk to him?"

"You can talk to him, but he can't talk to you," Caleb knew the next question.

"Why?"

"The gunshot hit him in the jaw, the doctors weren't able to save it. His jaw is gone, he can't talk, eat or drink."

"Oh, pity," Paul said. Anna, Alberto and Caleb were surprised by Paul's answer. Paul had always shown such concern for others, but the best he could muster for a man who had his jaw blown off was "pity." That wasn't a Paul-type response.

SAL'S VISITOR
2066

Over the next week Paul regained his strength, even getting out of bed and walking around the hospital hallways. He was talking, laughing, and giving his own HoloMate reports on his recovery in LFTP-939. His physical appearance looked completely normal except the healing wound on his head and his formerly blue eyes, which stayed black. The doctors couldn't explain it, but it appeared to be a small price to pay for Paul's coming back to life. Paul had seemed to forget about Sal, then one afternoon after he gave a HoloMate report he said to Caleb, "Let's go see Sal."

"I'll check with his doc." Caleb left the room, found Sal's doctor and asked if he could take a visitor. Caleb came back to Paul's room. "He said you can see him."

"Good, let's go, where's my phone?" Paul asked.

"I've got it," Caleb said.

Paul held out his hand, Caleb gave him the phone.

The two walked out of Paul's room, with two of Paul's security detail in tow. They got on the elevator, Caleb pushed the button for the fourth floor. The elevator was quiet, Paul staring at the door not saying or doing anything, as if he were the only one on the elevator. The doors opened at the fourth floor and they got off, turning to the right where Sal's room was next to the nurse's station. Caleb walked in first, seeing Sal lying in bed. His head was heavily bandaged with a feeding tube down his nose and a breathing tube attached to his trachea below the Adam's apple. Despite the heavy bandages, it was obvious there was no shape where Sal's angular jaw had once been.

"I've got a visitor," Caleb said to Sal. Then Paul walked in the room. Paul took one look at Sal and started to cry.

"I'm so sorry, Sal," Paul said as he walked up to his bed and grabbed his hand. All he could see was Sal's eyes, which started welling as Paul spoke. Caleb moved a chair next to Sal's bed. Paul sat, holding Sal's hand, both of them crying, Paul not saying a word, Sal not able to. Paul saw the leather straps on Sal's wrists holding him to the bed.

"Why the straps?" Paul asked.

"He kept pulling the tubes out," Caleb said.

Paul sat there for a couple of minutes, just holding Sal's hand. "Guys, can you give Sal and I a few minutes alone?"

"Sure," Caleb said. Caleb and the two security agents left the room, closing the door behind him.

After the door closed, Paul turned back to look at Sal. The tears once in Paul's eyes were completely gone. Paul looked at Sal, Sal for the first time seeing Paul's black irises.

"You've always come in second, you've been a loser your whole life, no one's loved you, not even your mother. Oh and Zola, you knew she was a DarkRoom whore right? She was a favorite amongst the senate." Paul tossed lie after lie at Sal just to torment him. Sal's eyes widened, a hissing sound coming through the trachea tube from his increased breathing. Sal's hands pulled at the bed, restrained by the wrist straps.

Paul continued. "You think I didn't know how you tried to VF me?" Sal started to shake, the hissing increased, the straps rattled against the bed as Sal tried to get free, his eyes like saucers peering out from the white bandages. Paul then leaned over to Sal and whispered in his ear, "I want you to hear this." Paul then made a call on his phone.

"Yes, Mr. Chairperson," the voice said. Sal recognized it, it was Mario.

"Do it in one minute," Paul said.

"Yes, Mr. Chairperson," Mario said.

Paul hung up, staring at Sal with his black eyes, smiling as he watched Sal struggle, knowing what was coming. Paul then leaned over Sal and kissed him on the forehead. Paul mustered up some tears before leaving the room, Sal still struggling in his bed.

"I feel so horrible for him," Paul said to Caleb as he walked out of the room and closed the door behind him.

They walked to the waiting elevator, then heard an alarm and nurses running to Sal's room as the elevator door closed.

Paul continued to recover over the next five months, but those around him noticed a change. His once patient demeanor had become testier, his kindness replaced with anger and disdain. His black eyes made him more intimidating, instilling fear in those who he interacted with. All compassion seemed to have left him, seemingly not caring about the thoughts and feelings of others. He became the anti of who he was years earlier. As the world would discover, they'd yet to see the worst of his depravity.

LINK THE ACCOUNTS
2066

After facing certain death just five months earlier, Paul had now fully recovered and was back at work in Rome. Most people who saw Paul after the assassination had similar responses--happiness then startled at his eyes. His doctors suspected the black replacing his usual blue iris pigment was only temporary. After five months the black was as prominent as it was when he first emerged from his brain death. Paul didn't seem to mind it, he kind of liked the new look.

Through Paul's recovery, Caleb became more integral to Paul's staff. Paul insisted that any communication be carried out by Caleb and no one else. Caleb was still head of HoloMate, but his CEO responsibilities took second seat to supporting Paul. With Caleb taking on more government responsibility, Paul injected greater influence over HoloMate, dictating broadcast content and ordering the shutting down of any HoloRooms he deemed not in the Europe Ethnarchy's best interest. While Paul allowed the DarkRooms to continue with no changes, he forced the shutdown of any HoloRooms speaking out against Paul and the Europe Ethnarchy. All forms of religion were banned on HoloMate. Anyone caught conducting any kind of religious service or study would be subject to execution. After Sal's death, Paul decreed MD Biometrics as property of the Europe Ethnarchy, with Mario as its CEO now working under Caleb. Paul used the VF capability that Mario created at MD Biometrics to order executions of those who spoke out against him. Trying to speak reason to Paul was met with strong retaliation. He even ordered his old friend Senator Dalia Backus VFd because she tried to appeal to Paul's now warped sense of logic. The three people Paul wanted most to VF were chairpersons Popov, Zhao, and Maghur. But like Paul, they were not MDChip wearers, so it was impossible to VF them. Paul's name became synonymous with some of the most notorious dictators in history--Stalin, Hitler, Hussein, Kim. The only two people in Paul's inner circle were Caleb and Natalizio. Paul needed them both for what he had planned.

Each morning Paul met with Natalizio and Caleb. Natalizio gave updates on military activity and Caleb prepared the day's propaganda messaging to be broadcast through HoloMate. The three would sit at Paul's desk, Paul in his leather chair and Caleb and Natalizio on the hard, wooden chairs across the desk from Paul. On this particular morning, Paul put out a request neither was expecting.

"I want you to link HoloMate subscribers to their MDCentral chip accounts," Paul said.

Caleb and Natalizio looked at each other, not sure where this was going. "You want what, Mr. Chairperson?" Caleb asked.

"Link HoloMate and MDCentral together."

"Why?"

Paul was growing impatient and was ready to lash out at the two but remembered that he needed them. "I want HoloMate to be able to control a user's MDChip. When can you have it done?"

Caleb was at a loss as to how to go about doing it and how long it would take. HoloMate and MDCentral were two of the largest and most complex databases in existence. It could take months to get it right but he didn't want to tell Paul something he didn't want to hear.

"Two months," Caleb said, not believing his own estimate.

"You've got two months," Paul said. He then went into more specifics on what he wanted. "I want an MDChip wearer to accept the StigmaChip through HoloMate, and I want the StigmaChip to only be activated once a user accepts terms through HoloMate."

"What terms?" Natalizio asked as he shifted in his chair.

"I'll give you the terms later. Right now, just build the capability. A StigmaChip should only be activated through checking an accept box."

"Yes, Mr. Chairperson," Caleb said.

"OK, now what about Zeus?" Paul turned to Natalizio for an update.

"Popov is targeting launch this coming February." Natalizio said.

"How's our mole doing?"

"He's still giving us code drops and development updates. We're able to compile the code and can simulate Zeus in our labs."

"Do you still need Riccio?" Paul asked.

"Yes," Natalizio said.

"As soon as he's no longer essential, VF him." VF had become a favorite phrase of Paul's. He thought nothing about killing off anyone who wasn't helpful.

"Yes, Mr. Chairperson." Natalizio's dedication to Paul ran deep, but even he was growing fearful of Paul and his erratic behavior.

"Caleb, arrange a trip to Jerusalem next week to meet with Dichter. Tell him to be at the airport where we will meet at the Europe Ethnarchy hanger for a brief meeting. We'll leave for Rome immediately after the meeting." Paul said.

"Any particular day?"

"You choose."

"OK," Caleb said. Both he and Natalizio were puzzled as to the purpose of such a short meeting but didn't want to question Paul.

"Nothing more." Paul said as he turned his chair around, away from Caleb and Natalizio. The two got up and walked out of the office. Caleb looked to the left and noticed the shadow box on the floor. It had been smashed and the dented folding stool was missing. He then looked to his right and saw it crumpled on the floor, with huge dents in the wall where the chair had been repeatedly slammed.

"What happened to the stool?" Caleb asked.

"Not your concern." Ever since his brain-death incident, Paul had angry outbursts prompted by even benign triggers. Earlier that day Paul got angry during a call with his sister when she asked about his eyes. He hung up the phone and saw the stool in the window box. It reminded him of his mother and how much he hated God for taking her, fueling his anger. He took the window box from the wall, smashed it to the ground, grabbed the stool and repeatedly banged it against the wall before throwing it to the ground.

After the two left, Paul turned his chair back toward his desk and grabbed his water, took a sip, and sarcastically said to himself, "Dichter's going to love this."

THE HANGAR MEETING
2066

Early on Monday morning Paul, Caleb and Natalizio left Rome for the three-hour flight to Jerusalem. Paul had already briefed Caleb and Natalizio on the purpose of the meeting with Dichter. Though they disagreed with what Paul was about to do, they were unwilling to confront him about his decision. Paul sat in the first row of the plane, with Caleb and Natalizio sitting behind him. They had already had their regular morning meeting prior to takeoff. In Paul's mind, there was nothing further to discuss. Natalizio was busy thinking about what he needed to do after Paul told Dichter of his plans. It was going to be a shock to the system and there were thousands of troops and tons of materiel that would be impacted. Caleb was doing the same, thinking through how to communicate the action the way Paul wanted it communicated. Both Caleb and Natalizio were dreading what was about to happen. Paul sat in the front row, calmly sipping espresso and looking out the window over the blue of the Mediterranean.

The plane landed in Jerusalem. Whenever Paul would come to visit, Dichter would personally greet him at the tarmac. Paul would walk down the stairs from the plane with Dichter waiting below, giving each other a kiss on each cheek when Paul reached the bottom. They had done this on every visit since Paul had brokered the peace treaty over three years ago. As Paul's plane landed, Dichter took his usual spot on the tarmac. He thought it odd that Paul could only stay for a short hangar visit but decided that he must be busy and needed to cut this visit short. He was just thankful Paul could make time for him.

The plane door opened, the stairway wheeled to the plane, then Paul emerged, followed by Caleb and Natalizio. Dichter was surprised to see Natalizio, as the visits were typically only Paul and Caleb. He watched as Paul descended the stairway, how Paul appeared to be looking out over the runway, not establishing eye contact like he typically did with Dichter. As Paul approached the bottom, Dichter attempted to kiss him as they customarily did, but Paul extended his hand for a formal handshake. Dichter again was taken off guard but awkwardly extended his hand to meet Paul's.

"Hello, Mr. Chairperson," Dichter said.

"Let's talk, Mr. President."

"Certainly." By now Dichter knew something was wrong. Paul always called him Ari.

Paul, Caleb and Natalizio walked the 40 meters to the Europe Ethnarchy hangar, with Dichter walking behind. They went in the hangar where there was a table with four chairs in the center. The four walked to the table and sat down, the sound of footsteps bouncing off the hangar walls.

Paul started the conversation. "I'll get to it. Popov is preparing to strike. We need troops and materiel in Finland, Belarus, and Latvia. I'm ordering the vacating of Israel and Palestine beginning immediately. You've had over three years to build up your forces, you need to defend yourself."

Dichter just sat there. It was one thing to re-prioritize forces and materiel, it was something different to abandon the region completely. He looked at Paul and his emotionless face and black eyes.

"Mr. Chairperson, please can we discuss this?" Dichter did nothing to hide his panic. No protection from the Europe Ethnarchy meant an immediate resurgence of the Palestine Coalition. An unprotected, Israel would fall into the coalition's hands.

"I've made my decision." Paul said, his tone an icy cold.

"Caleb, talk to him!" Dichter was grasping at anything he could to get Paul to reconsider.

"I'm sorry Ari," was all Caleb could muster.

"Director?" Dichter worked his way around the table to see if anyone would come to his aid.

"We'll conduct an orderly withdrawal," Natalizio said.

Paul got up from his chair. "We need to get back to Rome," he said as he started walking out of the hanger and to his waiting plane. Caleb and Natalizio got up and walked out, not saying a word to Dichter, who sat at the table, head in his hands, wondering how it could possibly be any worse for him. He was about to find out.

Caleb took out his phone and called Mario. "Do it," he said.

Dichter, still sitting at the table with his head in his hands, suddenly grabbed his chest and fell out of his chair to the hard cement floor in the hangar.

As they boarded the plane, Natalizio's phone rang. "When will you be out?" the voice asked.

"Five days," Natalizio said, then hung up the phone.

The voice on the other end of the phone was Palestine Coalition leader Zaid Rahn. Earlier in the week, Natalizio had told him of the Europe Ethnarchy's exit and that one of Rahn's lieutenants was really a Europe Ethnarchy agent.

Rahn ended his call with Natalizio. He and his lieutenants were in their bunker in the Jordanian Highlands, sitting around a makeshift wooden table. Rahn stood up, walking around the room behind each sitting lieutenant, telling them of the ethnarchy's exit in five days. He then stopped as he was behind the ethnarchy agent posing as one of his lieutenants, pulled a knife from his belt, grabbed the agent by the hair, pulled his head back, and slit his throat from ear to ear. The rest of the lieutenants sat there in horror watching Rahn kill one of his cadre.

"He was one of them," Rahn said. "We take back our homeland in five days." His lieutenants sat there staring at their colleague's dead body, too stunned to celebrate the eventual annihilation of Israel.

Paul, Caleb and Natalizio boarded the plane from Jerusalem back to Rome. Caleb and Natalizio talked about where all of this was going, and whether the once-brilliant Paul had turned into nothing more than a psychopath. If so, how could they stop him? At all times, Paul carried a device that Mario had built which enabled him, at any time to VF anyone in his inner circle. A single flip of his finger, and any of Paul's closest advisors, including Caleb and Natalizio, could be VFd.

Paul sat alone in the front row of the plane, thinking about what he would do next when MDCentral and HoloMate's account databases were integrated.

CHRISTMAS DECREE
2066

MDCentral and HoloMate account integration was complete in November 2066. To the world, integration was sold as a benefit in that they could see a history of their MDSolution treatments and order StigmaChips all through their HoloMate account. For Paul, it was a way to coerce billions of wearers around the world to follow his orders through "accept" terms. For any law Paul decreed, he had Caleb create an accept term that all subscribers were required to read and digitally sign. Each accept term had an expiration date. If the term wasn't accepted by its expiration date, a consequence would be invoked. Paul's favorite consequence involved the StigmaChip. Failure to accept would turn off the subscriber's StigmaChip function. The chip on the subscriber's forehead would blink red, a form of scarlet letter telling everyone that the subscriber not only went against one of Paul's decrees but, more importantly, was now prey to the Stigma blood cancer. Because the cancer was contagious, others avoided the subscriber. If a subscriber had yet to receive the StigmaChip, then failure to accept meant the subscriber would not be allowed to get a StigmaChip. Only those with clear chips on their foreheads bearing the three Stigma symbols were safe. Others with either a blinking red chip or none at all would be presumed contagious and not only shunned by others but would endure the painful blood cancer.

Paul's first test of the accept process was to outlaw the word *Christmas*. He issued a decree that the word could not be used in advertising, be displayed anywhere in a public place, or be used to describe any activity associated with the December holiday. Any songs typically sung or played during the holiday season containing the word either couldn't be used or needed the word Christmas changed to some other word. On November twentieth the decree was broadcast to all HoloMate subscribers. There was both confusion and skepticism over the decree, with millions around the world ignoring it. Each time a subscriber logged into HoloMate, they were presented with the decree and the requirement to digitally sign by December first or face the consequence of a deactivated StigmaChip. On the second of December, millions of StigmaChip wearers awoke to blinking red chips on their foreheads. Pharmacies were flooded with complaints about the chips, who were powerless to do anything. If a subscriber was caught disobeying the decree, they would be un-accepted and the chip consequence invoked. With Christmas day coming up, there was frantic activity by retailers, advertisers, movie studios, and anyone who used the word Christmas to strip the word from its language. Songs containing the word simply weren't played, and public signs with the word were replaced with other words that didn't violate the decree. Christmas trees were called holiday trees. Classic movies shown during the Christmas season weren't shown. Christmas presents became holiday presents.

Paul's Christmas decree test accomplished what he wanted. He was able to use HoloMate to issue an order with what amounted to a death sentence for those who didn't comply. The Christmas decree showed Paul was serious and those who defied him would pay the price.

Decree after decree was issued by Paul, all with the same consequence for non-acceptance. Those with no chip or a blinking red chip were shunned by clear chip wearers. Even though clear chip wearers were impervious to the contagious blood cancer, communities began segregating, separating into "clear" and "contagious" categories. Those who were contagious were increasingly snubbed by clear people. Bathroom usage became segregated, with "clear" and "contagious" replacing "men" and "women." Restaurants had clear-only sections. Employers were resistant to hire contagious applicants, due to fear of retribution of their clear customers. Contagious safe spaces cropped up where those with blinking or non-existent chips could gather for support, fellowship, and encouragement.

Paul, Natalizio, and Caleb continued to meet each morning to review war status, Zeus progress, and any new decrees Paul wanted to implement. Paul actually enjoyed that the world was at war. He loved seeing the prolonged pain being inflicted on people. He lusted for war, and the more he had of it the more gratification it gave him. He could have easily VFd enemy armies, but that would bring a stop to the war rush he got. Ending war would mean depriving his pleasure center.

He simply had to keep it going.

For six months after the Christmas decree, their morning meetings became more and more about Paul's self-exaltation, comparing himself to the greatest leaders in the world, proclaiming himself as the greatest mind that ever lived. He obsessed over the most trivial issues, the latest being the two HoloChurches that kept cropping up. Every time he had Caleb shut them down they managed to reappear on another channel. "Can't you find them?" He'd ask Natalizio.

"Chairperson, we've got bigger problems than two HoloChurches," Natalizio would try to reason with Paul.

"Find them and kill them!"

Natalizio eventually found the two, each run by Christians who accepted Jesus after the rapture. At Paul's orders, he had them killed then put their dead bodies on display in their own HoloChurch rooms.

HoloMate became one big propaganda machine, with Paul's message of self-glorification interrupting millions of HoloRoom meetings. Caleb and Natalizio became numb to Paul's self-aggrandizement, going through the motions, being mindful of Paul's ability to VF either of them at a moment's notice.

The three were in Paul's office where Paul had just finished his latest self-serving sermon. Caleb and Natalizio squirmed on their wooden chairs, waiting for the opportunity to leave. Once Paul was done, Caleb took the opportunity to wrap up the meeting.

"Anything else, Mr. Chairperson?" Caleb asked.

"I want a new decree," Paul said.

"What would you like?" Caleb wasn't surprised at Paul's wanting yet another decree.

"I want a decree telling people to accept me as God."

"Accept you as God?" Natalizio asked.

"You don't think I'm every bit as powerful as God?" the leading question making it difficult for Caleb and Natalizio to disagree without retribution.

"Why do you think you're God?" Caleb asked, cautious not to irritate the already erratic Paul.

"No one in history has had the same power I now have. I can annihilate entire populations with a single command. I can issue any decree and force people around the world to comply or pay the consequence. Doesn't that sound like God to you?"

Caleb saw the futility in arguing with Paul. "Yes, Mr. Chairperson."

"Nothing more." Paul said as he turned his back to them. This was how they ended all their meetings. Caleb and Natalizio got up and left, wondering when this nightmare would end.

That afternoon HoloMate subscribers logged in to see a new decree. Many just went to the line where they digitally signed without reading the decree. This one was different than the other decrees, only having six words, I ACCEPT CHAIRPERSON AMBROSI AS GOD.

ZEUS
2067

Chairperson Popov took the podium and began his speech to his cabinet. "Comrades, this day, June 22, 2067, will forever be known as Russia's greatest day." His long-awaited project, Zeus, was ready for launch. Zeus was a network of 15 satellites which, from 5,000 kilometers above the earth, could fire a laser or hypersonic missile and hit a target the size of a car with pinpoint accuracy. When in position, the satellites could reach a target anywhere on earth. The network of 15 satellites was controlled from Zhitkur, a fortified underground military base beneath the Kapustin Yar research laboratory in Astrakhan Oblast, Russia. Complex software controlled the movement and firing of the satellites, with commands being sent from Zhitkur through encrypted digital signals to the satellites. Each communication sequence between Zhitkur and the satellite had a digital identifier which ensured the communication was authentic. The digital identifier was designed to prevent a hostile actor from sending unauthorized signals to the satellite, thus taking over the weapon. The digital identifier sequence changed every five minutes to further protect the satellite network against a takeover. The digital identifier sequence was highly confidential and known by only a select few, one of whom was Riccio.

Popov and his cabinet personally visited Zhitkur for the ceremonial launch of Zeus. Standing on the stage of a packed auditorium of cabinet members, military leaders, and Zeus program managers, Popov took a puff of his cigar and continued. "For years we fought against the Europe Ethnarchy and its allies, with millions of Russian lives lost. Chairperson Ambrosi and his hostile act in the

Palestine region laid bare his deliberate plan to rule over all the ethnarchies. The Africa, Asia and Russia Ethnarchies had no choice but to meet Ambrosi and his allies with force to send them a strong message, that we won't be subject to his rule, we will be independent and free!" Applause erupted in the auditorium. Popov took out a handkerchief, wiped the sweat from his forehead, took another puff of his cigar, and continued. "Today the most powerful weapon in history will take its place 5,000 kilometers above the earth to ensure the Russia Ethnarchy stays independent and free from tyrants that threaten the wellbeing of our citizens." More applause.

Popov looked around the room, taking it all in. The moment was about him and his baby, and he wanted to savor the adulation. He continued, "Zeus suffered many setbacks over the years as Russia worked to defend itself from Europe and its allies, but as our forefathers before us, we persevered to this day, the day where Russia secures its freedom forever!" As the audience gave its thunderous applause, an assistant wheeled a small platform with a black box onto the stage and set it next to Popov. As the acclaim subsided, Popov dabbed his forehead, took another puff, and raised his hand to quiet the audience. "I have waited for this day for a long time, the day Zeus breathes life." Popov pushed a blue button on top of the black box. Behind Popov was a large screen broadcasting from the launch location in North Siberia. A camera was fixed on the first of 15 rockets, each containing a Zeus satellite. After Popov pressed the button, the first rocket roared to life, then achieved liftoff. The remaining 14 rockets launched one after another, each launch shown on the large screen to boisterous whooping from the audience. Popov stood with his back to the audience, watching each rocket leave its platform. As they launched he started singing *Be Glorious, our Free Motherland.* Soon the entire auditorium was singing the national anthem from the former USSR, the singing so loud it could be heard outside the auditorium throughout the building.

Riccio was in the room, singing with his Russian colleagues. After the last rocket launched, he sent a cryptic message to Natalizio in Rome, "Catch any fish?"

Natalizio saw the message on his phone, they had agreed on the cryptic message earlier that meant Zeus had been launched. Natalizio walked down the hall to Paul's office. Caleb was already there, being subjected to more of Paul's self-righteous ranting. "It's launched," Natalizio said.

"Are you ready?" Paul asked.

"As soon as they're in position."

"Good," Paul said. Natalizio gave Caleb a quick glance, who just rolled his eyes at Paul's blathering, being careful to make sure Paul didn't see. Natalizio turned and left, Paul resuming his sermon to Caleb.

Natalizio replied back to Riccio, "Two." Riccio saw the message telling him the takeover would happen soon. He put his phone back in his pocket and joined the singing.

COMM ACCEPTED

2067

Six hours after launch the satellites were in their 5,000-kilometer orbit, at which point Riccio would send the digital identifier sequence. The sequence was a 300-character string that was transmitted by both the satellite and the command center. An algorithm at the receiving location decoded the digital identifier. If the decoded result matched what the receiving location was expecting, then it considered the message as valid, returning a COMM ACCEPTED message to the sender and processing the instruction. If it didn't match, the instruction was ignored and COMM REJECTED message returned to the sender. Natalizio's cyberintelligence unit, thanks to Riccio's weekly code drops, was able to create software that changed the algorithm. A changed algorithm meant codes that were previously expected to work would be rejected. Both the sender and receiver had to have the same algorithm for communications to be accepted. Once the algorithm was changed, Natalizio then needed to upload software that sent false accept messages back to Zhitkur so the Russians wouldn't realize their messages were being rejected by the satellite algorithm. As far as they were concerned, Zhitkur and the satellites were communicating normally, but in reality the software that Natalizio's cyberintel unit installed was sending fake messages back to Zhitkur. All Natalizio needed was a valid digital identifier sequence to change the algorithm, and Riccio was going to get it for him.

After the satellites were in position, a message was sent to each of the satellites with a new digital identifier sequence that would be valid for the next five minutes. Any communications occurring during that time needed to have that same digital identifier sequence.

Riccio sent the sequence to Natalizio's cyberintel unit. In Rome, Natalizio was in the cyberintel command center when they received the sequence. The command center had three large screens on the wall, with three tiers of horseshoe-shaped tables and chairs facing the screens. The room was bustling with agents wanting to see the Zeus takeover.

"We've got it, Director," Carmen Acosta, Natalizio's assistant director of cyberintelligence said.

"Thanks, Carmen," Natalizio said. "Upload the algorithm, you've got five minutes before the sequence changes."

Acosta inserted the sequence Riccio sent into the first message which opened communication with the satellite. On the center screen the communication sequence between cyberintel and satellite one was displayed. Acosta prepared the message.

"Sent, Director," Acosta said. The room became quiet, everyone fixed to the center screen, waiting for an accept message from the satellite. Five seconds, nothing, then a COMM REJECTED message showed on the screen, followed by a collective groan. Natalizio was disappointed, but even more, was fearful of Paul's reaction. Natalizio took out his phone to message Riccio of the failure but noticed an unread message from him with the words, "Send it backward." Riccio was told to implement a last-minute change which reversed the order of the 300-character digital identifier sequence before the algorithm read it. He didn't have time to do a new code drop to Natalizio, so cyberintel would have to reverse the sequence on their own.

"Reverse the sequence order!" Natalizio said.

Acosta then went to work reversing the order of the 300-character sequence, re-inserted it, and sent the message before a new sequence was generated. Again, the entire room went silent and watched the center screen. Nothing for five, ten seconds, then COMM ACCEPTED appeared on the screen, to collective sighs. They all knew that comm acceptance was only the first step, they had to upload the new algorithm and the program that sent false accept messages back to Zhitkur.

Acosta sent the next message, which uploaded cyberintel's algorithm.

COMM ACCEPTED appeared on the screen. Two down, one to go.

Acosta sent the third message, a new program that sent false accept messages back to Zhitkur. In this program, Zhitkur would get a COMM ACCEPTED message, even though their message was rejected due to Natalizio's cyberintel algorithm replacing the Russia algorithm. Natalizio's cyberintel unit would then get the message and mimic harmless functions, such as movement of a satellite or testing of a feature, to make Zhitkur think they had control of the satellite. For Zhitkur, their commands all appeared to work fine because of the COMM ACCEPTED messages and the satellites responding to the commands, even though it was cyberintel in Rome controlling the satellites.

Acosta sent messages to the remaining 14 satellites, putting them all under control of Natalizio's Europe cyberintel. For the next two months, the only commands Zhitkur sent were about repositioning satellites and software updates. Then an interesting sequence showed up at cyberintel. Acosta picked up the sequence and called Natalizio at home.

"Director, we've got activity, you should get here immediately," Acosta said.

"I'll be right there." Natalizio and his wife were having dinner. Work interruptions were frequent, she was used to it.

"Gotta go to cyberintel," he said.

"Stay safe." That was more than a cliché for her. The world had become more and more dangerous in the past five years and being the head of cyberintelligence for the Europe Ethnarchy put a target on his back with the ethnarchy's enemies, never mind the constant threat of Paul VFing him for whatever reason.

Natalizio kissed his wife and left the apartment. "These damn bugs," he said to himself as he raced to his car to avoid the stings. Locusts, scorpions, and tarantulas larger than manhole covers were everywhere, inexplicably showing up, bent on attacking people. They'd been tormenting for months, not letting up.

He made the ten-minute drive to cyberintel. He walked into the command center where Acosta was waiting. He could see command sequences from Zhitkur on the left screen. The commands were for satellite six's laser to strike the Europe Ethnarchy government building in Rome at eight the next morning. Because the commands were intercepted by cyberintel before they could be executed, satellite six never received the command. Zhitkur received their typical COMM ACCEPTED message. As far as they were concerned, the eight in the morning strike was locked and loaded.

"What do you want to do, Director?" Acosta asked.

Natalizio wanted to confer with Paul before acting. He pulled out his phone and called Paul.

"What." Natalizio heard Paul's terse voice on the other end of the phone.

"They ordered a strike. What do you want to do?"

Paul didn't hesitate in his response. "Let's have some fun," Paul said.

VOLGOGRAD
2067

Popov ordered the first strike on the Europe Ethnarchy government building for August 25, 2067 at eight in the morning. Paul ordered Natalizio to change the strike coordinates for Popov's hometown of Volgograd. Popov's family had lived there for generations, seeing its name change from Tsaritsyn to Stalingrad then to its current Volgograd. Feeling confident, Popov decided to go to Zhitkur to view the strike from his fortified command center. At 7:30 that morning Popov arrived at the command center, an unlit cigar in his mouth. Several of his lieutenants were already there along with Zeus' operations staff. Satellite six was the one to fire the strike, and all communication with the satellite seemed to be working perfectly. Popov could see the latitude and longitude coordinates on the screen, targeting a clear strike for the government building. At 7:50 a final confirmation message was sent to satellite six, with a COMM ACCEPTED appearing on the screen. "Ambrosi will never know what hit him," Popov said as they watched the screen.

At cyberintel command center in Rome, Paul, Caleb and Natalizio watched their screens, seeing something very different than Popov and his lieutenants. The center screen showed the actual messages that cyberintel was transmitting to satellite six, with the coordinates locked on to Volgograd. The right-hand screen showed what was being transmitted to Zhitkur, the fake coordinates locked on the ethnarchy government building. Paul smiled as he looked at the two screens, "That fat bastard Popov is probably blowing smoke rings right now," Paul said to Natalizio. "He's in for the scare of his life."

Paul decided to have a bit more fun with Popov. "Set the strike for five past eight," he ordered. Paul wanted them to sweat this out a bit more, by having the strike occur five minutes later than they commanded.

Back in Zhitkur's command center, Popov stood with Alexeev watching the screen in the command center countdown to eight o'clock. On another screen was a satellite picture of the ethnarchy building. He wanted to watch it blow.

Ten. Nine. Eight. Popov watched the countdown on one screen, then the ethnarchy building on the other screen.

Five. Four. Three. His eyes shifted between the two screens.

Two. One. Zero. Then silence.

And the ethnarchy building was still there.

"What happened?" Popov asked.

"I don't know, Mr. Chairperson," Alexeev said.

The activity in the room grew frantic, with commands being sent to satellite six, only to get the phony COMM ACCEPTED messages.

"Try another satellite." Alexeev said. He looked over at Popov, who had chewed the end off his cigar in frustration.

"Satellite four in position, General," Alexeev's operations commander said.

"Execute!" Alexeev said.

The operations commander sent the command to execute, receiving the COMM ACCEPTED confirmation. The ethnarchy government building stood just as it always had on the beautiful sunny day in Rome.

Back at cyberintel command center in Rome, Paul laughed out loud as he watched the commands from Zhitkur on the right-hand screen. "They switched to satellite four!" Paul said, not even trying to contain his glee. "He's probably chewed through his cigar by now!" Paul knew Popov well enough to know that this would be eating him alive. And that Popov would probably execute someone over this.

Paul watched the countdown to the strike on Volgograd, from a satellite picture on the far-left screen. The real commands to satellite six were on the center screen, with the bogus Zhitkur commands on the right. He watched the frantic scrolling of commands on the right screen as Alexeev tried to figure out why the strike was unsuccessful. Paul's black eyes shifted to the center screen where he watched the countdown.

Fourteen. Thirteen. Twelve. He looked at the satellite picture of the unsuspecting Volgograd, its citizens having no idea they were going to die in the next seconds.

Seven. Six. Five. Paul's eyes shifted to the still-frantic command scrolling on the right screen.

Two. One. Zero. Paul looked to the left screen and saw a bright flash then a plume of dust and smoke engulf the city. Natalizio and Caleb watched the screen where the now decimated Volgograd once stood, acknowledging the military success, but at the same time saddened by the loss of innocent lives. Paul was giddy with excitement as Volgograd descended to rubble. "Yes!" Paul yelled as he left the command center. He ran back to his office at the still-standing government building, closed the door, made an espresso, and watched the recording of Volgograd being blown up over and over again.

Ten minutes after the failed attack on the ethnarchy government building, Popov got a call that Volgograd had been struck. He threw the phone to the ground.

"What?" Alexeev asked.

"Volgograd, you hit Volgograd, you idiot!"

Alexeev couldn't believe it. All the commands were accepted, he had verification from the satellites, the coordinates were locked. Hitting Volgograd just didn't make sense.

"Find out what happened!" Popov stormed out of the command center back to his office in Zhitkur. As he got to his office, he threw his chewed-up cigar against the wall and sat in his chair. He picked up his phone and called his mother, no answer. Sister, no answer. Brother, no answer.

The rest of the day was filled with confusion, frustration, and mourning in Zhitkur. Popov had every one of his generals on the phone or in his office, interrogating them about how this could have happened. Seeing Volgograd get decimated was too much for Riccio to bear. He watched innocent people die because he gave code drops and plan updates to Natalizio to protect his DarkRooms encounters. Riccio approached Alexeev, "General, I need to talk to you."

"What, Riccio," Alexeev said, perturbed at the interruption.

"I have information about the satellite misfire."

"Come with me." Alexeev took Riccio to a nearby conference room, where Riccio told him of everything, how he was blackmailed by Natalizio, how he gave him code drops and plans, how he feared what Natalizio would do to him if he didn't comply. Alexeev seethed as Riccio spilled his guts. "You're going to explain this to the chairperson," Alexeev said.

"No, I'm not." Riccio pulled a gun from his jacket, put it to his temple, and pulled the trigger. Alexeev tried to get to him before he shot himself but didn't make it. He walked out of the conference room, blood splattered on his uniform, the dead Riccio lying across the conference room table, his blood dripping off the table onto the carpet.

Alexeev went to Popov's office, still speckled with Riccio's blood, and explained everything Riccio had done and how he killed himself before having to face Popov. Popov was furious and wanted to execute Alexeev on the spot but knew he needed him. He charged Alexeev with fixing the Zeus mess as if his life depended on it, because it did.

In the following months, control of Zeus changed hands almost daily. With each control change, Paul and Popov used the opportunity to strike populous cities in each other's ethnarchies and those of their allies. Rome, London, Moscow, Shanghai, Paris, New

York, Singapore, Tokyo, and Delhi--all severely damaged. A Zeus laser strike triggered the eruption of Mount Vesuvius, coating Paul and Caleb's Naples hometown with meters of lava and volcanic ash. Millions around the world died, their rotting corpses strewn about, decomposing in full sight of the living. Some died from the Stigma blood cancer, some from famine, others from Zeus's strikes. Ethnarchy chairpersons and their cabinets were forced to go into hiding in secured bunkers. With so many code patches being deployed by Europe and Russia to control Zeus, it became more and more unstable, seemingly firing with a mind of its own. Zeus was striking oceans killing its inhabitants, striking faults triggering earthquakes, and hitting nuclear installations causing meltdowns. Neither Popov nor Paul could stop trying to gain control over Zeus, if one gave up it meant certain annihilation for the other. They had no choice but to continue their destructive actions, which Paul took great delight in.

THE MARCH ON ROME
2069

Popov called Zhao and Maghur to Moscow to plan how they were going to stop Paul and the European Ethnarchy. For two and a half years, Zeus continued its unpredictability, firing in every ethnarchy without rhyme or reason. Keeping basic services running like electricity and clean water was nearly impossible. Corpses were piling up on city streets, remote villages, and country farms. Anything broadcast on HoloMate, for those who could still connect to it, was propaganda about how Russia, China, and Africa were causing the destruction and how Paul was the only way out of it, that he was the savior the world needed. MDSolution supplies were depleted. Once a chip wearer's SK cells died off, something as innocuous as a cold became as lethal as the Stigma blood cancer. MDCentral too became unpredictable, randomly VFing chip wearers as electrical pulses from Zeus strikes interfered with communications between MDCentral and MDChips. What was most terrifying was that Paul didn't want any of this to stop. The chaos, pain, and suffering were like a drug rush to him. He needed to keep it going to stay on this high he was on.

Popov, Maghur and Zhao met in Popov's command center in Zhitkur. Popov took them into the room where Alexeev and his agents were furiously working to regain control of Zeus and stop the random strikes. Alexeev would gain control, then Natalizio, then back to Alexeev, and so it went. Popov wanted to end the conflict, and Paul wanted to keep it going. Maghur and Zhao saw first-hand the struggle and how it would never end unless they took a different path, which is what Popov wanted to discuss.

Popov took them to the same conference room where Riccio had blown his brains out two years earlier, the outline of his blood stains still on the carpet. The three of them sat down at the table. Popov took one of his last remaining cigars from his coat pocket and began. "Chairpersons, we can't continue this way. As long as Ambrosi is walking the earth, this devastation will continue. He doesn't want it to stop. We need to stop him if we're going to survive."

"How?" Maghur asked. "We can't rely on Zeus; our air and nuclear capability is obliterated. Supplies and manpower are decimated."

Popov pulled the unlit cigar from his mouth. "All we have left is ground. With anyone we can muster, with sticks and stones if necessary."

Zhao sat silently, staring at the blood stains on the carpet. "How these get here?" Zhao interrupted, pointing to the blood stains.

"We killed the person responsible for the Zeus mess." Popov wanted them to think he was in control of the situation with Riccio and that he killed him on the spot. If Popov told them Riccio killed himself it would have made him look weak. Zhao nodded his head, suspecting Popov was lying.

Popov continued. "None of us can do it on our own, Ambrosi is still too strong. We need to do it together."

Maghur and Zhao knew he was right. They would have to march on to Rome and take Ambrosi through a coordinated ground attack. "What's your plan?" Maghur asked.

"Africa by sea from the south and west, China from the east, Russia from the north. Start movement with whatever you've got and pick up anything or anyone along the way who'll help."

"Many won't make it, with this heat," Maghur said. The earth's average temperature had risen 10 degrees Celsius due to massive increases in greenhouse gas emissions. Maghur continued, "And it's always dark because of the smoke, thanks to your baby Zeus."

Maghur continued his rant. "I can't believe we've resorted to this. In this day and age, with all advances in weapons, we're about to fight a battle like the Battle of the Metaurus," referring to a battle between Rome and Carthage fought centuries earlier. Rome won the battle decisively.

"We hope different victor this time," Zhao said.

The three continued their plan of when the attack would commence. They agreed to get their armies in position and to begin their march on Rome in three weeks. They all knew the stakes--if they were successful in capturing and killing Paul, they would have a chance to rebuild. If not, then the world's misery would continue.

"Ambrosi will be waiting for us," Popov said. "We must persevere."

The three chairpersons got up from their chairs, somber at the reality of their situation and what they were about to do. They had no choice. It had to be done.

TETELESTAI
2069

After leaving Zhitkur, the three chairpersons finalized plans with their respective lieutenants. It was a case of all-hands-on-deck--whoever they could get, with whatever weapons they had, would march on Rome. Zhao was able to persuade the Asia Chairperson Chiyo Ikeda to join in the march. Ikeda was distressed at having to do this to her old friend Paul, but she also recognized the Paul she knew years ago bore no likeness to the current-day Paul who was causing so much pain in the world.

Zeus strikes had long ago obliterated the Europe Ethnarchy government building that held Paul's office, so he had moved, along with the cyberintel command center, to a fortified underground facility in Vatican City. Before moving in, Paul ordered the names of every pope interred in the Basilica be chiseled off their monuments, starting with that of his old boss Pius XIV who died two years prior. In Paul's mind, none of the popes in history approached his greatness and didn't deserve to have their names in his sight.

Paul, Caleb and Natalizio continued their daily meetings, which ran as long as eight hours depending on how much Paul wanted to rant that day. They had been discussing the march on Rome for days, as one of their few remaining agents in the field tipped them off to Popov's plan. Paul wasn't at all concerned about the march, he welcomed the conflict, delusional that his Europe Ethnarchy would ward off any attack. After all, in his mind, he was God. No one could possibly stop him. Caleb and Natalizio didn't share his optimism. On the day before the planned march, the three sat in Paul's office with Paul barking out orders to be carried out in between rambling lectures on how he would never be defeated because he was God.

"Chairperson, there are millions heading to Rome. We're outnumbered. We can't sustain this," Natalizio said. He and Caleb had been trying to convince Paul for weeks to back down. Their requests fell on deaf ears, with Paul growing increasingly agitated every time one of them mentioned backing down.

"You have *me*, a hundred-million couldn't defeat me," Paul said. He truly believed he was invincible; no army of any size could bring him down. Caleb and Natalizio had heard these words countless times from Paul. Trying to convince him otherwise had grown futile. Caleb and Natalizio knew this was a death march for them but could do nothing to stop the maniac that was their chairperson.

Paul continued, "We will meet The Three Fools with nothing like they've ever seen. They won't survive the day." Paul blathered for another hour about the Europe Ethnarchy would annihilate anyone who tried to topple it, and how no army was greater than Paul the God.

The day of the march came. In his command center, Paul, Caleb and Natalizio could see pictures of a sea of men, women and children, some holding guns, some riding on horseback, some with slings and stones. The darkness continued, with it looking like night even at noon. The air was filled with smoke and volcanic ash due to a Zeus strike on the Alban Mountains, triggering a massive eruption. Nothing was going to stop his determined enemies, not even the darkness of night or the smoke and ash filling their lungs. For those attacking Rome, this was a fight for survival as a human race. Caleb and Natalizio watched the screens as the swarm approached. Perhaps they would be killed instantly, or their enemies would torture them first. It was too much for Natalizio. He left the command center, went into the bathroom, pulled out a gun, put it in his mouth, and blew the back of his head off.

Paul and Caleb continued watching the screens, oblivious to Natalizio's exit. The agents in the command center watched as even some Europe Ethnarchy citizens who were fed up with Paul joined the mob. As they hit the rubble that used to be Rome they were met by Paul's army. Paul's own forces were distressed when they saw the vast crowd moving in on them.

Just as the first shots were fired and rocks slung, a bright white light appeared in the sky. Caleb assumed it was yet another rogue Zeus strike.

But this light was different.

It lit up the entire sky, brighter than the sun but not painful to the eyes. Then there was the same deep-bass voice the world heard seven years ago. It wasn't saying *now* like during the rapture. It said *tetelestai, tetelestai, tetelestai,* meaning "it is finished," the same word Jesus uttered right before dying on the cross. After the third *tetelestai,* the same Middle C trumpet sounded, gradually getting louder. Paul saw his army stop fighting, staring up at the light, frozen with fear, remembering what happened the last time they heard the low-bass voice and the trumpet. Just as during the rapture, the trumpet sound turned into a screech painful to the ear.

This time, though, the screech continued, then an image of a horse with a rider came down through the light. The screech got louder as the rider descended on the earth, getting loud enough to burst eardrums. Oddly, Paul was unaffected by the screech, which he attributed to his Godhood. As the rider continued closer, the light emitted a pulse, which then triggered VFs in all MDChip wearers and caused the StigmaChip glued to each wearer's forehead to burn away, leaving a square of burnt flesh on the forehead where the chip had been. Paul turned to Caleb and watched him grab his chest after the VF, then saw what looked like a lit fuse on his forehead.

Paul then looked up and saw the rider approach him, the rider's eyes like a blazing fire. Paul knew who the rider was, and he knew the rider came for him. He didn't know how he knew, he just did. Paul felt a wind at his legs, lifting him and Caleb together from the command center floor. Paul closed his eyes as they rose up through the roof, traveling through it as if the roof wasn't there. In all his

Godhood, Paul was powerless in the clutches of the rider. Paul opened his eyes to see himself and Caleb in the air, as if they were riding on an invisible pillow, traveling southeast through Rome. Paul looked at Caleb, now unconscious, blood dripping from his ears, his hands on his chest, the skin on his forehead burned away.

Paul and Caleb continued their southeast journey. He lay down next to Caleb, unable to change his fate, his life's movie reel playing in his head. He thought about his father telling him to not let life get in the way of love. He thought about his mother and the dented folding stool he kept in his office, his daily reminder of her dying on the one day he didn't walk with her to the mausoleum. He thought of his sister, how she was there when he awoke from his brain death. He thought of Pope Pius XIV, how he gave Paul his start in politics as a senator representing Vatican City. He thought of Caleb and his loyalty to Paul right up to his death. He thought of his friend and fellow senator Dalia Backus whom he had VFd for no reason other than to put his power on display. He thought about his best friend growing up, Bert, and how he so admired the life he had with his wife Laura and their son JT.

He then looked out to the southeast and saw the smoldering Alban Mountains. Knowing that this was his final destination, he just looked up at the sky waiting for the drop to happen. Paul could smell the sulfur of the crater below them, the intense heat burning his and Caleb's skin and clothes. As the two dropped into the waiting crater, Paul saw the face of his old friend Bert looking down at him, a tear coming from his eye, sad for the fate of his only true friend growing up. His clothes burned off and his skin black from the intense heat, Paul's black eyes closed as he and Caleb passed the mouth of the crater, into the waiting lava below.

EPILOGUE

After Paul and Caleb were thrown into the volcano in the Alban Mountains, the rider, also known as Jesus Christ, established his kingdom on earth for a thousand years. Satan, who entered Paul when he was brain-dead, was bound for a thousand years in a place called the Abyss. Believers, both dead and alive, lived with Jesus Christ in his kingdom. This aligns to the book of Revelation, chapter 20 in the Christian Bible.

While the story of Caleb, Paul, Sal and Bert is purely fictional, the activities represented in Paul's rise and fall as the Antichrist parallel biblical references found in the books of Daniel, Isaiah, Zechariah, Matthew, Mark, first and second Thessalonians, and Revelation.

Regardless of your beliefs, my hope is that you found the book to be an interesting and worthwhile read. If you'd like to learn more about autism or what the Bible has to say about the Antichrist and the end times, go to LawlessOne.com for additional resources and Bible references.

--Lonnie Pacelli

ACKNOWLEDGEMENTS

This book has been on my bucket list for over ten years. On May 22, 2018 (My birthday no less!) I started the planning for *The Lawless One and the End of Time*. My aim was to write a fictional account of the rise and fall of the Antichrist while staying true to how he and the End Times are represented in the Bible. There were many people who helped bring this story to life. My deepest thanks to Joe Amato, Rick Blossom, Mike Burkhalter, David Gill, Susan Caldwell, Joel Wycoff, Holly Wycoff, Henderson Mar, Joe Pacelli, Janis Mar, Amelie Oeschger, Pete Osman, Fred Gill, Bette Osman, Louis Pacelli, Phil Peterson, Ray Waldmann, Sharis Watson, Mary Waldmann, and Jim DuBois for their guidance, advice, and critical feedback. Special thanks to Dani Ley and the crew at Capital One Café in Bellevue, Washington where much of the writing was done. Also, thanks to Rachel Ronan with Kiwi Creative for the great work on the cover art. Special thanks and love to my daughter Briana Sanger who did a thorough review and helped with the medical sequences, my son Trevor Pacelli who provided expert advice on the autism sequences, and my wife Patty for the hours of editing and listening to me drone on and on about plot lines, time jumps, and characters.

Also by **Lonnie Pacelli**

The Project Management Advisor
The Truth About Getting Your Point Across
Six-Word Lessons for Project Managers
Six-Word Lessons for Dads with Autistic Kids
Six-Word Lessons to Avoid Project Disaster
Why Don't They Follow Me?

See more at LonniePacelli.com

Made in the USA
San Bernardino, CA
22 December 2018